PANTHERS PLAY FOR KEEPS

Previously published Worldwide Mystery titles by
CLEA SIMON

PANTHERS PLAY FOR KEEPS

CLEA SIMON

TORONTO • NEW YORK • LONDON
AMSTERDAM • PARIS • SYDNEY • HAMBURG
STOCKHOLM • ATHENS • TOKYO • MILAN
MADRID • WARSAW • BUDAPEST • AUCKLAND

Recycling programs
for this product may
not exist in your area.

Panthers Play for Keeps

A Worldwide Mystery/August 2016

First published by Poisened Pen Press.

ISBN-13: 978-0-373-27952-4

Printed in U.S.A.

For Jon

ONE

To a dog, a dead body has some intrinsic value. To me, it was just one more hassle.

We were out for a walk, deep in the woods bordering the little town I now call home, when we found it. When *he* found it, actually. Spot, that is. Yes, that is a stupid name for a dog, especially a big work dog like the shepherd mix I was with that day. It wasn't his fault; humans can be stupid, particularly about those we love.

Which would prove true often that week—but back to the body. The walk had been peaceful up till then. A late afternoon hike in the local preservation land, the last bit of forest safe from the developers who even now seem to see everything as a marketable opportunity. Exercise for him, a break for me in what had become an increasingly hectic day, when Spot—poor fool—started in. Whining, with that softly insistent "oh, please" tone that even the best-trained canine can use. Spot has some hound in him, and he can't help getting excited about a scent. I figured on an opossum, or maybe a deer. Whatever it was, it sure had the animal at my side excited.

I shouldn't have encouraged him. I know that. Being a companion animal is all about discipline. And while most dogs are good about the positive training—paying attention to any signal from their person, obeying the commands—a reliable guide dog has to maintain the negative discipline also. That means ignoring other stimuli—other animals. Even intriguing scents. You don't want Grandma's four-legged helper dragging her after the neighbor's cat, for example. But Spot had been working hard—too hard, maybe. So I'd let him go, giving him the nod as I unsnapped his lead. Anything out there would be more than a match for his housebroken ways, I figured. If not, it had more than a half-trained guide dog to worry about.

He'd only gone about ten yards when I heard it. An odd yap—half warning, half whine—that made me freeze. Dogs, even domesticated creatures like Spot, have more senses, more instincts than us poor bipeds will ever dream of. And the tan and black animal just visible through the bare trees was telling me that something was very, very wrong.

"Spot?" I kept my voice soft and low. Although we like to use words, the animals we work with respond more to our tone than to the syllables we utter. The dog before me would hear the question in my slight upward inflection—and in the thoughts that reached out through the shadows, where I could see him stiffen at attention. "What is it, boy?"

Another whine, one I couldn't decipher. And no, that's not as crazy as it sounds. I usually can get something from the animals around me: a scent, an image. Something of how they perceive the world. It's a strange sensitivity, my so-called gift, but it's usually reliable. Usually.

"Spot?" I took a step toward him, my own ears straining to catch whatever it was that held him. The hiss of a bobcat. The rattle of a snake. The first spring thaw had exposed the dead leaves of autumn; I didn't know what else had come to light.

"Danger?" It's not a question I usually ask. It's a training word. A command that tells a guide dog to stop, to put himself in front of his person. To stay, rooted, until we humans figure out what's what. He responded, though with that whine. I could see his tail again. It whipped once, hanging low to the ground. Not in happiness. Acknowledgment, rather, and something else, too, that I tried to read as quietly as I could while creeping up behind him. He was focused on something, all right. I could sense need—a singular drive—to go, to get *something*. I needed to see what it was, too.

"No! Back!" I froze as the command—*his* command—reached me. Listened. Somewhere, not too far off, ice melt rippled down a stream. A few late afternoon peeps and mutterings signaled bird life. Undisturbed bird life. The yell I'd heard had been in my head. A warning of sorts.

"Spot?" That whine again, high-pitched and unrelenting. But now I was getting something else, too. A scent, if that meager word can be used to describe the nearly three-dimensional sensory experience of what a dog smells. Something raucous and wild. Scared and fierce. What had the dog cornered, anyway?

The time for fear was gone. All of my own scanty senses on alert, I crept forward, slowly enough for my brain to kick in. Spot's hindquarters were partly obscured by a large maple, but there didn't seem to be anything in front of him. No tree. No rock or ledge. He couldn't have anything cornered. Of course, I paused as it hit me: he'd come across something wounded.

"No!" I saw, rather than felt, the tearing, the biting. And then I knew. I hurried the last few feet to where Spot stood at attention. Body ramrod stiff, he kept guard, sniffing the air. But already his nose had told me what I'd see before me on the ground. A woman, on her back. Arms thrown open as if to embrace the fading light, the gold and green of her long-sleeved blouse evoking the spring that had yet to come. It wouldn't for her; that blouse was torn, its thin fabric shredded from the collar down. The bleeding had already stopped from the blow that had torn her scalp half off, the dark hair that remained not quite covering one brown, unseeing eye.

TWO

THE WOODS AROUND Beauville aren't primordial forest. At some point, back when the town stream powered a mill or two, those original trees had been cut down. Maybe they went for lumber; those great hardwoods were once in great demand for ships as well as housing. Maybe they went for fuel. I didn't know. But the woods we'd been walking through were what came next, if *next* includes some semi-negligent forestry and the occasional fire, controlled or not. That meant tall trees, but thin, lower branches losing out to the canopy in search of our scarce New England sunshine.

This time of year, the ground below was pretty bare. Small hills and hollows let you know where the big, old trees fell, and once, out walking, I came upon a rotted stump that I could have parked my GTO on. Come summer, this lower level would be knee-deep in ferns, maybe some jewelweed and skunk cabbage in the damper hollows. But although younger forests are supposed to allow for more underbrush, I didn't see it here.

Granted, I wasn't looking that closely. I'm not squeamish; working with animals you can't be. But finding that body had thrown me. Some of it was the color. That blouse just looked out of place against the dull browns of the season. Some of it, to be honest, was the violence. Nature may be red in tooth and claw, but that woman was no more a part of the ecosystem than

I was. No more than I wanted to be, anyway, I thought, as I quickened my pace. Lying there, she barely looked human, so torn and still, and it had taken me a moment to recognize what she was, never mind who. Something about her was familiar, though, and the image of her face—what was left of it—was ricocheting through my brain as Spot led me back to the car.

As we got closer, we slowed. Down by the parking area, where more sunlight gets through, the flora changes, and I had to watch my step. We were getting to the brambles, a big hedge of them serving as a backstop to the open asphalt. Come summer, the south side of those bushes would be full of blackberries, a feast for the birds that I might muscle my way into. Now, though, they were drab and ragged, last year's leaves still holding clumps of ice and other debris that had blown their way. With the sun behind them, the leafy accumulation looked solid. A wall, or another dead thing, lying in my path.

No, not dead. Not quite. I'd been spooked; I knew it and fought the reaction. Still, I found myself holding my breath, my heartbeat quickening as we approached. Dark, low, and large in the shadows, the compact hedge reminded me of nothing so much as a crouching animal, waiting to pounce. I panicked, just for a moment, freezing in my tracks. Spot stopped in guard position, right in front of me, senses alert.

"Command?" He waited, good dog that he is. I'd stopped so suddenly, he knew that there might be a problem.

"Walk," I replied, keeping my voice level. I'm not the nervous type, and the moment would have embarrassed me in front of any human companion. For Spot, it was all one. I'd stopped, so he had. An animal needs no explanation for caution, I told myself. What Spot thought, he didn't tell me. At work, he was as silent as usual, and for once I was grateful. Still, he kept himself between me and the hedge as we passed it. He would be a good service dog, if I didn't sabotage his training. As I opened the car door, I rubbed his ears and felt his heavy tail thump against my leg.

At the very least, this had been a good test for Spot, and he'd delivered, I'll give him that. He'd obeyed my command to return to the car and had barely whined at all as I drove back toward town, looking for a cell signal. His only utterance hadn't even been audible, just a low-level cry—half query, half complaint—that I picked up because it matched my mood as I steered down the highway, one eye on my cell.

"It's okay, boy. We'll go back." I kept my voice soft and low as I drove. "I promise." Animals respond to the tone of your voice, not the words, as I've said. With us, though, it could have been more: Just as I could pick up that soundless whine, I suspected Spot was getting more from me than audible reassurance. This thing I have, this sensitivity—call it a psychic connection—with animals means that not only can I hear what's going on with them, but most of the time, I can reach them the same way. It's freaky, sure. But it has its uses.

"We'll go back." I was still talking as the bars lit up, and I pulled over to the shoulder.

"Detective James Creighton." Even on his cell, Jim answers like a cop.

"Hey there." My voice dropped an octave. Yeah, I was calling with an emergency. What could I do? He gets to me that way.

"Pru." I heard a sigh. I didn't think it was a good sigh. "Can this wait? I'm kind of in the middle of something."

"Sure, Detective." Spot's head whipped around at the change in my voice. "I just thought you'd want to know about a dead body I found in the woods."

"What? Pru…" Maybe it's me, but it did seem odd. I tell the man in my life about a dead body, and he suddenly takes on an accusatory tone. "What did you do, Pru?" Okay, it wasn't just me.

"I called you, Jim. As soon as I could get my phone to work." That wasn't what he was asking, but I was no longer feeling particularly helpful. Being spooked had put me in a mood. "Isn't that what a responsible citizen does?"

"Pru…" Creighton was talking, but it was Spot who was commanding my attention. He was looking at me, concern in his doggie eyes. I didn't know if he could hear the growl in Creighton's voice or was picking up on my own rising temper. It didn't matter. Seeing those big sad eyes brought me back to the reality outside my own flawed romance.

"Get ahold of yourself, Jim." I was talking fast now, eager to get the story out before he—or my own temper—could interrupt. "I was out in the preservation land with a dog I'm training. Okay? He started acting odd, and I gave him his lead. He led me to a body. A woman. She's probably about a mile and a half from the road."

I gave him directions to the parking area and agreed to meet him there. It wasn't me he wanted to see, that was clear. But Spot would be able to bring him back to the body, and both the dog and the woman deserved that much closure.

He got there only a few minutes after I'd parked again and let Spot out. Flanked by two cruisers and an ambulance, he parked his unmarked car right behind mine. Anyone else, I might have thought that was co-incidence.

With all those people, though, we didn't have time for conversation. Instead, we talked as if we were on stage. "Ms. Marlowe, can you direct us to the body?"

"I can do better than that, Detective." I matched his tone. "I—and Spot here—can lead you to it."

I ignored the smiles. Beauville is a small town. Jim's officers knew we were an item. The EMTs probably did, too. Instead, I knelt at Spot's side and spoke softly in his ear. That was partly for effect. He knew what I wanted, and he wanted to get back to that poor woman, too. Even Creighton could probably see that he was quivering with anticipation, his mind focused. *"Find! Find! Find!"* The low-pitched whine vibrated from every fiber of his muscular body. But, theoretically, I was training him for someone who wouldn't have such a direct connection with his canine brain.

"That's right," I tried to fit my words to the soundtrack in his head. "Find her, Spot. Good boy." I stood and un-clipped his lead, and he was off.

"What the—?" Creighton took a moment to glare at me before he took off after the dog whose brown and black fur was quickly fading into the growing shadows.

"Relax, Jim." I called as I trotted after him. "Spot won't let us lose him. And he'll call when he finds her again."

"He'll call?" He'd stopped and I caught up. The oth-ers were either slow or intentionally giving us space.

"You'll hear him." I kept walking. "Why the attitude, Jim?"

He shook his head but adjusted his pace to mine. This early in the season, we were walking on dead leaves, and I could just make out Spot as a blur of movement up ahead.

"What?" I reached out and took his arm. He didn't shake me off. "Jim?"

"You have, shall we say, a cavalier attitude toward death." He spoke as much to the mulch as to me. "And to the law, which is not only what I do, Pru. It's who I am."

"It's not who—" I stopped myself. I'd been about to tease him. That's easy enough. Jim Creighton might look like a boy scout, with that close-cropped hair and those blue eyes. There was steel in his spine, though. It was part of what attracted me. The challenge. "I do respect you, Jim." Time to be serious.

"Do you?" He flashed a look I couldn't read, no matter how well I knew those eyes. And then we heard it. One bay, as much like a human wail as a dog's hunting cry. Ahead and to our right. Creighton and I both broke into a run, and only his outstretched arm stopped me from stumbling over the body that Spot now guarded.

"Over here," Creighton called to his crew. A bit unnecessary, I thought, before I realized: this was a dominance play. I looked down at Spot. He looked up at me and wagged that big flag of a tail once more. He knew it, too, and he was cool with it.

After some pets and praise, I snapped Spot's lead back on and led him back toward the car. He'd done his job, and neither of us needed to stay as the EMTs checked out the corpse. Already, one of Creighton's minions was cordoning off the area. They'd be here all night. Spot and I had already had a full day, and see-ing it—her—there with the techies and the crime-scene tape going up was disturbing, almost as if they were all making her less of a person. Less of a woman, even as they did their job. Letting Spot into my car, I managed to pull up onto the soft leaf mold and escape the box my sometime-boyfriend had put me in. I wasn't going to hang around waiting. I couldn't. Creighton knew how to reach me if he wanted more.

THREE

_____

"WHAT DID YOU EXPECT?" The question was rhetorical, the tone biting. *"Keeping company with...a dog?"* The pause may have been for effect. It was also functional. Wallis, the tabby who shares my house, was bathing. And even though her thoughts came to me silently, I heard them in her voice—well, what would be her voice if her mews and chirps were translated into sardonic English.

"I don't know, Wallis." I looked over at her. I'd come home only a few minutes before and sat, now, in our big country kitchen, a tumbler of bourbon before me. "I don't know."

She looked up, whiskers on the alert. I knew why. As much as I'd wanted to ignore the subtext of her question, I couldn't take it at face value. Not with those green eyes on me. Not with her ability to hear my thoughts—even those thoughts that I'd rather not be thinking.

The image of the woman's face was hard to banish, and the whiskey had only muddled my initial sense of recognition. Wallis' scorn had a bracing effect, however, and I focused on that. Death wasn't a big deal to a cat. Not to any animal, really, except for us. But scents— clues, causes—they could matter. That's what she was telling me, in her own way. She had a vested interest in my survival, and so did I. That was reason enough for me to focus.

First, there was the question of what Spot had been trying to tell me. Not that there was a body—*that,* he had shown me. But before. The scent I'd been getting from him wasn't of decay. It wasn't even human. It was wild. Fierce. And while the death of a human may be traumatic to a dog, I didn't think that was what I was getting. I'd picked up fear, or at least a sense of heightened alertness. That's what had made me so jumpy as we'd gone through the woods. A dead body doesn't fight back.

Then there was the problem of Spot's caretaker. Although I worked with the dog almost every day, he didn't live with me. He lived with—was being fostered by—a newcomer to town. She'd been waiting when I brought the dog back. Not worried, exactly. She was too cool for that. But attentive, as I gave her the briefest rundown of our day. Not that strange signal—that strange scent—but the outline of what he had found. Of what we had seen. It was important for Spot that I do so. He'd had an unusual experience. If he acted out, if he had experienced more stress than I was aware of, I needed her to notice. To care for him, and to let me know.

As much as I disliked her, I figured she could handle it. Laurel Kroft—Dr. Laurel Kroft—was a therapist, a professional. Smart and city-trained, a shrink who saw the possibilities that service dogs had in our area, especially as the number of retirees began to boom. Maybe she was being generous, taking in an animal who would eventually go help someone else. I suspected more venal motives. Then again, she was also a honey blonde and had recently become chummy with a certain detective I knew.

"Jealousy is such a cruel emotion." I looked up to meet Wallis' eyes.

"Hey, you were the one talking about dogs just now." I had made sure that the good doctor knew that I had already spoken with Creighton. She didn't have to know that our interaction was barely civil. "I was only taking care of business," I said out loud.

"That's just..." She went back to licking. The one forepaw was going to be spotless. *"Common sense,"* she said, her voice full of fur. *"I wasn't talking about myself, anyway. When I'm..."* Lick. *"...discontent, I take action."* Another lick. *"Pounce, bite."* Here she stopped to sink her teeth into a mat. *"Done."*

"Good to know." I looked at the glass briefly before emptying it. "But not exactly useful." She knew what I was talking about. Creighton and I were good together. We had been for over a year now. But for so many reasons, I couldn't see myself committing to more than we had. A few nights a week. Some laughs. He was law and order. I...wasn't. Even if I could ever find a way to tell him about my special gift—that is, tell him and not have him back away before calling the funny farm—I wasn't sure if I could ever live within his rules. Hell, I had thought he liked it like that: no strings and a chance to visit on the wild side. I should have known that he was too conventional at heart.

"You act like it's a done deal." Wallis again, reading my thoughts. Before I could object, however, she pushed her point. *"He hasn't said anything yet, and he still keeps calling. You have to make your move, though. While there's still time."*

"Still time..." I thought about that. Dr. Laurel Kroft had only come to town two months ago. She can't be more than a year or two older than I was, but she'd done well for herself. Bought one of the nicer old houses and had it fixed up before moving in. She had taken some kind of administrative job with the new "retirement community" at the edge of town, but I'd heard she was thinking of opening a private practice as well. Who had I heard it from? Creighton, of course. He'd kept a close eye on the new development, partly because of some trouble we'd had with an assisted living place a few months before. I'd thought he was interested in the licensing, looking for potential trouble spots.

That was before I met our new shrink. I'd been just leaving the town shelter, when I'd caught it—not a scent, but a signal. Every animal in the place had just gone on alert, and I've learned enough over the years to take that seriously. I'd stepped into the foyer, looking around for the skulking or the furtive. Instead, on the other side of the glass enclosure where the police station lets out, I'd seen shearling, and the kind of creamy wool that costs more than an entire sheep.

"Thank you so much, Jim." The voice had been as expensive as the coat. Warm and as smoky as Scotch, it made her few extra years an advantage—the seduction of experience. "I look forward to it."

"My pleasure." That was what had raised the alert. Creighton, and he was definitely not using his business-as-usual voice. "I'll give you a call."

I'd stood in the doorway then, watching as she smiled and slowly sauntered away. Only when she'd gotten into her SUV—a Range Rover, naturally—did I turn toward my sometime-beau.

"What's that doing here?" No, it wasn't nice. Wasn't

smooth, either, but I'd been cleaning cages. Even when I wasn't, my hair never swung like that.

"Afternoon, Pru." Creighton didn't miss a beat, and I had to wonder if he'd seen me there. "Looks like you've been busy."

I am not often at a loss for words. I was then, though, and as he stepped back into his side of the building I found myself thinking.

Since then, I'd made a point of meeting the good doctor, director of therapeutic services for the LiveWell Community. I had already started working with the regional service-dog group, and I was looking for volunteers, people to foster likely animals. At the time, it had seemed a reasonable solution. Keep an eye on the problem. Get to know it. Befriend it, even. Now, as the spring thawed and Creighton's visits became as scarce as the snow, I wondered if I should have done something different.

"Huh," Wallis had very clear opinions. *"Like you'd want to be that kind of pampered house pet."*

"No, but…" I did enjoy Creighton. Enjoyed him as long as it could be on my terms.

"Well, do something then."

I stared into space. Considered more bourbon. "Like what?"

"Kill it." Wallis is first and foremost a predator, small but fierce. My mind jumped back to the impressions Wallis had shared earlier: the sharp snap at the neck. The quick shake. The piercing bite. *"Kill it before it grows into anything. That's what one does."*

I couldn't help it. I flashed back to the body. "You may be right, Wallis. You may be right."

FOUR

WHETHER HIS OFFICIAL duties or some other cause kept him away, I didn't know, but Creighton didn't stay the night. He'd only shown up after I'd fallen asleep on the sofa. He'd probably tasted the bourbon on my breath; he certainly knew my body rhythms. That might have been why we didn't talk as I led him upstairs, our union quick and practically soundless but no less satisfying for its economy. He slipped out sometime after, having waited till I drifted off in the wake of pleasure. I knew him well enough by then to suspect that he'd told himself his visit was medicinal, a means of comforting me after a rough day. I also knew him well enough to wonder if it meant good-bye.

The latter thought haunted me more than I'd have liked, and once the sky started to gray I became restless, though the image of that body kept creeping into my mind as well. In part, I blamed Wallis. She had joined me in the bed once Jim had left—a holdover from the coldest part of the year—and I knew the image fascinated her. The scalp half off, leaving the flesh raw underneath. That one eye.

"You've got a bloody mind." I was barely up to making coffee when she sauntered into the kitchen.

"And you're suddenly squeamish?" Tail coiled neatly around her feet, she sat waiting. I ignored her long enough to get the coffee started, before cracking open

the four eggs we'd share between us. *"Besides,"* she licked her chops as I sliced a healthy pat off the butter. That had been intended for the pan, but I put it on a saucer for her. *"You need something to occupy your mind."*

"I have a job." While the second pat melted, I salted the eggs. Wallis had trained me to hold off on the pepper until I had divvied up the portions, but the Tabasco was already on the table. "Several."

"Huh." She'd made quick work of the butter and looked up, appetite whetted for more. *"Dog walking— and more dog walking."*

"It isn't..." Why did I bother? Yes, my newest gig had me spending more time with canines than the motley assortment of animals I might usually help in my role as unofficial animal behaviorist of Beauville. It was also potentially steady work, and it got my main sponsor— Doc Sharpe, the local vet—off my back. And since the idea of writing a thesis had about as much appeal as scabies, I didn't seem any nearer to getting full accreditation, so this would have to do. I reached for her plate, sliding half the scramble onto it. "Hey, it keeps us fed. And it kept the heat on this winter."

"Barely." Despite her tone, I picked up the purr as she lapped up the eggs. My own I blasted with hot sauce, just because I could. Besides, I needed to wake up. I was already running late for my appointment with Growler, a butch little bichon I walked on weekdays. He didn't require much exercise, but he could be temperamental.

"At least that puffball has sense. Not that you bother to ask for his help."

I nearly coughed out my coffee. "Can you not do that?"

"Huh." She hadn't even looked up.

"Besides, what do I have to ask him about?" Growler was a smart little dog, a lot sharper and more mature than his harridan of an owner gave him credit for. He could be grudging with his insights, however, even with me—his one human ally. And particularly because of his sexual orientation, I couldn't see asking him for romantic advice.

"Jesus." Wallis looked up, licking her chops. She'd been picking up more human expressions from me, and the effect was disconcerting. *"What is with you today, Pru? I'm not talking about Creighton. I'm talking about that body. You know you're going to get involved."*

I didn't even answer, just pushed the rest of my uneaten eggs onto her plate. She sniffed at the Tabasco, but withheld comment as she carefully licked around it, and I went off to get dressed and start my day.

Twenty minutes later, I was trying not to inhale. The woman in front of me smelled of stale smoke on the best of days. Today, she seemed intent on breaking some kind of EPA record as she leaned in, malice in her eyes.

"Makes you wonder what the connection is, doesn't it?" It wasn't a question, not really. She squinted as she waited for my reaction, and I realized that unless I gave her one, I'd never get away. So I did.

"I don't think there is one, Mrs. Horlick." I fought off the urge to blink as she exhaled in my face. "I took Spot out for some exercise after an intensive afternoon of training. It was pure coincidence that he is being fostered by Dr. Kroft."

"Fostered, huh? And I thought she spent all her time with those rich people, looking out for what she can get." For a moment, she sounded like Wallis. Only Wallis would never let her neat tiger stripes become as shabby as old lady Horlick's housecoat. "Trying to make them as crazy as she is."

That was it. "Is Bitsy not up for his walk today?" I used Growler's human name, the belittling moniker his woman had bestowed on him, and kept my voice level. The first rule in training is not to reward bad behavior with a reaction. "Because without twenty-four-hour notice, I will still be charging you for the day."

"No, no. Hold your horses." She turned back into her dark hallway, leaving the door open for me to follow. I stepped up into the doorway, where I could reach the lead that hung on the coat rack, and waited. I value my lungs. "Come on, Bitsy."

I heard the scrabble of claws on a hard surface and one excited bark as she opened the door to the basement. The white dog bounded out to greet me, tiny tail wagging in spite of himself. I clipped on the lead and made eye contact with those black button eyes. One nod and we were in agreement.

"Sorry 'bout that." I let the little dog set the pace as we walked back to the sidewalk. Neither of us could get away quickly enough, but his legs had their limits.

"It's nothing," I said under my breath. I could feel Tracy Horlick's eyes on me.

"She's been bad lately." We turned onto the sidewalk. *"Worse, ever since—"*

"Don't you let him run all the way down the block." Tracy Horlick was yelling and waving her cigarette for emphasis. "I don't want him getting hurt."

"Not to worry." I forced a smile as I waved back. "I won't let him overexert."

"Huh." The white dog slowed his pace. He was get-

ting older; it was true. But I didn't have the heart to hold him back on his one real outing of the day. *"Old bitch."*

I waited. Growler—his chosen name fit him a lot better than the cutesy one Tracy Horlick had given him—would have his say on his own time.

"Hmmm... Gary's been out." The white dog stopped to sniff at a fence post. *"Sean, too."* I was curious as to what the bichon had been about to say about his person, but I didn't feel I could interrupt. When I wasn't around, she let him use the tiny, fenced backyard as a lavatory, which meant that our rounds together did not only constitute his only real exercise, they also had to fulfill all his social needs as well. As gruff as he was with me, I knew the little fellow liked me. Didn't matter. I wasn't a fellow dog.

"The old kidney trouble..." I tagged behind him as he moved onto a tree and then a hydrant. It seemed rude to interrupt. Instead, I let my mind wander. But as I found myself picturing my hunky local detective with that honey-blonde head on his shoulder, I caught myself. Better to wonder about the dead body—and its effect on my canine charge.

"So you want a consult, or what?" I looked down to see those button eyes staring up at me. I didn't know how long Growler had been trying to get my attention, but there was no use denying my interest.

"Yes, I do. About—" I stopped myself. The body. Spot. Laurel Kroft. Whatever was going on with Tracy Horlick. It all was of interest. "About anything."

He cocked his head, and I tried not to smile. Growler knows we humans think he's adorable. He hates that about us. I didn't know how successful I was, but I figured I'd get credit for trying.

"That big guy will be okay." I was right. *"He's got the imagination of a cat, but he's solid. I can smell it on you. He'll file all that information and someday he'll get to use it."*

I bit back my own response to that. Spot would have other opportunities with bodies? Should I be looking into corpse-retrieval programs?

"Don't need to. All the same skills." The response came even though I hadn't voiced the question aloud. I had to remember how transparent I was.

"You said it." The bichon had moved on, and I was following him as he trotted, more slowly now, down the sidewalk. The movement didn't seem to impair his reception in any way. *"What got him was the panic. The—how would you say it?—the desperation."*

I didn't want to think of that body as anything but a puzzle, but Growler's observation made me. Panic. Desperation. I sure didn't want to see that still, torn flesh as a person. Now it hit me, hard. That poor woman.

"No!" Growler's response was as loud in my head as a bark. The lead had gone tight, and I realized that Growler had stopped in his tracks. I'd stepped past him. *"Not her,"* he said again, looking up at me with obvious frustration.

"Sorry." I halted. Desperation…that could cover a lot of things. A lot of people. "You don't mean me, do you?" I didn't like to think of myself that way. Certainly not about men, about Creighton.

Growler seemed to consider his point made. *"Clueless,"* he muttered, doggie style, but he started walking again.

"Okay, so she was scared. I get that." I didn't know if I had that right. Growler wasn't helping. A sniff, almost a growl, was all he gave me, so I kept talking. "Do you have any ideas about that body?"

"She's pissed off because she lost him." I started to object, when Growler barked. One short, sharp yelp. *"Not you, walker lady. Focus!"*

"Sorry." So this was about Tracy Horlick. "Whom did she lose?"

"Whom, ha!" Another little bark. I thought perhaps Growler was getting tired but squelched the thought as quickly as it appeared. The bichon did not like being patronized. *"Next block."* He'd heard me anyway. I silently voiced an apology. *"Old sharpie."*

"Excuse me?" I would imagine Growler would have appreciated company. But maybe he was more competitive than I'd thought. "A shar-pei?

"No! Pay attention, walker lady." A little snort and a shuffle. He was getting tired. *"A sharpie—Mr. Sharpie, that's what she calls him, you know, in her mind."*

Now we were getting somewhere. "What happened?" I'd never known Tracy Horlick to have any kind of intimate relationship, though she must have a source for her gossip. From her lacquered hair and those constant smokes, I'd assumed that Beauville's old-style beauty parlor and maybe the convenience store were it.

"He wasn't there for games."

"Games?" I was beginning to see the appeal of gossip.

"Huh." The bichon was nearly panting. Well, if I had to, I'd carry him back. *"Just try it."* I looked down in time to catch his glance. *"Old Sharpie wasn't there for her. He's gone now."*

I let that one sink in as we reached the corner and Growler paused, panting. In general, I trusted the bichon's take on the world—ours as well as his—but I also knew he had a particularly grim view both of heterosexual relationships and, more deservedly, of his person, Tracy Horlick.

"Was he old?" I asked finally, once the little dog had turned and started walking back. "Sick?" Any smoking buddy of Tracy Horlick's was a good candidate for a coronary.

But now that we were on our way back, Growler was saving his flagging energy for his own pursuits. I got images of a retriever, a beagle, and—strangely—a large and well-endowed opossum in rapid succession as he trotted, nose to the ground to pick up the various scents. Another short bark let me know I wasn't supposed to have seen that last one, and a final stop to water an ailing rhododendron.

"I didn't say he was dead, walker lady." The bichon was growing testy. Some of that might have been fatigue. *"He's too wily to fall for that. More fox than bird."* He paused. We'd returned to the corner by the Horlick house. I could feel him gathering his resources and felt my heart go out to him. No matter how tough he might style himself, Growler was still a little dog at the mercy of a bitter old human.

"We all have our leash and collars." I nodded in silent agreement. *"What you've got to ask yourself is how much would be too much. And how far...?"* He was panting. *"How far could jealousy push you?"*

FIVE

IT WAS A good question, and one I made myself ponder as I drove back into what passes for the heart of our town. Growler might have been talking about Tracy Horlick, and I had to confess, I was getting a vicarious thrill from the idea that the old bag both had an admirer of some kind—and that she had lost him. Then again, the little dog could have said the same about me. Not only did he bear no love for women in general, his own liaisons had been, of necessity, brief, temporary, and all-too-often unconsummated, a sacrifice to the so-called domesticity he was trapped in. If sometimes he got a little catty, so to speak, I could understand it.

However, I couldn't help but wonder if Growler had been trying to communicate something else, something about the body in the woods. Animals, as I've said, aren't sentimental, and there was no reason for Growler to focus in on the woman that piece of carnage had once been. But he had—at least, I thought he had—given me a distinct impression of panic, of a desperation that probably transcended even his rudest attempts at describing my romantic plight.

This was good because Spot had been unusually silent, even for him. Service dogs, I'd discovered, tended to be uncommunicative. The dedication and focus that allows a creature to bury his individual identity in the role of helping another, particularly one of a different species, didn't make for a chatty animal. And the excitement of the day—the walk in the woods, the discovery, and then the opportunity to use his dog-given skills to find the body a second time—had occupied his entire consciousness. At least, that part I could access. If there had been more the bigger dog might have picked up, I wasn't getting it. I suspected there was, though. Not just about the body itself, but about the circumstances that had left that poor woman there. Had Spot been trying to protect me, letting me share that sense of something wild, something truly dangerous, but no more? Had he been trying to shield me from the fear that Growler had picked up? The utter terror?

I simply didn't know. There was so much those more acute animal senses could have told me. Maybe he had been sharing the scent of another animal, a scavenger who might have found her before we did. The lingering aroma of any drug or other intoxicant that might have led a woman off, alone, into the forest. Even—Growler's words came back to me—the presence of another. Someone who had taken the woman in love or in rage, and left her, broken, in the wilderness.

No, for that kind of information, I'd need a more communicative beast. Barring that, I'd have to settle for Creighton.

Jim's unmarked cruiser was in its usual spot when I arrived, and I took a moment to do some uncustomary preening in my rearview mirror. Unlike Dr. Kroft, my hair is neither smooth nor orderly and instead falls in a cascade of rowdy black curls when I don't have it tied back for work. I freed it now, running my fingers through it to loosen those curls and let the spring dampness plump them up. That's about all I could manage, in a car. It had been enough in the past.

"Hey, Pru." I hadn't even made it to the front door when Albert hailed me. As portly as a hibernating bear, and just as shaggy, the Beauville animal-control officer barreled across the parking lot, one hand holding either his belly or some other precious thing inside his down parka.

"Albert." I nodded, brushing one unruly lock from my eyes. "You've got something there?"

"What? Oh, yeah." He fumbled with the snaps of his vest. "Bandit—uh, Frank."

I had to smile. Albert kept company with a ferret. You can guess which was the brains of the operation. And maybe, for me, useful.

"Hey, Frank." I kept my voice low, reaching out with my thoughts to the small mustelid I could now sense, curled inside the grimy vest.

"Cold." His sleepy voice reached me.

"You better take him inside." I looked up at Albert, trying to skim over the part of him covered with beard and duct tape. "I'll be by in a bit."

"Ok, uh, Pru?" I turned back. "Could I get a consult about something?"

I raised my eyebrows. "Consult" implied payment. "A job?"

He shrugged. "It would be for the town. So, maybe."

That could be promising, so I rewarded him with a smile and watched the color flood the chapped skin above his beard. "Cool," I said, and watched the heat go up to his receding hairline. Head down, he shuffled off to the right.

I waited, before following him into the glassed-in

entranceway that the shelter and our local cop shop shared. As he headed toward his desk—and passed it for the kitchenette beyond—I reached for the left-hand door. It would have been nice to consult with Frank before I bearded this particular dog, but I'd been fighting my own battles long enough to know I could do this.

"Sandra." The officer at the desk smiled in acknowledgment. She knew enough to let me walk past.

"Just a minute there." She also knew who her boss was. I was halfway to Creighton's private office when I heard his voice behind me. I turned in time to see Sandra throw herself into some paperwork. Creighton, standing beside her desk, must have been in one of the small side offices used to interview guests, both willing and not. He was out now, and staring at me.

"Jim." I smiled. It's not hard to smile at him, especially when he's glowering. "May we talk? In private?"

Sandra bent lower over her papers at those last two words, and Creighton squinted at me. There was nothing to see except my smile, however, and so I led the way into the back hallway and the small private office with his name on the door.

"Have a seat," he said, redundantly. I had already tilted the guest chair back. In deference to his mood, I refrained from putting my boots up on his desk. "So," he said when he'd taken his own chair, "to what do I owe the honor of this visit?"

"Jim, really?" I'm not good at playing innocent, but I raised my eyebrows in the attempt. "We didn't really get a chance to talk about her last night." I paused, it was a cheap attempt, though, and he didn't fall for it. "The woman in the woods?"

He nodded. "You want info."

"I am involved." I floundered for a moment, trying to come up with a more compelling explanation than sheer curiosity. "I was working with a dog—with Laurel Kroft's dog—and I was getting some very strange signals from him." Nothing, so I kept going. "Anything you can tell me might help."

"The dog has a good nose." He was watching me, looking to see if I'd give him more.

"He does, but he's being trained to pick up more than scent. To pick up signals, human signals." That was as far as I dared to go. Creighton knows me pretty well by now. In fact, if he weren't so damned rational, he'd probably have figured out my little secret.

"Well, she wasn't giving out any." He reached for a folder on his desk. "Not anymore."

"Come on, Jim. Give me something." I leaned in. Usually that has the desired effect. He didn't even look up. "Who was she?"

He shook his head, though whether that was supposed to indicate that he didn't know or that he wouldn't tell me, I couldn't tell. "Sorry, Pru."

"Okay, then. How did she die?"

Now he looked up, smiling. "And you call yourself the animal expert?"

I sat back, confused.

"The victim was mauled, Pru. The top of her head was nearly torn off before something opened her throat and she bled out."

"Couldn't be a bear." I was thinking out loud. "I mean, there might be some mothers and cubs out there, but black bears are usually all bluster. Though a young male, coming out of dormancy…"

He was shaking his head. "It wasn't a bear. It was

something smaller, and the claw marks aren't right. The ME's doing some tests, but his first hypothesis was a mountain lion attack."

"We don't have—" I stopped myself. We don't, but we could. "There's been no evidence of cougars returning here."

He didn't respond and instead watched me, waiting. Whatever he had expected, it wasn't that. There was something else. Something wasn't making sense. I put my hand to my head and heard Creighton chuckle. But the gesture wasn't about my hair—or even about flirting with him. I was trying to remember, to recall something I'd gotten. From Spot? No. It was what I'd seen. "She was wearing slacks. A nice shirt. What had been a nice shirt." I remembered silk. A pattern, dark green and gold. "That's not hiking gear. That's not—"

I looked up at him, serious, finally. No thoughts of flirtation in my mind. "What was she doing in the woods?"

"A better question would be, how did she get there?" He was definitely examining me, watching my face for…something.

I was lost in my own thoughts. It had been a hard winter, one of the worst in years. Everything out there was hungry, and a woman alone…

As much as I didn't like the idea, it could have been a bear. That was more likely than what he was calling a mountain lion. Mountain lions—cougars, our native American panthers—are solo hunters, rarely seen in the wild. And although the tawny cats—*puma concolor*— might once have been common, they had been run out of most of the Northeast by hunters and developers. By a more dangerous predator: humans. There was even some debate about whether or not there were any native animals left in New England. The last confirmed cougar in Massachusetts—confirmed as in shot dead and identified—was over a hundred years ago.

There had been a sighting in the late '90s, though, and cougars were known to migrate: an animal that was eventually traced back to Western stock had met its end on a Connecticut highway a few years back. So it was possible…but not likely. He—or she—would have left traces. Scat. Claw raking on trees, like so many scratch marks on a sofa. Of course, if nobody had been looking for a big cat, those signs might have been ignored. They wouldn't be now. Cats, big or small, are creatures of habit, which meant that once located, they are easy to find. If there were a cougar out there, he or she wouldn't last long. There'd be traps. A hunting party. It was inevitable, not that it was fair. Beauville, like so many tourist areas, was in the middle of a building boom. We invade their space; we become prey. It would be a tragedy, and not just for one lone woman.

Creighton wasn't having any of it. He was shaking his head. "Pru, you're slipping." There was a note in his voice I didn't know. He was mocking me. "Yes, the ME says the wounds are consistent with an animal mauling, but as you were clearly about to point out to me, we haven't had any reports of mountain lion attacks for as long as I've been on the job. I don't know what happened to her, Pru, but I don't think she was killed in the woods at all. Didn't you notice? She wasn't even wearing a coat."

SIX

"THAT DOESN'T MEAN what you think it does." The words slipped out. I could sense Creighton sit up, but I couldn't stop myself. I was imagining those woods, that hunger.

"Maybe she had a fight, and decided to walk home from some lover's lane. Maybe someone pushed her out of a car. At night, lost in those woods." I'd had a bad night out in the woods not that long ago. I knew how scary it could be, and how deadly. "Maybe she died of exposure, and some animal came upon her." I looked up. "You've had the full autopsy?"

He shook his head. "I won't hear till later, but you're missing the obvious. She didn't die there. Didn't you notice the lack of blood?"

I shook my head. I hadn't. Then again, she'd been lying on a thick bed of leaves.

"Some animals drag their prey." Bears did, I knew. Did cougars? I was trying to recall everything I'd ever read about the big cats. "To cache it, to save it for a later meal." I swallowed, my mouth suddenly dry. That meal had once been a woman. "Maybe Spot and I interrupted something. Did you look for drag marks?"

He shrugged, and I remembered: the thaw had been brought about by three days of heavy rain.

"How long has she been…" I paused to swallow. "Out there? You're sure the blood didn't just get washed away?"

He nodded. "Look, Pru, I probably shouldn't have told you what I did. But it seemed you needed to know. For, ah…closure."

"Closure?" Now it was my turn to fix him with a gimlet eye. "Closure, Jim?"

He had the decency to flush, ever so slightly. It made him look younger, more vulnerable. It didn't make my next question any easier.

"You've been spending time with our new shrink, haven't you?"

He looked up. I met his eyes. I didn't like this, and I wasn't a masochist. What I am is a realist, and this was the tear-the-Band-Aid-off moment. Trouble was, he didn't say anything.

"Never mind." He didn't have to. That flush said it all. "Look, it's been fun. But you've got a case to solve. I've got a dog to train. And, hey, she's a nice lady." I couldn't help the extra emphasis that crept into those last two words. She was, and neither trait would ever be applied to me.

I turned to walk out, willing my heart to be still as I heard him say my name.

"Wait… Pru?"

I set my jaw. Turned.

"I am going to need to talk with you again." He had the grace to look a little embarrassed as he clarified that. "To get your statement about exactly what happened, how you found her. When." He smiled a little. "Maybe you can tell me what the dog said, too."

I let the door slam as I wheeled out.

"No reason to panic." The voice sounded right beside my ear. Without thinking, I wheeled around. *"Not here."*

And caught myself. I'd made it to the foyer, where I could see into the animal shelter. Albert was slumped over his desk, but Frank was standing on his hind feet, staring at me. Even from here, I could see his nose twitch as he sniffed the air.

"Hey, Frank." I didn't know if he could hear me, but, as I reached for the door, I figured it was not only polite to greet him, but also politic. Creighton might not want to give me much information. I may as well hit up the building's one other intelligent male.

"Oh, he's not that bad." Frank sank down to all fours as I approached, nose still actively reading the air. *"He's—how do you say it?—trainable."*

I caught myself from laughing out loud. Albert, it seemed, was asleep, the combination of his beard and his belly making a comfortable pillow for his shaggy head. Was Frank picking up lingo from me? Or was the idea of a pet just that universal?

"Pet?" The button eyes looked up into mine, and for a moment I was flustered. Then I got it: Albert might have some annoying habits, but he fed Frank regularly, gave him treats and toys to play with, and kept him safe from larger predators. We humans may not always be the ideal caregivers, but for many of our companion animals, the deal was a good one.

"Not all are good."

I nodded. Frank had a point, as I knew well. But as I silently agreed, he brought his tiny, agile front paws together at my response and stood up again, bouncing from paw to paw. I didn't need that little dance—a ferret sign of distress or agitation—to get Frank's point. The snoozing man behind the desk was an obvious object lesson.

CLEA SIMON 41

"Hey. Some of us just aren't meant for domestication."

He hopped again, still agitated, and Albert stirred. Well, I'd do what I could for the little fellow. Besides, I'd said I'd drop by. I dragged a chair over toward the desk, letting the grating sound of the legs on linoleum startle Albert into full consciousness.

"Bacon!" He sat up with a start. "Oh, it's you."

I smiled. "Pleasant dream?"

"I was—I was planning my shopping list." Albert reached for a pencil and jotted a note. "Didn't see you."

I let it lay. "You said you wanted to speak with me?" I had questions of my own, but if I were lucky, his would negate any need to ask.

"Uh, yeah." I saw him spell out the word "eggs." It took a little effort. "You're working with that special dog program now, right?"

"Yeah." This wasn't what I'd expected, but I waited. I didn't think the regional service-dog association would have any use for Albert, but I was curious.

"You think they might, you know, have a dog for me?"

I felt my eyebrows go up. Albert is not the sharpest tool in the woodshed. Nor the most attractive. He does not have any obvious impairments, however, beyond his personality. And as his presence behind that desk made clear, someone had judged him fit for full-time employment. Granted, Albert was more old school dog catcher than modern animal-control officer, but he served a purpose.

"What are you thinking about, Albert?" Maybe he had a health issue. Considering his diet and apparent disdain for exercise, it was possible.

"I was thinking it would be useful to have a dog who could, you know, help with my duties."

"Your duties?" Albert's mandate entailed rounding up unwanted or nuisance animals. After that, I was the one who usually dealt with them—either relocating them, as I had a troublesome raccoon a few months ago, or finding some other way to repair the ruptured human-animal bond. The unloved pets, they were harder to deal with—largely because of the people involved—though Doc Sharpe and I did what we could, which usually meant working to place them in better homes.

"Yeah, you know. If there's a wild animal I have to take care of." He was doodling now, and Frank was eyeing the pencil eraser with a covetous glance. "Like, something I have to track in the woods."

"You want a hunting dog, Albert. Not a service dog." This was my opening. "But what kind of animal are you talking about? Has someone said something to you?"

He shrugged, but kept hold of the pencil. I didn't think Creighton would confide in this shaggy bear of a man. For better or worse, though, Albert was part of Beauville's bureaucracy. Not even my alpha dog lawman could keep him entirely out of the loop.

"I heard some of the guys talking, over at Happy's last night." Of course. Creighton might not hang at our local dive—for at least the part of the night he'd been with me—but some of the crew he'd brought out yesterday did. "Heard there's something out there. A mankiller."

"Woman-killer is more likely." The words slipped out before I'd thought them through, but when Albert looked up—startled—I realized I might as well take advantage of the moment. "Those guys get any kind of ID off her?"

I tried to sound nonchalant. Not like I'd just asked the same question of Creighton. I got the same answer: a shake of the head. Considering that it was Albert I was dealing with, I was willing to believe he honestly didn't know.

"Kind of funny, isn't it?" I didn't want Albert to see my frustration, so I kept talking—and held out another pencil for Frank to play with. Not that I wouldn't sympathize, but it wouldn't help matters if the little beast gave up and bit Albert in frustration. "I haven't seen any wildlife reports of a nuisance animal, have you?" Officially, the state reports are available to all animal welfare professionals. In reality, I have no standing— and no means of getting access to them.

"Of a mountain lion or whatever it is? Nuh-uh." He shook his head vigorously. "That's what's so spooky. No warning, just…whoosh…like a ghost in the night. Like those lions in Africa? The mankillers? They get a taste for human flesh, you know."

"We don't know that's what happened." Now it was my turn to fight frustration. "Very few animals kill humans by choice." It had been a while since I'd studied the big cats, but basic animal behavior is pretty much the same the world over. "We've pushed into their territory. We're the intruders. But—"

I stopped, unsure of how much I wanted to share with the shaggy man before me.

"We don't even know if that girl was killed by a mountain lion, Albert." I didn't tell him she'd been moved. Or that Creighton wouldn't have been so curious if the death was a simple case of person-meets-panther.

He was shaking his head. "Deputy Johnson said she was, for sure," he said. "Joe Carnovy did, too." He looked up at me. "They had to look for evidence around the body, you know, before the medics took her away? They said it was pretty obvious. She had claw marks all down her front, like from an angry cat. Joe said she looked like this." He faked a rictus. It wasn't attractive. "Like it was really bad."

"Great." Whether or not this was true, it wouldn't make my job any easier. I'm for moving nuisance animals, not killing them, and I had the law behind me. Cougars were protected. However, a lot of contingencies would allow for an animal to be destroyed. If there were a public outcry, the best I could hope for was that the damned cat had moved on.

"Watch out!" Distracted, I'd quit wiggling the pencil, and Frank had grabbed it. I smiled and pulled on it slightly, the better to give him a bit of a tussle. *"This isn't a game."* Those agile paws clasped the pink rubber of the eraser and his teeth bit down. But the dark button eyes remained on mine. *"And big cats aren't the only killers out there."*

SEVEN

MAYBE IT DIDN'T matter who she was. The woman in the silk shirt was still dead. Now that she'd been moved from the preservation land to a hospital morgue, someone would identify her. Make the necessary preparations for her. Mourn her.

I'd done my part, or Spot had. It was time for me to get back to work. Of course, those two things weren't mutually exclusive. Especially, I thought as I eased my baby-blue GTO out of the parking lot, if one pursuit helped further another.

Service dogs are new to me and that made the job more interesting. The training itself is pretty basic, in that it involves accenting—and cementing, in a way—the basic role of the domestic canine. Dogs tend to be human-centered; we've bred them that way and, as Wallis would be quick to point out, they've accepted that. It's what they want now, believe me. Most times I get called in to help with a "problem" pup it's not that he's consciously misbehaving. It's that he can't figure out what his person expects of him. He's getting mixed signals, often positive feedback for negative behavior. Or, less often, he's bored. A dog, unlike a cat, needs a job.

So basically what I'm doing is an extension of regular dog training. I'm teaching the animal to recognize and respond to the slightest clue: The small gesture that a wheelchair-bound person may be able to make with one finger. The hesitation a blind owner may feel approaching a street corner. On the flip side, I'm also teaching the animal to tune out any outside influence. Squirrel? Doesn't matter. Cat? Forget it. Even the friendly advances of well-meaning bystanders should not be acknowledged by a well-trained service animal. The dog must become an extension of his person—his eyes, his legs. At times, his physical representative in the world. People with disabilities might as well be invisible, I was learning. A large dog, though? When one of those pushes against you, you make way for the human who follows.

What was new for me was the extent of it—the total immersion. Some of that is because of my so-called gift. When you can hear what another creature is thinking—sense its needs, its fears and desires—then you care less about wanting to inflict your will on that creature. I mean, it's just too much fun knowing *why* Fluffy is scratching at that one chair. Of course, that's partly me. I've never been what you might call leash-trained, so I've never felt a particularly strong drive to inflict that discipline on others. But with service dogs, total obedience is a must. And the dogs who are best at it are the ones who *want* to lose themselves in their person. No wonder Wallis scoffed at the whole idea. Then again, it paid. More to the point, it kept Doc Sharpe from fussing too much about me, and that meant I had a little more freedom.

Not that all collars are visible, I reminded myself as I turned onto one of Beauville's nicer streets. Laurel Kroft lived here, her renovated Victorian a direct reflection of what my tumbledown old house could be, if I ever had the money to fix it up. I'd only been inside the first floor of her home, but I recognized the care and labor that went into refinishing those old, wide-board floors. I wondered, of course, how much nicer the rooms upstairs were. But as I pulled into her neatly paved driveway I tried to block the images that came to mind. I didn't want to be tied down, and that meant giving up the right to tie down anyone else. But, hey, like dogs, some men want the leash. Nothing I could do about that. In that way, I was like my father, who had taught me more about playing cards than he did about familial responsibility. Before he took off, that is—leaving me to bear the brunt of my mother's resentment.

We were simply different types of animal, my mother and me. And there were a lot more like her in the world, I thought, as I pulled up in front of the glossy green door. Laurel Kroft opened it and stepped out as I emerged from my car, giving me one more reason to be grateful for my poker face.

"Hello, Pru." Whatever kind of animal she was, her coat was sure sleek, and her long, lean legs spoke of breeding, as well as the gym. "I'm glad you're here."

"Oh?" I tried to keep my voice light. I was here because I had a contract to work with the dog, not as any special favor to her. She needed to understand that, and I needed to understand what was bothering her.

"It's probably nothing." She tossed her hair, shedding any trouble that would dare cling to those dark blonde tresses. "A little stress."

"Is Spot acting out?" I'd get more from the dog himself about what was bothering him. I didn't often get an entrée into the woman, though. "Would you like to talk?"

"I don't really have time right now. I'm scheduled for

a session." She retreated back inside the house, and I followed into a glorified foyer painted the kind of dark green you see in magazines. She was as tall as I am, which is rare. Her height all in those legs.

"A session?" I was imagining a designer. Maybe a colorist. All those city affectations were making their way back here.

"At LiveWell." Her tone said she'd guessed my thoughts. "I run socialization workshops aimed at keeping the residents integrated into the larger community. It's quite rewarding. In fact, I have been trying to engage Spot's..." She hesitated, and I wondered which word she'd chose. "Spot's charge." That was good. Neutral. It meant she felt some reluctance about giving the dog up. It meant she was capable of bonding, which had both good and bad points.

"It's too easy for those with disabilities to become isolated," she said as I followed her into the living room, waiting while she rummaged through a drawer. "Perhaps especially those who have other resources."

Rich people, I translated. Because, of course, those were the ones who could afford her services.

"Richard Haigen undoubtedly has friends." I tried to keep my voice neutral as she pulled out a small box—it looked like a deck of cards—and put them in her bag.

"Oh, I know." We were playing one-up on each other. "In fact, I believe I've engaged at least one of them for our session today."

She won, if ingratiating herself into Beauville's elite was winning.

"This will be important for Spot, too." She must have seen something on my face. "With a happier, healthier person, he'll be a happier dog, won't he?" She didn't pause for an answer. "I want him to go to a good home, you see."

I did, though I wasn't sure why this was her concern. "People underestimate service animals," she went on. "They see a dog and think, 'oh, it's a pet.' They see a cat and they think…"

She gave a dismissive wave of one manicured hand, and I bit my tongue. This was all new to her, and she was an enthusiast. That wasn't a bad thing, really, but I was beginning to tune her out when what she said next made me focus. "People underestimate the range of a living creature," she was saying, and I turned to look at her. She couldn't know, could she? Laurel Kroft was an intelligent woman. She'd observed me working with Spot. And she was spending time with Jim Creighton. I didn't know what he knew—or what he suspected. And I didn't think he'd betray me. But people let things slip. Especially in moments of intimacy.

I felt my eyes narrowing, and could imagine how Wallis would respond, the fur along her spine beginning to rise. Maybe Laurel sensed it too, because she then went off on a tangent, nattering on about money or something. "What these animals do is priceless, and if I'm ever in a position to really help them, that's what I'd do."

Maybe she'd been talking about making a donation all along. Bully for her. I had work to do. "Shall we?" I wanted her to do the signaling, for several reasons.

She had turned from me, though, so I couldn't see her face. "Spot." She cast her voice low, but fairly loud. "Come." I heard the clicking of nails on the hardwood floor, and resisted the urge to kneel down to greet the dog. "Leash."

"Very good." I was watching her, but I wasn't thinking simply of the commands. Spot was going to have to learn to obey whoever was in charge, and that meant people who didn't have any special connection. What I was hoping for, as the dog approached, was some insight into the woman before me. She seemed off-balance, for her, and I was still waiting for an explanation.

"He was restless last night." She said finally, after clipping on the leash and handing it to me. "Whining in his sleep and kicking. I think he was having nightmares."

"You let him sleep with you?" This was information. I tried to separate it from thoughts of Creighton, and how he'd fit in bed with the hundred-pound dog. I'm good at keeping my face blank. I know I am. But Laurel Kroft wasn't one of the barflies at Happy's, and she was trained to read people like I did animals. I thought I saw a smile, but I couldn't be sure as she reached once more for the door.

"Sometimes," she said. And that was all.

EIGHT

"GREAT." I LET Spot into my car and hit the gas, a little harder than was probably wise. Often, I begin a session with Spot at his home. Today, I couldn't wait to get gone, and since the pretty shrink was heading out, too, it was easy enough to act like today's regimen had to involve the great outdoors. I'd focused on the dog, so I couldn't tell if Laurel was smirking. I really didn't want to know.

"Where to?" I turned toward Spot, wanting to clear my head. Wanting to make contact. I honestly did have a job to do, and once again I was reminded of why I prefer animals. They're direct. Honest. If they have an agenda, they let you know right away. Even if that involves eating you for lunch. Once they pounce, they don't try to make small talk.

Spot turned toward me, his big ears pricking, and I realized that he was catching some of this. Maybe all of it. Like the other service animals I'd met, he was so focused, I sometimes forgot how smart he was. How aware of his surroundings, and those included me.

"What?" I couldn't help smiling at those big, dark eyes. His tail thumped on my leather seat. "Aren't you ever territorial?"

At that, he turned and pressed his nose to the window, and I sensed a moment of regret. No, he couldn't be, could he? Not with what I was training him for. He

was a working animal, born for it. But was this asking too much?

"What you said." The voice was quiet, but I heard it.
Spot was staring out the window as the thought came
to me. *"Not the scent, not the..."* I got that feeling of
frustration again, like tugging on a leash to go another
way. *"Listen."*

That's what I got for anthropomorphizing. Spot was
reminding me of what I already knew. I was the one
who wanted freedom. He'd be happier as a service dog
than a lone wolf. Or—I couldn't help a bitter smile—
as someone's pampered pet.

Blocking the thought of Laurel Kroft and her glossy
grooming, I homed in on what she and I had planned.
Spot was almost ready to be tried out. Two weeks ago,
Laurel had told me about a potential client: one Richard
Haigen. Haigen wasn't that old, she'd explained, but he
had severe macular degeneration that hadn't responded
to treatment. He'd be blind within the year.

I'd gone to meet him after that, to get a feel for where
he was—and what Spot would need to do. I hadn't
known Haigen before. He was one of the new crowd:
moneymakers who move here once they've sucked their
native playground dry. They're predators, same as any
raptor, and I don't blame them for past crimes. Besides,
the estate—there was no other word for it—might have
become a housing development otherwise, situated as it
was on a gentle hill abutting the state preservation land.
This way, the big old farm had been preserved, more
or less, the open land turned into landscaped gardens.

The first time I'd visited, I'd felt bad for Haigen, despite an introduction that bordered on hostile. I knew
the type, from my city days. Tall, broad rather than fat,

and with a booming voice that demanded to be heard, he was a former master of the universe now exiting the known galaxy. His coke-bottle glasses were the obvious indicator of his changing status, despite boxy frames just a little too hip for his jowled face. Whatever crimes he'd left behind, he was trying for a new start: country gentleman in a bucolic setting refurbished with all the mod cons. That faded as I watched him barking at a wife, who clearly was in over her head, and grumbling at the pretty maid when she startled him with a tray.

He had a lot to hold together, and I'd bet his command had ranged over significantly larger turf back in town. But the two women he'd growled at? Not their fault, and since both were considerably younger, I guessed he'd chosen them for reasons other than their efficiency. And he wasn't that miserable. I didn't see any staff, none of the usual factotums you'd expect around the rich and powerful. But he'd had a buddy with him when I'd visited, a superannuated good old boy who'd probably served as his wingman back in the day. Nick, I thought he'd called him. Nick Draper. "Here's Nicky," he'd said, propelling him toward me with a wave. Like I might find the dark-haired lunk more attractive with a boyish name. I didn't, and I worried for that little maid, but I was glad the man had a friend.

At least Haigen had perked up when I started talking about Spot. Partly, I figured, that was because he needed a project. Partly, I hoped, it was because he liked animals. That could have been wishful thinking; I wanted the best for Spot, if not this rich guy. Still, getting him used to working with a service dog would be good training for both of them, not that it would soften the blow as his world went dark.

"Caught in a box..." It was a wisp of a thought, accompanied by a faint scent of trees and leaf mold. Too faint. I cranked down the window a crack. I'd been driving aimlessly, enjoying the ride. For Spot, however, the enclosed car must have been dull as—well, a dog could find something of interest even in the plainest dirt. The air that came streaming in was cold, frosty even. But the thaw had held, and the air had to be rich with information and intrigue for an animal like Spot. Sight was the least of it.

"You must think we're so limited." I knew Wallis did. "But because of that, your new person will need you."

That's when it hit me. All the answers I couldn't get from Creighton, maybe I could get from Spot, now that he was making the effort, communicating with me telepathically in phrases I could understand. It was a rare opportunity, and even as I warned myself that this kind of communication tended to be limited—even as I reminded myself that I had to be careful against misinterpreting, against *over*interpreting the canine's half-phrased thoughts—I made my decision. I had to try. I hung a hard left and headed toward the highway.

Spot's ears pricked up as we cruised along the edge of the preservation land. And when I pulled into the service road we'd driven up the day before, I could feel his other senses on alert. Yes, he was all dog, made to work. But revisiting a trail like this one had to be a challenge.

Unless... I paused. What with the tension between me and Dr. Laurel, I'd never followed up on what she'd said about Spot. Dream chases and nighttime whimpering could be a sign of distress. They could also signal involvement, unfinished business—much as human dreams may. As we pulled into the parking area, I reached out to place one hand on Spot's broad back.

"Is this okay?" I wasn't sure how to translate my concern, and hoped that the physical contact would help. "Is it too much?"

"Out!" He didn't pull away exactly, but even without any special connection I would have been able to tell what he wanted. I walked around the front of the car and opened the passenger side, taking the lead in my hand.

"Heel." I was being paid for this, I might as well do it. Besides, I needed to exert some control over what happened.

Spot's training was good, and he waited, body still. His mind was racing, though, shooting off a rapid-fire series of images, chronicling the woods and its inhabitants. After about forty-five seconds, I gave him the go-ahead signal and he started toward the woods, pausing at the edge of the pavement for one backward glance.

"Follow?"

"Yes," I said, not knowing if I had agreed to tag along or if he was asking permission to seek out that rich, strange scent once again. "Follow."

With that he was off, and even as I let out the lead, I had to trot to keep up. All around us, I could hear the sounds of the awakening woods—a litany of chirps and chatter that fell into muted silence as Spot and I approached. Spring was coming, after another hard winter, and everyone was ready to get down to business. To eat, to find a mate. To do what one could before some terrible jaws came clamping down.

"Wait!" It was a command, so clear I stopped short without thinking. Spot, about twenty feet ahead of me, was frozen.

"What is it?" I didn't dare speak the words out loud, but my question must have been clear.

"Careful..." I saw his black nose twitch, but I relaxed. It takes a discerning creature like Wallis—who knows me well—to separate out the signals I'm sending from the ones she—or he—wants me to hear. Spot had picked up that I was listening to the birds and squirrels, and these had been startled by our arrival. He was echoing back. Interpreting. Nothing more.

Either he got that too, or he reached the conclusion by himself, because he started on again, going a little more slowly as we went deeper into the woods. The silence was almost complete here; the deep leaf cover, damp and soft, muting any sounds our feet would make. Even some of the larger animals—I got a sense of a possum and at least three nesting raccoons—seemed to be holding their breath. It was a little too much for one human and one good-sized dog to have provoked, and I felt the hairs along the back of my neck go up.

"Spot?" I voiced the question this time, even though my mouth had gone dry. "What is it, Spot?"

How could I have been so careless? We weren't the largest predator in these woods. Creighton might have his doubts, but something had savaged that woman.

Spot had stopped, and I came up to him. Better that we should stay close together: one big creature instead of two smaller ones. Me standing and tall with Spot by my side made a less appealing target for a hungry predator.

"Gone." The one word had me breathing again. Of course, he had never forgotten what we were dealing with here. *"This way."*

I let him lead me a few hundred feet farther, and then

waited as he sniffed some leaves. They could have been the ones cradling the body we'd found. To be honest, with the changing light and the sameness of the brown leaf bed, I wouldn't vouch for it.

"She was here?" I reached tentatively for Spot's head. I wanted the contact, but I also didn't want to kneel down, to make myself look lower or smaller, just in case he was wrong.

"Here, I found her." Of course, the scent remained. The body, however, had been removed only after we'd gone.

With that confirmation, it was easier to see the signs of Creighton and his crew. Some of the leaves seemed to have been raked; they were probably taken for further analysis. One of the trees seemed to have had some bark scraped away, although whether that was done intentionally by the cops or by some photographer backing into a damp oak was anyone's guess. But while Creighton's people would have taken anything that a human would consider a clue, I had another tool at my disposal. Now that we weren't facing a dead body—or an angry detective—I could give Spot his head.

He didn't need a prompt, and as soon as I let the lead out again, he began investigating, nose to the ground, ears pitched forward as if to capture more of the scents and the scene.

"What is it, Spot? What do you get?"

More sniffing. Leaf mold. Something warm, with charcoal fur. A mole? A squirrel? Then—bingo!—he was on it. Blood, fresh enough, and suddenly the images started pouring forth. Fear, acrid as smoke. Pain just as sharp. More pain. Blinding pain and sounds—not human. Or, well, not that of a rational human anymore. Then the rip and tear of teeth. Huge teeth. The warmth of blood and then…cold silence.

When the images faded, I realized I was leaning back on that oak, panting as if I'd just been chased. So this is how Spot saw the world? I looked down, a little dazed, to see the shepherd mix looking up at me.

"I smelled that here." Yes, I'd gotten that. But there was something more. *"In the blood, here."*

And I remembered. Yes, those emotions—the fear, the pain—they might well remain in the blood when it was spilled. It didn't mean the attack, for there was no other word for it, had happened here. Had it?

Spot looked at me and tilted his head. It was a complex question, one I wasn't sure how to phrase. I thought of a woman, here in the woods, her hands outstretched in a useless last-ditch attempt. I pictured her falling in the shadows of these trees. It was horrible.

What I got was sunlight. Warmth. An echo of the calm that had preceded the attack. Did that mean the woman had been killed on a brighter day—or closer to high noon? The morning shadows were leaving us now, but in an hour or two, this leafless bit of forest might be fairly bright. Or was I just picking up an emotional state as interpreted by a dog: the last bit of peace before the kill?

"The blood is silent." Yes, I knew it was, now. Spot seemed to be trying to tell me something, but I was stuck on my own memories now. Those images had been so vibrant, so harsh.

"Run away, quick, quick…" I sensed a bit of a struggle. Spot was a well-trained dog, a domestic animal. Still, he called it as he saw it. *"Trapped."*

She might have been happy, out here for a walk. Not

that she was dressed for it. And again, I wondered, how did she get out here? Who was she? I pressed as hard as I dared, concentrating on the depths of those dark eyes.

"Who isn't important." I got it, finally. Not that I understood. *"Who didn't do it. She was in the way. In her way. That's how she got killed."*

NINE

IF I DIDN'T know better, I'd have said that Spot had just given me motive. She got in her way. That sounded like jealousy to me. The disposal of a rival, in a particularly permanent way. That didn't fit, however, with anything else that I knew. Even in my blackest mood, for example, I doubted I could tear Laurel Kroft's sleek coif half off and let her smooth throat bleed out on the leaves. And if I couldn't, well, no matter what the handsome Creighton might believe, it did look to be the work of an animal.

There was something wrong here, though. Something I wasn't getting. And as Spot went back to sniffing, I worked at phrasing my question correctly.

"What did this, Spot?" I didn't want to picture a cougar. The tawny fur, the broad muzzle. The fangs. That would be the animal equivalent of leading the witness. I didn't want to think any more about Laurel Kroft, either. No matter what was going on between us—or between the pretty doctor and Creighton—she was Spot's caregiver, at least for now. No, I tried to blank my mind out, and when that failed, I recalled what I could of the victim's wounds.

I'm not squeamish. Never was, and living with Wallis has weaned me even further from it. But I hadn't taken a really good look at the body we'd found. Now I closed my eyes and took a breath. That blouse, that was a good starting point. A gold pattern—interlocking chains? Maybe—I could picture them running down her arms, bright against the deep green background. Quite lovely, really, if it hadn't been for the dark staining on the front. No wonder I hadn't noted that she wore no coat. Maybe that's what had been bothering me. I couldn't tell, yet I had to make myself try.

It wasn't fun, but with my eyes closed, I made my memory move up her arms to her chest. To her throat. At first, I saw black—the darkness of terror. The dark hair and the raw flesh beside it, dark with clotting. That one eye. Dried blood staining what remained of her shirt. A touch of gold, where a shred of her shirt had not been soaked through. Where a claw—

"No!" I couldn't help it. I'd felt it. That moment—the panic, the realization. The giant paw. The jaws. I yelled out loud, jumping back in terror at the image that had leaped into my head.

"Master?" Spot was looking up, worried.

"No." I forced my voice down, into its normal register. "Everything is fine. We are good."

A tilt of the head. "Good boy." I wanted to give him what reassurance I could. In response, he gave his flag of a tail a half a wag. More acknowledgment of what I was trying to communicate than true happiness.

"Good boy!" I put some heart into it. After all, as far as I could tell, Spot really had done everything I'd asked of him. By sharing his impressions—the scent of blood left on leaves and his acute canine interpretation of it—he had fleshed out my memory. I didn't know if he had smelled a killer, or if some chemicals in that spilled blood—adrenaline, maybe, or something stronger—had triggered my own reaction. But he'd allowed me to see what might have happened. How this killing might have gone down.

I should go for more. I still had no sense of what exactly had torn that poor woman's throat out. And I had no idea how jealousy or ambition—how "getting in her way"—might figure into it. But I didn't know how much else he could give me. We had come back here. Spot had done his best with the scene. Truth was, I didn't have the heart for more.

I liked to think it did Spot some good. Revisiting a scene might not give a dog "closure," as Creighton had called it. Not in the human sense. But I'd pulled him away yesterday before he'd had a chance to really explore. That unsatisfied curiosity might be what had caused his dreams the night before. I really didn't know. But Spot came willingly when I told him we were going, and I believe both our moods picked up as we approached the clearing where I had parked.

"Heel." Once I could see the brightness of the sun ahead, I realized I should really use the time as I was paid to. "Good boy," I said as he responded instantly.

"Walk me." I shortened the lead and watched him step up so it was just taut. "Let's go," I said, and he began leading me. Not too fast and very careful, coming back to my side to halt me with his body when we came up to a large branch in our path.

"Good boy."

I turned and began walking again. This time, I had my eyes half-shut, just as an experiment, but I could clearly see the brush ahead of me. Out from under the trees, at the lot's edge, it had grown thick and brambly. And I walked toward it as if those thorns would mean nothing to me.

"No!" Spot was in front of me, leaning his considerable weight against my legs. *"Stop!"*

"Good." Spot was perhaps a tad premature, but his reaction was basically correct. Besides, I was ready to go home. "My turn now." Letting out more of the leash, I signaled that I would take the lead. "Walk," I said out loud.

"No!" Ignoring my lead, he stepped in front of me. *"Get back."* He flicked his ear away from me and turned slightly. Body still blocking me, he turned toward the hedge-like undergrowth.

"I've got it, Spot." I reached down to get his attention and to remind him I was in charge. As soon as I touched his head, however, I realized there was more involved than canine overexuberance. Something was going on here. Something that countermanded his training, and I needed to find out what it was. "Are we a little excited?"

Wallis hates it when I use first-person plural. She finds it infantilizing, or, in her words, "treating me like some foul-bottomed kitten." Spot was upset, though, and I wanted him to know I was with him. We were together.

"Did we do too much today?"

"Danger!" As I've said, this can mean many things to a dog. This time, however, Spot's body language made his meaning clear. His back was stiff, his muzzle pointed at the dense undergrowth, and I felt a chill run down my spine.

"What is it, Spot?" I was still talking out loud, I was pretty sure. But my voice had dropped, as if in fear of being overheard. "What's in there?"

Maybe it had been my moment of panic in the woods, an emotional reaction so strong it had been communicated in human form to another creature. Maybe Spot was still processing that. Protecting me.

Or maybe I was fooling myself. Maybe I just didn't want to believe that whatever had attacked that young woman was still out there. Maybe between us and my car. It was high noon. A crisp and beautiful spring day, but I was shivering. All I could think of was the body we had found less than twenty-four hours before. The shock of raw fear—that secondhand terror—still chilled me. I didn't know what had torn her like a papier-mâché doll, but something had. And I had a horrible feeling that whatever had done that was now waiting, watching us, from the shadows.

TEN

WE STOOD THERE for what seemed like an eternity, although I could have calculated the time by the audible beating of my heart. Spot stayed on alert, and I stared for all I was worth, trying to decipher the mass of shadows in the brambles, to distinguish the shape of a potential predator from last year's leaf fall, while we both stood as still as statues. It was the sensible response, one young animals know by instinct. Movement gets noticed, and getting noticed—if you're prey—gets you dead.

Unfortunately, I'm not a bunny. I'm a human, and as the seconds—or maybe they really were minutes—ticked past, I became aware of two distinct urges. The first was for a bathroom. And while I'm not above squatting in the woods, I know enough to not make myself look smaller—more vulnerable—to a predator. If I'm going to be jumped, I sure as hell don't want it to be with my jeans down. The second urge was to strike out—or at least to talk back to whatever it was that was out there. I'm not saying humans are superior creatures. I've learned that much in my time with this supposed gift. What I am saying is that I was getting angry. Here I was, acting on another's trauma reflexively, when the one thing I had going for me was my brain. Not that I could out-argue an alpha predator. But if I couldn't

find a way to think my way free of this situation, well,
I deserved to die wetting myself.

It was time to act.

"Spot." I kept my voice level but low. The command
firm. "Come here, Spot. Heel."

There was a moment's hesitation, more something
I sensed than saw. He didn't want to step beside me,
where he couldn't protect me. I got it. "Heel," I reiterated, putting a touch more steel into my voice. He came
and stood beside me but not willingly. Every fiber—
every hair on his coat—was on alert. If I didn't already
feel alarmed, his resistance now would have clued me
in.

"Watch out." It was a warning, the equivalent of a
whisper. I got it, and reached down to lay my fingers in
what I hoped was a comforting fashion on Spot's head.
But I was focused on the bush. Somewhere in there was
something that had raised Spot's hackles and should
have raised mine. Something in there had attacked the
woman we found. Something that was, most likely, an
animal. And here I was, the animal psychic. Wasn't
it possible that I could reach out and make some kind
of contact with it? That I could, if not communicate,
at least eavesdrop on whatever it—he, she—wanted?
Shouldn't I be getting something?

I tried to focus on what a predator would feel. What
would make a large animal attack? *"Fear?"* Not for
oneself, maybe, but for one's cubs or kits. I mulled this
one over, trying to envision little ones—a den of some
kind. Not my scene; I couldn't get a handle on it.

"Hunger..." That was easier, and I did my best to envision my own appetite growing, wild and ravenous. I
got so far as to feel my belly grumbling before the silli-

ness of the situation got to me. The absurdity—my fear, my other impulses. Nothing from the brush, though. If Spot hadn't been on alert, I'd have been tempted to believe that it—whatever it was—had gone. Slunk off while I was doing my best to throw mind darts in its direction.

This was crazy. My temper started to rise, and I tried to ride that: *"Anger, rage?"* That one wasn't hard: I don't like being scared. *"Grrr..."* I rumbled out a growl, loud enough to cause a slight twitch in Spot's ear. *"Challenge..."* I pushed it further. This was getting a bit crazy. I was sick of being stuck here. I could see the parking area, my car. I wanted to go home.

"Home." There! It was so faint, I could have missed it. Thought I did, for a moment, until I sensed Spot looking up at me, as if waiting for a command.

"Home? Spot?" I had to check, but no, the word—that slight echo—had not come from the dog by my side.

"Home." I said the word out loud now, trying to conjure up all the images the word provoked. Warmth, a soft chair. A fireplace.

"No!" I stepped back, the force of that monosyllable was so strong. Beside me, Spot shuffled backward a bit too, the slightest whimper barely breaking the air.

Was there something about a fireplace—about fire? It was true that wild animals had no reason to love flame. More often than not, fire meant destruction, rather than warmth. But that didn't have to be: I thought of the coziness of my own living room, especially when the rest of the house was set to an economical chill. I thought of the warmth on my feet. How the logs smelled, and how Wallis would stretch out by the hearth, her paws outstretched at her most cat-like.

"Cat?" There it was again. Strong and…could it be? Curious? For a moment, my stomach clenched in panic. Of course, a house cat like Wallis would be of interest to something big and wild and in the woods. My little tabby might fancy herself worldly, wise, and tough as nails. In reality, she'd be at best a tender morsel to a creature big enough to take down a woman. To a…

"What are *you?"* It was useless, and I knew it. We humans are cursed with self-awareness. A few of our domestic animals have it. I thought of Growler, who had battled with his person's interpretation of his gruff nature from Day One. Most animals, though, are blissfully unselfconscious. They eat, they mate. They do what instinct and training urge them to do to continue to exist in a harsh and thankless world. They do not ruminate on their very natures, or on the relative gifts and liberties granted to other species. At least, not often. Growler had made his own kind of rough peace with our kind, with our domination of him and his world. Wallis, on the other hand…

"Cat!" There it was again, only this time I was ready.

"No!" I yelled back. I didn't care that Wallis was at home, miles away, and theoretically safe inside our old house. I didn't care that I had provoked this reaction, calling up some primal urge with my own mental image of my soft and warm pet. Maybe it came from being a certain age still childless. Maybe from my uncommon bond with my longtime tabby companion. Maybe it was the simple orneriness of my nature, a trait that has gotten me in trouble many times before and was now compounded by fear, by stiffness, and the growing pressure in my bladder. I'd had enough. "No! No cat." I yelled, waving my arms as if in a shooing gesture. The thought in my mind went out as loud and as hard as I could send it. "No cat, no. Not for you."

I got something—a flash, a feeling. A connection. I'd been heard, if not understood. And then suddenly, nothing. I'd been staring at the underbrush for so long, I didn't trust my eyes, but surely there was a motion, a rustling of the old, dead leaves, a swaying of the over-hung branches. I should have been afraid—riling a wild animal is not generally smart policy. Maybe it was my anger that was keeping me afloat, maybe it was in-stinct. I felt…okay. And then the rustling stopped. The branches settled back into stillness, and I knew, even before Spot leaned his warm presence up against my leg, that whatever had been in there had gone away. Either my outburst had scared it off, or my denial— no cat—had sent the message. We were not prey. Not today. It was gone.

ELEVEN

I COULDN'T WAIT to get home. No matter what my rational mind was saying, my animal brain was urging me home, to Wallis, in the most urgent tones. Spot seemed to acquiesce: I had the strangest feeling that he was puzzling things over as I raced us both back to my house. And when I left him in the car, promising to be quick, he barely responded.

"Cat?" I thought I heard.

"Yes." I slammed the door behind me and ran up to my own front door.

"Watch it!" Wallis pressed both white front paws against my chest and pushed as I hugged her close. *"I am not a..."*

"Toy, I know," I said, nuzzling into the thick ruff of fur around her neck. "It's just that...you don't know what I'm dealing with, Wallis."

I wasn't sure how much to go into. After all, as much as I wanted Wallis to be wary, I didn't need to frighten her with an image of a killer who would never come within miles of our front yard.

"Oh, don't I?" That's when I got it: the flash image of jaws, clamping down on the back of the neck. In Wallis' case, it was a mouse's neck, the tiny spine firm against her teeth, but I could feel it as if they were my own. She held on—*I* held on—until the pressure had suffocated the smaller beast. In my heart, I knew joy,

my only frustration being that I hadn't managed to crack the mouse's spine, or even its skull, with that first bite.

"That's how it's done." The image receded, and I found myself staring at Wallis, her eyes glittering with the thrill of the memory she had just shared.

"Thanks, Wallis." I pulled back and looked at her, my heart swelling. Only Wallis would compare herself to a killer and be proud of it. I thought of that mouse and did my best to block the other image—the woman, half her head laid bare.

"What?" Her green eyes stared into mine, cool and calm. *"You think we're that different?"* There was a mocking tone in her voice, and for once I couldn't tell—not for sure—if she was teasing me or having a laugh at my human frailty. *"Go back to that...dog."* Now the voice dripped contempt.

It did, however, remind me of whom I had left in the car. "Okay, then." I released her small body. "But I won't be out late. And I could use a consult." It wasn't simply flattery. Maybe she sensed it, because she drew herself up, wrapping her tail around her front paws, and didn't complain when I reached to stroke her smooth striped head.

Spot was staring out the window when I got back to the car.

"Sorry about that." It hadn't gotten that cold, but I still felt bad about leaving him for what must have been close to fifteen minutes.

"Cat." One syllable, that was it. I turned toward him, but he was staring out the window, at my house. Some things never change, I thought, and put my baby-blue baby in gear.

I got any additional proof I needed as I glided up

Laurel Kroft's drive. There, parked right in front, was Creighton's unmarked car. It wasn't a surprise, or shouldn't have been. And I reminded myself that I had made my choice as I parked and walked around the car to open Spot's door.

"Hunt?" The query was more a general question than a specific request. I read it as the dog's way of asking what was going on.

"No need." I reached to stroke that broad head. I needed the comfort, even if he didn't, and with that I walked Spot up to my rival's front door.

"Dr. Kroft." I nodded as she opened the door and handed her the lead. Spot stayed by my side even as she took it, and I tried not to think of the symbolism of that.

"Pru!" I didn't need the extra emphasis in her voice to let me know she was gloating. But before I could turn to leave, I heard another voice say my name.

"Glad you made it," said Creighton, stepping out from behind her. "I wanted to speak with you both."

I bit the inside of my lip, nodding at him as Laurel held the door open. As she led the way into the living room, I allowed myself to imagine what Wallis would have done with that nubby cream sofa.

Spot, however, was a very different animal. Without any cue that I could catch, he trotted over to a small brown rug by the window and sat. Whoever ended up with him was getting a well-trained companion.

Which I wasn't, by any stretch of the imagination. Then again, that wasn't a job I wanted. "So, what's shaking?" I stared at my onetime beau. "Jim?"

Creighton hadn't sat either, though he motioned for me to take my place by the lovely Laurel on the couch.

She had sat, crossing those long legs. I didn't, and he nodded, as if in confirmation.

"Hey, if you're not going to tell me why you want me here, I've got clients to take care of." That nod had pissed me off.

"Maybe one less than you thought, Pru." That stopped me. "We're not sure how this is going to shake out yet."

I didn't say anything. I didn't have to. Laurel, by my side, was staring at him with an intensity that demanded an answer.

Still, he could have kept us waiting.

"The dog," he said, after only a short pause, "the one you're training?" I nodded. He turned toward Laurel. "You own him?"

"I'm *fostering* him." Laurel's voice retained its control and warmth even as she corrected him.

"But you both know that he's going to Richard Haigen, right?"

"I don't think that's been determined." It was my turn to speak up. "I've begun to work with him, to see if he's a good fit. Just because he could use a service dog doesn't guarantee that he'll get one." I paused, thought about who Haigen was—or had been. "Or not this one."

Creighton nodded, as if he'd heard what I'd left unsaid. "I don't imagine Haigen misses out on a lot that he wants. Certainly, his wife doesn't seem to think so."

That was an eyebrow-raiser, and I waited for more. Laurel, however, was getting impatient.

"You may be making an invalid assumption, Detective." I liked her for that, even if the formality seemed a little strained. "True, Mr. Haigen has more resources than many of us. However, that kind of bounty can make his growing disability feel even more unfair. As if he were being forced to pay some kind of karmic tax."

"Oh?" Creighton looked faintly amused.

Laurel took the bait. "Yes, he's rich. And, I gather, he can be difficult. But he's dealing with a lot of change right now. Not just with his eyesight, but with the decision to relocate and disperse his staff. And, really, the routines formed between him and his wife were established ages ago. I'm not going to comment more on this, although I gather you observed something of an unhealthy dynamic. All I ask is that you keep in mind that he's in pain."

"His eyes?" Creighton started to speak, but Laurel waved him off.

"Psychically. For a man like Haigen, a man who has had everything—and who has surrounded himself with great beauty—to lose his eyesight is devastating."

"Yeah, it's not like he's a working stiff." I couldn't resist. "Like a truck driver or someone who actually needs to see to make a living."

"Pru?" There was a lift in his tone now. Creighton was enjoying this. Lucky for him, I had the bit in my teeth now.

"Richard Haigen is a spoiled brat. I'm sorry he doesn't have anyone else around to yell at anymore, but he treats his wife like crap, and she takes it. I don't know if it's because he's richer than Croesus, or because she likes it. Some women do. What I do know is that she's devoted to him. And if she could put herself in a dog suit and follow him around all day, he wouldn't need Spot here. But he does—or he's going to, soon. And whether or not Spot ends up being that dog, he's going to make someone a hell of a service companion."

It was as long a speech as I'd made before either of them in quite a while. Laurel looked surprised, but Creighton was smiling. Which didn't improve my mood.

"And so why, Detective, are you asking us about Haigen? And don't tell me they've passed laws against rich guys being obnoxious. Not in this country, they haven't." I paused. "I'd have heard." I didn't really have an ending.

At least that made Creighton's grin bigger. When he smiles really wide, he gets a dimple. I scowled, but that only made it more pronounced.

"What?" I was pissed now and striking out. "Are you going to tell us that a half-blind guy killed that woman, then drove her out to the woods to dump her body and try to make it look like an animal attack? Or was this supposed to be some kinky final exam to see if Spot is up to being his dog?"

"I don't know, Pru, but we're looking at the possibilities." The smile was gone now, but the softness of his voice stopped me cold. "Because we've identified our Jane Doe, and she is someone you've both come in contact with. Certainly through your work with the dog, maybe somewhere else. That's what I'd like to talk with you both about."

I don't know when it happened, but I could feel it. All three sets of eyes were on him now. Spot as focused as Laurel and I.

"The deceased has been identified as Mariela Gomez." He paused, and I knew he was watching both Laurel and me for any reaction. Spot, on his rug, was eyeing him just as intently. "And we were all partially right about how she died. She was moved, and there is evidence of human involvement. However, the wounds are consistent with a wild animal attack. A large wild cat, to be precise."

TWELVE

IF CREIGHTON HAD wanted to shut us up, and I wouldn't put it past him, he couldn't have done much better. Mariela Gomez. No wonder she'd looked familiar. When last I'd seen her, she was wearing a gray uniform that did what it could to play down some significant attributes. Mariela had been the pretty maid, the one who'd been working so hard to bring the Scotch, get more ice, where's the water, even as her boss sat there, all chummy with his buddy, acting as if his legs were going, along with his eyes.

At the time, I'd felt bad for her. Felt bad for the wife, too, but Mariela was getting a lot less for her services. I'd wondered about the buddy, too. The one who seemed ready to take care of all of Richard Haigen's rich-man problems. In retrospect, I had to wonder if those problems might have included the wife. Dierdre might not have had much more clout in that household than Mariela the maid, but she had the ring—and some kinds of women are not made to be alone. Mariela was younger than Dierdre. Mariela seemed to be trying harder. Now Mariela was dead.

So was the room. Even Spot seemed to look up with what passed for surprise, though given his sharp nose, surely the quiet canine had surmised the source of those wounds long before.

For me, Creighton's bombshell was interesting, but only a starting point. I had my questions about the relationships in the Haigen household, but I wasn't ready to start accusing anyone of homicidal jealousy. Glass houses, and all that. Besides, I was here in a professional capacity.

"Are you sure about the wounds?" I broke the silence first, focusing in on the one area I have some expertise with. "I mean, as the cause of death? Because animals, even large predators, will scavenge. If something found her and was hungry…" With my eyes on Jim, I felt, rather than saw, Laurel cringe. I didn't even take a moment to gloat: this was too serious.

"You want the whole rigmarole, Pru?" Creighton shook his head. "Coronary failure due to blood loss? Yeah, the wounds we saw were the cause of death. The coroner sent some slides over to Tufts," Creighton said. "He wanted a vet to look at them. Teeth. Teeth and claws is what we've heard. Consistent with a moderate-size wild cat."

"Did the vet say what kind?" I was wondering how much DNA would be left in those wounds. Maybe we had a migrant. That Connecticut cougar had been traced back to the Dakotas.

"She didn't." I sat back at that. At least the so-called expert wasn't jumping to conclusions. Creighton waited a moment, then seemed to make a decision. "We'll get more in a few days," he said. "But the vet confirmed what you said, Pru: There've been no verified reports of any large wild cats in the state. Not in years. And there's still the question of how she got there, so we're still looking at human involvement."

"Maybe..." Laurel sounded tentative. "Maybe someone was trying to rescue her? To get her away from... something?"

Creighton shook his head.

"But why would someone move her?" Laurel's voice had gone breathy, and not in a good way. I wondered if this talk of death and killing was too much for her. It was a happy thought. "I mean...after?"

"Sometimes predators will drag their prey." I tried to sound nonchalant. "They'll take a body to a safe location, a cache of some sort. To keep it safe from other animals."

I heard her swallow. "Even some of the smaller omnivores will gnaw at a body." I was trying to think of examples, just for the fun of it, when Creighton broke in.

"She wasn't dragged. She was moved—by a person." His eyes narrowed, just a bit. He must have seen that I was considering the situation. I was being put on notice.

"And that was definitely postmortem?" To my right, Laurel gagged, just a little. Who could blame me if I smiled? To cover, I turned toward her. "You can tell, because after death, wounds won't bleed."

"I am aware of basic physiology." To her credit, she kept her voice level. Her skin had gone sallow, however. I picked up a mild distress whine from Spot. He was worried. A good dog, with a better soul than me.

"You both probably want to know why I'm telling you this." Creighton broke in, but that whine had increased. Spot was more than concerned, he was distressed.

"What is it?" I was on my knees by his blanket. "The dog is upset," I explained over my shoulder. "He's probably reacting to the stress in your voice." I didn't know if that was true. He was quite capable of picking up some of Creighton's narrative from my mind. Maybe from his, too. Although I'm pretty sure I'm the only one in town who can hear animals, I've never quite determined how much they can get from even the most deaf of us. And I can't blame them for not wanting me to know, either.

"Spot?" I knew I looked a little crazy. Creighton has had his suspicions about me, as well, having seen some of my interactions with Wallis. But this dog was upset, and I was at least partially to blame. I'd wanted to rile Laurel and hadn't thought of who else was listening. Besides, he and I had been through something today—and he'd done what he could to protect me. In the guise of petting him, I lifted that big, triangular head and stared into those dark eyes.

"What is it?" I silently willed my question to him, then rephrased it as a command. *"Show me."*

"Cat." I saw the bush again, the dead leaves rustling with movement. *"Big cat. Scared."*

"Poor boy," I said aloud. To Laurel and Jim it would sound like I was responding to the whine, which had been growing in intensity. *"You're safe here. We all are,"* I tried to comfort him with that thought. Pictured the room, the walls. Our twenty-minute drive from the wooded preserve.

"No!" He jerked his head back from my hand with a bark. I'd done something. Startled him. What had been in my mind? This house? Was he not safe here?

"Is the dog all right?" Creighton was asking, which I thought was odd. After all, Laurel was his foster mom.

"Yes, he's fine." I reached again for his head, trying to convey that message.

"He had nightmares last night," Laurel chimed in. "Whining and kicking, like he was chasing something."

"Chasing?" That was a new thought, and I rephrased the question in my thoughts. After all, what might appear to be a bad dream to a human could be something very different. *"No need to hunt,"* his response was immediate. *"Not her."*

"No need to hunt... Mariela?" Was this grief? Was Spot mourning the damage we had witnessed? Yes, her death had been needless.

The big brown eyes that looked up into mine were blank, and they brought me back. Of course, animals don't think that way. Death has no moral or emotional weight in their world. It simply is. Need, however, comes in many forms. Spot wasn't saying Mariela's death was pointless. He was telling me that whoever killed her did not do so out of necessity.

"Who, Spot?" I didn't ask out loud. I didn't dare. *"Who didn't have to hunt?"* He'd been responding to me, sure, but also to what Laurel was saying.

Could he mean…*"Laurel? The food lady?"* Nothing. *"Blondie?"*

Only now did I realize I had little idea of how Spot saw the people in his life. It was an easy oversight— Spot was so focused on his training that I'd taken it for all he knew. It was also stupid. I rephrased the question: *"Is Laurel hunting?"*

I glanced up at Creighton. I couldn't help it. Men always see themselves as the aggressors. Stupid of them. But a wave of thought—the silent equivalent of a bark—

drew me back. Spot was calling me back, calling me to attention. I'd missed something.

"Scared," the dog repeated.

"Laurel? Is she scared?" I glanced at her, taking in her warm blonde hair, that creamy sweater. I tried to focus on what Spot would notice: her hands, with their long, tapered fingers and manicured nails. The clean stiffness of her ironed jeans. I got nothing. Either Spot wasn't talking about Laurel, and his silence was the canine equivalent of a denial, or he was tuning me out. It had happened before, and it always chilled me.

As much as I dislike the responsibilities that come with this gift, I've come to rely on it. It was more than an advantage. It was, at times, my only real connection to the rest of the world.

Spot wasn't playing along, and with a sigh, rested his head on the carpet. I responded by taking his muzzle between both my hands. I confess I was getting a bit desperate. Not only was I not getting anything, my edge on Laurel was proving useless. But as I raised his wide, dark head and stared into his eyes, something happened. Something I wasn't expecting from such a straightforward animal. I got a sense of frustration, as if he was reflecting my emotion back at me. Was he showing me what he was seeing in me?

Or was I getting a clearer picture of what he felt? Of…yes, exasperation. A…well…dogged sense of trying and trying and not getting through. Of wanting to give up, despite the necessity, the urgency of trying one more time.

"What?" I risked speaking aloud, my face so close to his I could feel his doggy breath on me. "What am I not getting?"

"Pru?" It was Creighton. I was making him uncomfortable. I didn't care.

"Detective, would you like a beverage?" Laurel Kroft wasn't letting the moment go to waste.

Disappointment—gone so quickly that I could have thought I'd imagined it. If only... *"What?"* I knew from Wallis how annoying we can be to the animals around us. How dense. Clearly, I had missed something—something big.

"Scared." There it was again—that word. Echoing the human word, but carrying with it a sense of stomach-tingling edginess. Not panic, but a sense of being on the alert. Alarmed. Ready to run.

"Scared." Only the image I was seeing wasn't of the house anymore. Or even the preservation land, where Mariela lay under the trees. It was the underbrush where Spot and I had been frozen for those long, tense minutes. Only those dull, dun leaves were up close, reversed. I was seeing the brush from the inside. And what I was looking at was us, Spot and me, and as we came closer, the alarm turned to fear.

THIRTEEN

IT WASN'T ANYTHING I could explain, and I had already spent enough time on the floor. With a quick pet to Spot, as a silent expression of thanks, I got back up and turned to face my two human companions.

"Everything copacetic?" Creighton looked amused. Laurel didn't. I could see why. She thought I was hogging the stage, so to speak. Showcasing my expertise in front of the man we both felt some animal attraction for. I have to admit, I enjoyed her discomfort. It took the edge off that strange vision, and I was smiling broadly as I settled back on the sofa beside her. The fact that Creighton had ignored her offer of a beverage helped, too.

It wasn't necessarily a contest, but I was in the lead.

"If we may continue…" Creighton had been leaning on the fireplace mantel. Now he stood to his full six-two. Since both of us females were seated, we both had to look up at him. I almost expected him to start preening. "I am here, I'm afraid to say, in an official capacity."

Maybe he was, I thought. Then I realized I should perhaps listen to what he was saying.

"We're trying to establish a time line," he was saying. I looked up at him. Creighton gets a certain set to his jaw. There's something about his eyes, too. It means he's telling the truth, but through his official cop fil-

ter. Which means it's not the whole truth, or not un-
varnished, anyway. I glanced at Laurel and wondered
how much of this she was picking up. She didn't know
him as well as I did. At least, I didn't think she did. She
didn't have my training as a behaviorist either. But she
was a shrink. I took in how she was staring up at him,
eyes wide. I didn't trust that look either. That much
adoration? She was trying to wash me out of the room.

"…pinpoint the time of death."

I cursed silently. Letting myself get distracted was
an amateur's mistake. Never watch just the tail when
you're trying to read the dog.

"Excuse me?" I smiled as I said it, though I resisted
the urge to bat my lashes. Not that Creighton is im-
mune to that kind of signifying, but he does know me
well enough that he might have gotten suspicious. "I
was thinking of Spot, here. What were you saying?"

I'd broken his flow, and he looked peeved. Maybe I
should have tried the eyelashes.

"Both you and Dr. Kroft were acquainted with the
victim. What I am hoping is that between the two of
you, you might be able to shed some light on who she
was, and that information might be useful to us in our
investigation."

He was lying. I couldn't pinpoint exactly why, but I
knew it was so. Maybe his voice was a little too even,
too restrained. Maybe it was the way he held my eyes,
like he was forcing himself not to blink. Whatever. If I
could keep him from being able to tell that I knew his
secret, then I had an edge.

"What would you like to know?" I heard the slight
lilt in my voice. Flirting comes easy around Creighton. And if I could put him off guard, it could give me

a further advantage. "Anything specific?" Besides, it was fun to piss off Laurel.

"When did you last see Mariela Gomez? Day and approximate time, please."

The questions came with the sound of a trap slamming shut. I'd been wondering about Dierdre, about Richard. Creighton was talking to me and Laurel. Were we both suspects? Was I? I had to think fast.

"Last week, but only in passing." I thought back. The younger woman had been in and out during my visit. Quiet, efficient, if her boss hadn't barked at her, I might not have noticed her. Then again, maybe that had been the point. "As you seem aware, I'm working with her boss—Richard Haigen. He's going to need a service dog, and he certainly can maintain one." That family had more money than Trump. "And we have a unique opportunity with him. Usually, you don't get to work with a client before he loses his sight."

"And the victim? Did she work with you, too?" The way he emphasized the verb worried me.

"No, not at all." I was as clear and direct as I'd be with Growler. "She was strictly support staff for the humans. Haigen, his wife. This friend of theirs—Nick something." I tried to picture her, but the image of her as I'd last seen her kept interfering. "I think she was wearing some kind of apron. Some kind of uniform."

That blouse: the one she'd died in. It didn't fit with who she seemed to be. I hesitated, trying to figure out if this was important. But I paused too long.

"Pru..." There was a growl in his voice. A warning note. Creighton wanted in.

"There was—I thought there was tension in the household." I was trying to figure out what I thought.

Trying, too, to figure out what I wanted to share. "Haigen kept barking at her, though as far as I could tell she was doing her job. He yelled at his wife, too, so maybe that was just his way of communicating." That shirt. Maybe it would mean something to him. For the life of me, I couldn't figure it out. "For what it's worth, that shirt, the one she was wearing when we found her?" He nodded, just enough to keep me talking. "It was nice. Silk, I bet. It wasn't like anything I'd ever seen her in. Not at that house."

He pursed his lips. "Interesting. Ms. Kroft, can you tell us when you last saw the victim?"

"Probably the same day. Thursday, was it?" Her voice was a little tight. She was hiding something. "I came by after the session."

This was news to me. I raised my eyebrows, so Creighton would notice.

"Were you part of the training?" He had, but he was being very careful.

"Oh, no." So was she. "But, you see, I've grown so fond of Spot that I felt like I wanted to see where he was going. I wanted to see if maybe I could maintain some kind of connection with him, once he went on to his new life."

No, this was wrong. Service dogs don't have friends. They have a job, that's it. That job means that all their focus, all their waking hours, belong to one person—the client. If they can't do that, then they flunk out of the program. For Laurel to try to do that was akin to sabotage.

It was possible. Simple, selfish, but possible. If Laurel Kroft really did want to keep Spot as a pet, one way to make sure he stayed would be to invalidate him for the service program. The tiny stipend she'd been receiving for his food and care would dry up, but I had a pretty good idea she was well enough off to care for one full-grown dog.

Or it could be that she was playing at something else. I tilted my head, willing Creighton to follow up on this line of reasoning.

"And are you friends with the Haigens?" He was. I could have given him a treat. Hell, I would, given the chance. "Besides your connection through the dog?"

"Well, I *know* them." That was it, she was flustered. Sitting next to her, I felt her shift slightly on the sofa. The color that had drained out of her at the mention of the body had come back, just a little too fast. "I know his wife, that is."

"Really." In Creighton's hands, the one-word statement was a question. It was one I wanted to hear the answer to, too. "Not Mr. Haigen?"

This would be something—if she were having an affair with the wealthy, soon-to-be-blind client. I thought of his bullying and his bulk, and what such an alliance might mean. Maybe we could kill multiple birds with one stone, so to speak.

"Well, in passing…" She was floundering. I was enjoying it. "I mean, of course, I *know* Mr. Haigen. Richard." She actually licked her lips. "I would have to because of our dog, of course. But not well."

I didn't have to look at Creighton. We were both seeing the same thing. Besides, I didn't want to be obvious. Because I knew one thing for sure—once we were done here and Creighton was satisfied with letting me go my own way, I was hightailing it to the Haigens. There was something going on here, and it wasn't all about the dog.

FOURTEEN

I PROBABLY SHOULD have taken Spot. Only I couldn't think of a good excuse since I'd just dropped him off. And while it felt odd to drive out to the Haigens without a dog in the passenger seat, I knew I could come up with something.

"Scared." What had Spot meant by that? I thought back to the vision he had shared with me. The implication was that the beast—whatever it was—inside the bush had been afraid of us. Or, more likely, him. And in a way I could see that. Most wild animals really do prefer to avoid humans and domestic dogs. We're just too much trouble, and they have enough good sense to know it.

And maybe it—she?—had felt cornered. After all, we'd been approaching at a good clip, heading toward my car. The car was parked in an open area, one that probably was still redolent of all the police activity of the day before. An animal caught there unawares might have believed itself cornered. Trapped.

But if that were the case, why had it attacked Mariela the day before? As my car ate up the road, I tried a few different scenarios.

Maybe Mariela had startled the animal. Without Spot to warn me, I might have walked right up to that underbrush. That could have sparked an attack. In fact, a frightened animal would be more likely to lash out. Mariela hadn't been eaten, after all.

I realized I was accelerating and eased off the gas. No matter how long I lived with Wallis, I still had a hard time thinking of everything as potential prey. And there was something about Mariela's wounds—something about the attack that didn't look intentional. That looked, well, wrong. Besides, that scenario raised another question: If Mariela had been alone and startled a jittery wild animal—okay, a cat—then who had moved her?

Maybe Mariela had been with a companion. That would fit with the nice clothes. Maybe even the lack of a coat, if her companion—I imagined a young man of a suitable age—had perhaps been holding it for her. Maybe they had separated and she had done something that made her vulnerable. I thought of stories about joggers out west who had been mauled. At least one had bent over to tie a shoelace, the act making the human seem smaller, more like prey. If that were the case, then maybe her companion had found her and, in the process of trying to help her, had moved her. And scared off the animal.

But if that were the case, then why leave her alone in the woods?

Several reasons sprang to mind, none of them complimentary. Someone was with her who wasn't supposed to be. A married man. Someone doing something wrong, anyway. Out in the woods with a well-dressed young woman.

"Scared."

The wave of feeling hit me so hard, I nearly swerved off the road. As it was, I could feel the sweat break out

on my forehead, despite the cool of the afternoon. I'd
been so blind. Spot had tried, but I'd misread once again
what he'd been trying so hard to show me. It wasn't he
who was scared. I'd gotten that. But maybe it wasn't
that wild animal, whatever it was, that had been hiding
in the bushes. Because what Spot had been relaying to
me was what that animal had been sensing. He'd been
showing me the view from inside the brush. The sense
of us, of where we were, getting closer and possibly
threatening. But what I was feeling wasn't necessarily
what the animal was experiencing. It may very well
have been what it—he, she—was picking up. I thought
of Mariela, dead and battered on the ground. I thought
of that lovely blouse, and the blood it had soaked up
from those horrible wounds. *"Scared."* Yes, a wild animal would have picked that up. Any animal would have,
and that might have been the go-ahead to attack.

THIS REALIZATION KNOCKED me back so hard, I nearly
drove off the road. Well, that and the fact that a little
red speedster had just sped by me as if it owned the
road. In reality, the highway was big enough for both of
us—nobody else was out here—but he'd come charging up the hill as if he owned it, riding the median like
a daredevil with a grudge. I'd swerved again as I felt
the wind of that little car, and found myself staring at
its bumper in the rearview for the few seconds before
it disappeared over the next ridge. I'm, as you might
have figured, a little bit of a car nut, and there was
something familiar about those wheels. I hadn't gotten a good look at the driver, but in truth the car might
have been more distinctive.

Especially this time of year. Fall—foliage season—

is when we get everything up here. Dodge Caravans and SUVs more fit for off-road trailblazing than highway driving clogging up the roadways, mostly trudging along five miles under the limit. They support the local businesses, or at least buy our knickknacks, so the authorities like them. Me, I'm usually live-and-let-live, but if I can scare a few of them off the pavement, I consider that my civic duty.

Winter, we get some skiers—either passing through or looking for cross-country trails. And some of those folks like the sportier models, not that any of them know how to drive in snow.

But it was too late for the slopes and too early for anything else. Stick season, which brings nothing but the runaways. Year-round, they show up: adulterers looking for a place to play. A few odd scofflaws who have their own reasons for leaving the city. My ex Tom was one of those, a former cop who had come around on a private job—and had tried to enlist me in some shady dealings. Not that I'm averse to a little easy money, but time hadn't been kind to him, and with Creighton around, Tom had been easy enough to ignore.

Still, it didn't figure. That crowd doesn't want to be seen. They certainly don't drive sports cars. And that little red model? It sparked something. I remembered a diner. An older gentleman… But with that thought in mind, I'd come to the turnoff for the Haigens. I'd be at their door in five minutes, so it was time to concoct my story.

FIFTEEN

"DIERDRE, GREAT TO see you." I plastered my biggest grin on my face as I climbed the front stairs. The petite brunette who stood at the top had already opened the door with a look like a deer in the headlights, and I needed to get inside. "I'm so glad you're here." Her makeup was impeccable. It didn't move at all as she returned my smile.

My story, I'd decided, was that I was doing a preparatory home visit. An almost-final run-through before we settled Spot on her husband. It wasn't a bad cover. In the weeks to come, it would even be true. Basically, I wanted an excuse to ask about her and her husband's habits, their visitors and friends. Figuring out how Spot's routine might fit into all of that seemed reasonable enough.

"Pru." I didn't hear anger in her voice. Annoyance, maybe, but there could be other reasons for that. Fatigue. For all I knew, she was cooking dinner. Having a fight with her husband. Or getting rid of the evidence. "What a surprise."

It's the kind of thing people say when they don't want you there. Since she was unlikely to growl, it was all the warning I would get. And one I could easily ignore.

"I just had a very good day with Spot," I started in. "I think he'll be ready ahead of schedule, and I wanted to check in with you and Mr. Haigen to see where you stand."

"Where we stand?" She was confused, which is what I intended. In the moment of silence that followed, I shifted from foot to foot. She got it. "I'm sorry," she said. She wasn't, but she was as well trained as that dog would be. "I was—We've had a visitor. Won't you please come in?"

"Thanks." I looked around for the other guest. Not seeing anyone, I stepped by her, into an entrance hall that could have doubled for my old apartment, only neater. White stone tile would've shown any mud that tracked in, if any had dared, and the little rug—I'd have bet Tibetan—clearly wasn't for wiping my boots on. I slipped them off. I didn't like feeling unbalanced, but I wasn't sure of my options as I stood there, uncertain. Waiting. The only other vehicle out front had been a Mercedes SUV with tinted windows.

I knew that car. I'd seen it here before, and had asked about it then, being a gearhead in my own way. "Richard's eyes..." Dierdre had said, by way of an explanation, though I'd been more interested in how the GL drove. "We've put it on the market."

"No takers on the Benz?" I asked today. I couldn't see her driving it. Then again, it would have made driving Spot around easier. For all its size, I bet it had pickup.

"What? Oh, we're not selling locally." I nodded, unsure of what to make of this non sequitur. "Nick has it over at his dealership in Amherst."

Nick, the rich man's factotum. Then again, it was probably a smart move. Blue book value on this model was close to fifty thousand, more than most folks around here made in a year—and they had to eat on that. Yes, I had checked.

"And I should be getting it back there." The voice, deep and resonant, startled me. For all his size, Nick Draper moved quietly, coming up behind Dierdre. "Richard's asleep now."

I watched as he walked by me, pulling on a heavy barn coat that magnified his bulk. "You're taking care of him?" I wasn't sure what the dynamics were here, or if the buddy were actually more of a dogsbody.

"I'm helping out." He smiled, showing his teeth.

I smiled back. It wasn't reflex, it was a mutual display and completely conscious on my part. Brawny and craggy looking, rather than wrinkled, with a mop of dark hair that still looked like his own, Nick was probably used to women returning his smiles. I wondered again about Mariela. For all her apparent devotion to Richard, she might have found this big guy attractive. Then again, she might have found him as smug as I did.

"Think you can sell the car?" I hadn't realized he had a dealership. Hadn't realized any of this set had anything like a job.

He shrugged, but the smile didn't dim. "Better chance in Amherst than here. I had some people looking at it yesterday. They might want it for their summer home, the four-wheel drive and all."

He made it sound like a beater. Richard hadn't thought of it that way. Back when I'd first seen it, he'd looked miffed when his wife talked about selling it. "So, you're a used car salesman?"

He chuckled, low and deep. "You can say I'm a facilitator. I have an interest in a dealership out there, and if I can help a friend…" He let the sentence hang there, but his meaning was clear. He was a useful leech.

Dierdre cleared her throat with a dainty little cough. I'd almost forgotten about her. Nick's smile must have had more wattage than I'd been aware of.

"Thank you for all your help, Nick." Her voice had gone all formal; she was dismissing him. It was the wrong move, and it made me look at her harder. Was he here for more than her husband? "Richard was really upset," she said, turning to me, her dark eyes wide. "The whole thing with the girl…"

I nodded, wondering again about the dynamic, as her voice trailed off. Mariela was hardly a girl, and Richard wasn't the only person in the household who would have known her.

I'd taken the Haigens at face value. Ailing older husband. Picked-on younger wife. Somewhat younger, I amended my thoughts. Dierdre was probably a trophy at some point, but the glittery leaf had been flaking off for some time now. Maybe it wasn't Mariela who Richard was trying to pawn off on Nick. Maybe it was Dierdre.

"Not a problem, Dieds." Nick's low voice cut into my thoughts. The diminutive was intentional, I was sure of it. I'd seen his eyes dart to me as he'd said it. I held my breath, waiting to see if he'd touch her. How she'd respond.

He didn't. Bouncing the keys in his hand, he nodded to me and sailed out the door. I watched him drive the big Benz away.

When I turned to Dierdre, she was watching, too. The light raked her face, highlighting the fine lines around her eyes and her mouth that nothing could erase. She was last year's model, all right, and I wondered if Richard had made moves to replace her. You don't need sight to be vain. I'd heard how he talked, how he'd treated her, never mind that his wiry mop had more gray in it than she would ever allow. With all the work she put into herself, I wouldn't have blamed her if she'd sought a little extracurricular attention, though I might have questioned her taste. Nick was younger than her husband. Taller, too, his size coming from bones and muscle rather than flesh, but that smile wasn't much of an improvement over Richard's permanent scowl.

Had I interrupted a tryst, or something darker? She'd had too much work done for her brows to furrow, but something about her mouth, about the way she clasped her hands together, made me think that she wasn't happy to see the big man leave. Dierdre Haigen, I thought, was afraid.

I studied her for another cool minute before she remembered I was there.

"Sorry." She reached for her brow in a girlish gesture, as if to fix her hair. Her smooth, dark 'do was lacquered in place, but the move served as a screen, and when she looked up, her smile was back. It could have been the Botox that kept it from reaching her eyes. "Richard has just been devastated by all of this."

"All of this" was a neat summary for a woman's death. I nodded, wondering again how Dierdre felt about it.

"WON'T YOU HAVE some tea?" Dierdre's voice was softer now that she'd decided to welcome me in. There had been something about Mariela. Something, I'd had the feeling, she'd been about to say. "Richard, as you heard, is napping, but perhaps I could help you?"

"Actually, I'm here to help you." I put Mariela out of my mind. What I needed to do now was regain the ground lost when I'd taken my shoes off. I needed to assert my dominance over the situation. "And, of course, to express my deepest condolences."

Dierdre blinked at that, and I had a quick flash of Wallis purring. My tabby would have enjoyed seeing me toy with this pampered little mouse of a woman. When she didn't say anything, I threw out another prompt.

"Mariela was part of your household, wasn't she?" We were still standing right inside the foyer.

Dierdre Haigen's unnaturally plump mouth opened and for a moment the mouse resembled a goldfish. When those dark red lips snapped back shut, I knew that whatever came out next would be a lie.

"Why, yes, and thank you." Her dark head bobbed and one manicured hand fluttered in acknowledgment. Noblesse oblige. "It's not as if she were a member of the family, but still…" With another limp wave, she dismissed the life of a woman.

"Even so, you must have been devastated." I doubted anything touched this woman that deeply. Then again, I have my own prejudices.

"It was a shock." She dabbed at dry eyes. "Mariela had been with us for years."

That wasn't an answer, and it didn't do anything to break down my preconceptions about this woman. She might as well have been speaking about me, and we'd only met a handful of times.

"She did live on the premises, though, didn't she?" It was a guess. From the sudden tightness around her mouth, it was a good one.

"Well, yes. In the staff apartments." One of the outbuildings, I figured. If only I could get a chance to look at them. "But you came about the guide dog?"

"Indeed." I'd have my chance later, I determined. "Because Spot will be living here with you and your husband, I wanted to come by and see if I could get ahead of any problems."

"Problems?" Her brows managed to rise. "I thought the dog would be fully trained."

I had to smile at that. "He is." I nodded toward the room behind her and took a step. After only a brief hesitation, she followed me in. "But often people who don't live with animals don't realize what their limitations are. Or," I paused, taking in the room, "what the limitations of a newly disabled person may be." I saw more white, a fireplace that looked like it was never used, and the kind of furniture you see in design magazines. This wasn't a cozy room, and I wondered if anyone ever sat here. Then again, she had paused for some reason. I was going to find out why.

"That grouping, for example." Under the big picture window, metal-frame chairs were pulled up close to a glass-topped table. "That may become more difficult for Richard to maneuver around, as his sight deteriorates. Spot will keep him from walking into things—he'll stand in front of him to stop him, if he needs to—but it's just as easy to change a few things around. Make more space for both of them."

A noncommittal little snort greeted that. I had the feeling that Dierdre would more likely ban both her husband and his dog rather than rearrange a designed grouping.

"Richard is used to things being a certain way." She

wasn't looking at me, and I wondered if she was telling the truth. "He's very...particular."

Maybe I had been unfair. If so, a barked shin—or a fall—would change that.

She turned back to me. "But you were talking about accommodations for the dog?"

"Not accommodations, exactly." I was watching her and decided to risk it. "After all, I assume Spot will stay with Mr. Haigen. Will sleep by his bed." I paused, waiting. "In case he needs the dog during the night."

Another little nod that said nothing.

"Will that be a problem?" I couldn't ask outright what their sleeping arrangements were. Hell, to an outsider, Creighton and I wouldn't seem much like a couple either.

"Oh, no. No." She was distracted by something. I'd bet anything it had to do with the dead woman.

"Was caring for the dog going to be one of Mariela's duties?" It was a reach. I couldn't come up with anything better.

"I thought—You said that Richard would be with the dog constantly." There was a question buried in there.

I nodded. "Yes, but of course a dog has his needs. He'll need to be walked. Unless—" I looked out the window. The grounds were huge. "Have you considered putting in a dog run?"

"What? No." She crossed the room and reached for the curtain before catching herself. She'd been about to pull it closed, I was sure. What I didn't know was why. "We can have Raul walk him."

She didn't have to say that Raul was the help. The way she said his name did that, as did her easy assurance that he'd accept additional duties without question. Hey, it was a job. And it might, I realized, be an entrée to someone who knew Mariela better than this ice queen.

"Raul…" I let his name linger. Gardener, I'd wager. Maybe handyman or groundskeeper? That was my in. "May we check out the grounds?" I softened my tone, put on the smile again. "They look lovely, and it might help me get a sense for anything Spot might need."

"Now? No, no." Despite the smooth mask, the faintest suggestion of a furrow appeared between her eyes. "In fact, I was just on my way out. Do you mind?" She wasn't going to say anymore, I could see that. But just as clearly, she couldn't take her hand off that curtain. Not with me there. So I nodded as if I didn't notice, and let her lead me back to the front door. I took my time with my boots—if she really had an appointment, she'd have donned her own coat by then. When I finally couldn't stall anymore, I stood to shake her hand. She took it, but I'd swear she wiped it off as soon as I was gone.

I DIDN'T GO FAR. I didn't think she had any appointment, but I was hoping that the lie would spur her to get out of the house, just as cover. Maybe she'd rabbit off in search of help or advice. Either way, I figured it was worth a little wait. Parked as I was, a half-block down from her driveway entrance, I'd see if she pulled out, and I'd trot back to investigate. Those outbuildings intrigued me, and Creighton had said that Mariela had been moved. Creighton's people would have checked her living quarters. Creighton's too good a cop to let the obvious things go. But the Haigens were a big deal in this town, and I'd bet they could limit just how much of their property would be inspected, at least without a court order. Besides, I knew Creighton. He was tougher than he looked, but he didn't flaunt it. Until—and unless—he had reason to pounce, he would wait. My boyish beau was like Wallis in that way. Smooth.

It wasn't a cat that I wanted here, anyway. Once again, I kicked myself for not bringing Spot. His nose would have picked up a lot that I'd miss. Not that it would necessarily be easy getting the taciturn beast to share any of it.

SIXTEEN

I WAS ALMOST ready to go get him when I saw her leave. A different Mercedes, one of the little sporty ones, edged out of the woods and took off, making full use of its power. I saw her as she drove by, head back, hands easy on the wheel, and for a moment I could relate. Fast cars bring their own kind of freedom, a sense of power at your command. I wondered how Dierdre Haigen felt married to a man whose life was becoming increasingly circumspect, who must, at some level, be becoming more dependent. A man whose money had paid for those nifty wheels. Then she disappeared in the deepening shadows, and I turned my mind to the task at hand.

I didn't exactly saunter as I made my way past the house. I didn't hide either. I was a local, a professional, and perhaps more to the point if I met Raul or any of his colleagues, someone else hired by the Haigens to do a task. If anyone asked, I'd stick with my original story: I wanted to check out the site of a possible dog run. Hey, maybe I'd even do it, and talk the lady of the house into building one.

For now, I took my time—and the scenic route. A slate path skirted the big house before splitting. One branch led to a barn-like building—the garage, I figured, since an offshoot of the driveway also headed that way and I hadn't seen the missus' little speedster out front. The other wound its way through what would probably be gardens in a month or two, and so I followed, doing my best to look as if I belonged. As I walked, I listened. Birds aren't the brightest, but they do serve as an efficient early warning system, and if I was going to have to explain myself, I could use a heads-up. I figured something was waiting: up ahead, behind a screen of closely planted evergreens, I could see a cluster of buildings. Everything looked still, but it sounded still, too, which was weird. Granted, it was late in the day, but someone should have been peeping. Someone should be making a last-ditch attempt to claim those arbor vitae as his own. Instead, there was nothing more than the occasional muted rustling.

I stopped walking, trying to focus in. There was something. An oppressive quality to the silence. A sense of fear, unlike anything I had ever felt and I wondered who or what was out there. Not a hawk. Even an eagle would cause some squawking—the sharp "Flee! Flee! Flee!" of warning. Coyotes, even bobcats, would provoke the same. No, this was something from beyond the ecosystem. An alpha-plus predator. Probably, I figured, a human.

As I turned the last corner, I saw him. Bent over a rake as he neatened up a gravel courtyard between three buildings, he didn't look particularly threatening to me. Even when he stood and turned, I didn't see it. Short, a little plump, with the dark hair and cheekbones of Mesoamerica, he looked like a comfortable part of the landscape, quietly going about his business. Then again, I was as tall as he was—and not covered in fur or feathers. For all I knew, his chores included trapping or poisoning whatever creatures the homeowners considered pests.

"Hello." I waved and smiled. No sense in looking for a fight. "Are you Raul?"

"Yes." He tilted his head, considering me. He wasn't returning my smile. Then again, he'd just lost a colleague. "May I help you?"

"Dierdre—Mrs. Haigen—said you would be helping with the service dog?" It wasn't a lie, and it both made me sound like an intimate of the boss lady and like she'd given me a reason to come down here.

He didn't respond.

"You know, the seeing-eye dog for Mr. Haigen?" Sometimes the old names are more widely recognized.

It wasn't my phrasing though. At least, I didn't think it was. The short dark man in front of me still wasn't talking, but he was shaking his head. I wouldn't have put it past the lady of the manor to not have informed him yet of his new duties, but surely, working for someone as entitled as Dierdre Haigen, he couldn't have been that surprised.

"Do you mind if I take a look around?" Still smiling, I kept my voice as even as I would with a skittish animal and took a step forward. "I was wondering if we could put a dog run—"

"No! Go away!" Dropping his rake, he stepped in front of me. "Go back!"

I paused. Around me the birds had gone quiet again, a tense silence. The held breath before the strike. "Excuse me?"

"You have to go." He made sweeping gestures with his hands, as if he were scooping me out of the gravel. "Go!"

He wasn't big, but he was solid and I found myself retreating. "Wait, Raul. It is Raul, isn't it? Can't we talk?"

"No. No talking." His earlier facility with the language seemed to have left him, and his face appeared frozen in a grimace of pain or horror. "You go. Go now."

He bent for the rake. I didn't need another cue. Nodding and smiling like an idiot, in a last-ditch attempt to salvage my dignity, I took another step backward and then another.

"Go!" He advanced, rake in hand.

I turned and ran.

SEVENTEEN

"WELL, THAT WAS INTERESTING." I was talking out loud. Not to myself, exactly. It's a habit I've developed from being around Wallis, although my feline companion was too far away to respond. I was sitting in my car by the side of the road, waiting for my hands to stop shaking. "Very interesting."

It wasn't the rake, I decided, as I took a few deep breaths. Nor even the repetitive demand—the threat?— that I go. No, what had spooked me was the look on the stocky gardener's face. I've seen grief. Experienced it myself, more than once. This was something else— some combination of pain and shock that didn't quite compute. Horror, I'd thought initially, and sitting in my GTO, I decided that I'd been right.

The man with the rake had looked into the abyss. That was what was behind his hoarse exhortation, behind the raised rake.

It had to be related to Mariela. Granted, working for the Haigens probably had its problems, and I had no doubt that they could be petty and mean. But to provoke that kind of terror? No, something more serious had marked that man. Something that had resulted in a young woman's head nearly torn off.

Sitting there, I found myself wondering what Mariela had meant to him. Mariela had been younger. I pegged Raul in his forties, easily fifteen years older than the

dead girl. That didn't mean much. They could have been
married. They could have been relatives. Even friends.
His reaction would have been reasonable. Coworkers
sharing their bosses' casual abuse. Then he'd have reason to mourn her death, even be shocked.

But terror? Unless Creighton was a lot colder than I'd
given him credit for, I couldn't believe he'd let a civilian
see the girl as I'd found her. And if he hadn't exposed
the man with the rake to the full savagery of what had
happened to the dead girl, then what was he reacting
to? Even if the man back there had had to identify the
mutilated girl, she would have been cleaned up before
he viewed her. Wouldn't she?

I thought of the birds. Of the nearly complete silence of the grounds, despite those lush trees and a
well-planted garden that rambled down into the wooded
valley. I thought of my initial impression, my feeling
that fear permeated those grounds. And I thought of another possibility—the man back there knew what terror looked like. Raul had seen it, firsthand. He knew
what had butchered that poor girl. Whatever had gone
down, it had happened here.

I STARTED MY CAR, the rumbling of its 450-cubic-inch
engine soothing the last of my nerves. It was a leap,
one I had no way of proving, I realized as I pulled onto
the road. I had made a lot of assumptions. Assuming
the attack—the killing—had happened here. Assuming
Raul might have seen it. It all felt right up to that point.
It fitted with what I'd seen. What I'd sensed and heard.
But after that, it fell apart. Raul witnesses an attack and
then—what? If he couldn't save her, wouldn't he have

gone for help? Wouldn't he, at least, have wanted Mariela decently cared for? Washed and buried?

I mulled that one as my baby-blue baby took me toward the highway. The gardener did it, I thought, and it hit me: he might not have had any say in his role. Raul was the help. He could, possibly, have been enlisted in the disposal of the body, if someone with power over him had put the pressure on. That would explain the look, the terror. But it still didn't explain what had actually happened.

A wild cat, maybe a cougar. That's what the vet's report was suggesting. And, yes, I was willing to believe that some big cats—maybe not native, but something similar—were coming back into the area. We've got bears and coyotes now. It was only a matter of time.

But they weren't the only alphas, the only beasts who saw our wide-open space as territory to be claimed. In some ways, the Haigens were like any other predator. They take what they want. They don't feel responsible. And while I wasn't sure how the first part of that would play out in an animal attack, I had a sure sense of how the second part would.

Call it entitlement. If a wild cat had attacked someone on their property, the Haigens would be the first to raise the alarm. Oh sure, it would be nice if it were out of concern. If not for the poor young woman, then for her family or friends. More likely, it would be for themselves. "There's a killer out there!" The cry would be raised. "Do something." Creighton, Albert—none of us would have had any peace until the animal had been run to the ground.

Only, they hadn't. We hadn't heard anything. And someone had moved the young woman after her death.

Creighton was saying it wasn't an accident. He wasn't saying what he thought it was, and he surely wasn't telling me everything. He seldom did, but this time I didn't think I could wheedle it out of him.

What was I missing? Could the vet have been fooled? Could a savage attack been camouflaged, a body ripped to look like the work of a beast? Stranger things had happened. Dierdre Haigen might have the heart for it. I doubted if she had the strength. And her husband, well, he could do it, probably. If someone pointed him in the right direction.

Nick? He was a friend, supposedly, and I'd bet he had free range of the grounds. He was helping with Richard, too. He did favors for the Haigens, and friends like him had been known to get rid of inconvenient women— mistresses, and the like. But I'd seen Mariela. I'd seen how she'd been brutalized. There were simpler ways of disposing of a woman. And I doubted even a sleaze like Nick Draper could brutally assault a woman and then cruise back into the house, ready for cocktails. That led me back to Raul. Which just didn't make sense.

I mulled that over as I made for the highway and home. Wallis, I knew, would have an answer. Not that she'd say anything, but she'd give me the look. The green-eyed, dead cold stare. *"You're going soft on the gardener,"* that stare would mean. *"He's a little guy. A worker. You feel bad for him."* That would be the gist of it, though if she voiced anything at all, it would be much simpler: *"Oh, please."*

She'd be right. As much as the man with the rake had unnerved me, I didn't want it to be him. Partly, yeah, because he was the help, kind of like me. Partly, though, it was the expression on his face. It might have scared

the birds, but it hadn't been the face of someone planning violence. It was the face of a unwilling witness.

What had happened? What had Raul seen?

As if on cue, my phone rang. And, sick of the circling
cycle of my own thoughts, I reached for it. "Hello?" I
hadn't checked who was calling, but as I answered, I
realized whom I was hoping for. Who I, well, missed.
Damn Laurel Kroft.

"Ms. Marlowe, what a pleasure." It wasn't Creighton. It was a man, and a voice I recognized, but not one
that I could place immediately. "Don't tell me you don't
recognize me?"

A little smoky and older. Very smooth, like whiskey or... I thought of the car that had passed me on the
highway. A flashy little red number.

"Bill," I said. Gregor "Bill" Benazi drove a red Maserati. Funny thing was, I'd have thought that he'd have
driven it far away by now.

"You remembered." A dry laugh, like the wind over
dead leaves. "I'm touched."

I didn't respond. Benazi had helped me out of a jam.
Helped a cat, too, which spoke in his favor. Then again,
I had reason to suspect that the soft voice on the other
end of the line belonged to someone much more dangerous than any errant gardener.

"I was so pleased to see that you have your vehicle
back up and running." He didn't take notice of my lack
of response. Then again, he wouldn't. A short man, im-
peccably dressed from the soft sheen of his silk jacket
down to his Italian loafers, he was as smooth as the silver
fox he resembled, and just as much a predator. "Though
I confess, I was curious where you were headed."

Why did I think he already knew? "I had business

with the Haigens," I said. Benazi might spend most of his time on the wrong side of the law, but I had a feeling he would be acquainted with my clients.

"The Haigens," he wrapped the name in a small sigh. I could have been imagining that, because just then I had come to the highway. I didn't think so. "Friends of yours?"

"Clients." The road was empty. I was, I admit, intrigued. "I'm training a service dog for Richard Haigen."

"Hmm." Another noncommittal sound. "I didn't think Richard was available this afternoon."

"As a matter of fact, he wasn't." My gut had been right, and I found myself growing more curious. Dierdre and Nick had said Richard was sleeping, but I had no reason to believe them. "Was he with you?"

That chuckle again. "I prefer more salubrious company, Ms. Marlowe."

"Then, how…" I paused, unsure exactly what I wanted to ask.

True to form, he ignored the interruption, albeit with perfect decorum.

"Which leads me to the point of my call." I waited. This had to be good. "I was wondering if you would care to join me for dinner tonight, Ms. Marlowe? I believe a meeting, under congenial circumstances, of course, would be of benefit to us both."

I had to hand it to him. Without any kind of threat, the dignified little gangster had shut me up.

EIGHTEEN

"HMMM...*INTERESTING*." WALLIS had her tail wrapped around her front paws as she inspected my outfit for the evening. She was commenting more on my indecision than on the tailored jacket I'd chosen to give my jeans some polish. At least, I thought so. With her subtle tiger stripes and neat white bib, Wallis never had to worry about inappropriate attire.

I wasn't so lucky. I mean, I know I'm easy on the eye. I get the attention I want, and I know how to deflect what I don't, without any of the bells and whistles too many of my gender resort to. For my work, what I wear doesn't matter, and I usually opt for jeans and denim shirts that can take a fair amount of fur and drool and repel some of the more frenzied clawing.

For this dinner, however, I was at a bit of a loss. I'd agreed to meet the owner of that Maserati for a few reasons of my own, and not only because of his soft-spoken insistence. Curiosity being the main one. I'd met Benazi when I was trying to place a cat—a Persian whose owner had been killed by a rare dueling pistol. Benazi had some involvement with the pistol, either as a broker or a middleman of some other sort, the exact nature of which was still unclear. I'd never gotten the whole story out of him, and when he'd taken off—with the cat—I'd been left with more questions than answers. To have him show up now only raised more. I didn't see

the Haigens as gun collectors. For one thing, I couldn't
see any antique in that chrome and glass house. But the
fact that Benazi knew I was there lent credence to my
suspicion that he was involved with the couple, too.
Though in what way, I didn't yet have a clue.

I was also curious about why he had called me. I
mean, I think I'm hot shit. But one of the things working
with animals has taught me is how disposable we all are,
myself included. I have more respect for Growler—hell,
I almost had more respect for Alfred—than I did the
Haigens. But in their world, I'm just one more service
provider. Yet Benazi must have been keeping track of
me; the timing of that call was a little too pat.

Those were my prime reasons for going. As I buttoned the jacket and turned, checking out my silhou-
ette, I had to admit to another, too. While I had little
firm idea of what exactly Bill, as he'd insisted I call
him, actually did for his livelihood, I did know some
things about him. Take that car, for example. And the
two-hundred-year-old pistol, with its silver filigree and
the beautiful grain of its wood grip. These were parts
of Benazi's world, his toys if not his stock in trade. In
our brief interaction, what had been obvious was that
he had a knowledge of, and a taste for, the higher end
of life. Even Fluffy the Persian could be seen as falling
into that category, if you chose to see animals that way.
From another angle, you could say that I was maybe
coming to understand why she had chosen to go off with
the man. Especially when my main squeeze might be
straying. Bill Benazi was a good twenty years older than
Creighton, but a girl appreciates being treated nicely. At
the very least, steak is a toothsome break from pizza.

However, I'm not anybody's pet. Nor am I likely to

become one. Once Wallis and I had both approved my outfit, I grabbed my car keys and headed toward the door. I'd vetoed being picked up in no uncertain terms. I didn't ask how my caller knew exactly where I lived, even as he insisted that my rambling side street was "on his way." Benazi was the kind of man who knew many things, and I took it as almost a courtesy that he'd shared this. Still, I had set him straight on that point, too. I would meet him under my own power.

"Bearding the lion in his den?" Wallis watched from the back of the sofa as I pulled my leather coat over the jacket. The night was cold, and the feel of the soft hide comforting. *"You think that makes you...safe?"*

I looked over at her. Sometimes, I think she doesn't care about me. That she'd see me taken as prey without blinking, at least if she could be sure someone else would come along to fill my place. Sometimes, I think she's hiding a deeper attachment, and right now I chose to hear her words as a warning.

"It's a restaurant, Wallis." I conjured up images of tables, of people and light. "We're not going off to wherever." I didn't know where Benazi lived. Not in Beauville, I was fairly sure. Maybe in one of those mountaintop houses I would occasionally spy, now that the leaves and the snow were gone, sunlight glinting off picture windows as I raced down the highway. An aerie. Yes, that fit Benazi. It had been months, but I could still see his eyes, piercing and dark; a profile like a hatchet; and a smile as cold as death, despite the cordial urbanity of his words. His fancy sports car might not exactly fly, but the man was a hawk.

"Exactly."

I blinked. Wallis didn't, and I had to wonder: had

she put that image in my mind? There are few things
Wallis feared. Death from above, the strike of talons,
was one of them.

"It's just dinner, Wallis." I reached to stroke the dark
patch where her stripes came together. She leaned into
my hand and I felt her begin to purr. My hand, after all,
had also just tucked my knife into my boot.

I'D GOTTEN TO the bistro early, thinking to check out the
scene. I had a perfect excuse. The little restaurant—six-
teen tables in a converted mill house six miles out of
town—was new, and I could always say I wasn't sure
exactly where it was.

There was no need. He was waiting, sitting at a table
by the window. As I walked up from the parking area,
I could see him, as I was sure he'd intended. The place
was French, the chef from the city. And the candles on
the table were supposed to give a romantic glow to the
room. From outside, though, they did little to soften
the angles of that face. If anything, the dim lighting
made for more shadows, and his deeply set eyes were
cloaked in darkness.

As I stood there, he turned toward the window. I
froze. It was dark out. The paved path lit only by a series of low Japanese lanterns. There was no chance he
could see me, little chance he could see anything beyond his own reflection. Still, for a moment, I had a sudden desire to flee. My car was only a short walk away.
I owed this man nothing. Just then he smiled, though,
and I had the strongest sense that not only could he see
me, he could sense my hesitation. My, call it what it was,
my fear. And that was too big a challenge. I took the
last few steps to the door and came in out of the night.

"Ms. Marlowe." He stood, of course, reaching to take my hand as the maître d' pulled out my chair. I used the chair as an excuse not to give it to him. In part, I thought he might kiss it, and I wouldn't be sure how to respond. In part—that scene by the window—I had an eerie feeling about him touching me. A feeling like he would be able to pick up too much of what I was thinking, as if he were more akin to Wallis than to a man like Jim Creighton.

"Thank you for joining me." He dipped his hand, turning the rejection into a gesture of welcome. "Please."

A waiter came over with a balloon glass, filling it from a bottle I hadn't seen.

"I took the liberty of ordering." Benazi raised his own glass. "The chef has a decent cellar. Of course, if you'd prefer a cocktail…"

"No, this will be fine." I took a sip. Nice. "Thanks." As I replaced the goblet on the table, the movement of the wine within caught the candlelight and pulsed like blood. "So, what brings you to town, Bill?" I wasn't going to be lulled by all these classy appurtenances. Benazi was as civilized as Wallis, underneath his smooth exterior.

His raised eyebrow acknowledged this. "Always business with you, isn't it, Ms. Marlowe?"

"Please, it's Pru." Something about his honesty was charming. "And, well, I have to admit, it was strange to hear from you. Or maybe not so strange…" I drank a little more. The wine was good, and it gave me a reason to stop talking and observe him.

He nodded, again, as if I'd confirmed something for him. "What is it you do, exactly, Ms.—Pru?"

"I'm a behaviorist, sort of." It was his eyes, rather

than the wine. It was hard to lie to them. "I work with people's animals. Kind of a glorified dogwalker, in a way."

He laughed silently at that, his shoulders hunching up in his good wool jacket. "Please, Pru—"

Whatever he was going to say was interrupted, however. The waiter had arrived, with menus and a list of specials that seemed to utterly engage my date. When we'd ordered—I noticed we both went for the meat—he turned back toward me, and I braced myself for his next question.

It didn't come. Instead, he raised his glass. "May I propose a toast?"

I couldn't see any reason not to respond, and so I raised mine.

"To health and long life," he said.

"Long life." For a moment, I flashed on my mother. Sometimes, dying is a good thing. A much longed-for escape, and when I looked back up, I could tell Benazi had seen something on my face.

"I'm sorry." He reached over the table, and I let him place his hand on mine. His was warm and dry, and I trembled a little, as if I were a small animal. "You have had…" He paused, before starting anew.

"I have had the benefit of a long and varied life, Ms. Marlowe." I noticed he had switched from speaking about me to himself. I'd also noticed that he'd reverted to his prior form of address. I didn't correct him. In this setting, at this time, his formality seemed appropriate. Courtly, even. "And I have been witness to some things that perhaps are best not spoken of."

I waited, curious as to what he was going to say. Before he could continue, however, the waiter arrived with our salads, and I reached for my fork, automatically. With the first bite, it hit me then how hungry I was, how little I'd eaten all day. Which could, I thought while crunching down on the bitter romaine, explain the strange feeling I'd had. Those first few sips of wine must have hit me hard.

"I won't go into details," he began again once we were alone. The hand that had held mine now waved away the past, like an importunate moth. "But I have seen some unusual sights and met some highly unusual people."

He paused, as if expecting me to pick up the conversational gambit. I only nodded, chomping away. The passing thought that perhaps it was rude to keep eating as he bared his soul occurred to me. I dismissed it and speared more romaine.

He took a break, then, to address his own salad, though I had the distinct feeling that he was motivated more by a desire to put me at ease than by hunger. Well, I could wait. "And this has given me the capacity to recognize others who, well…" I hadn't thought to see Gregor Benazi at a loss for words. It was refreshing. "Let me just say that I believe you and I have more in common than either of us may have previously thought."

I looked up from the last bit of anchovy, curious as to what he was getting at. And, before I could follow up, our steaks arrived. As the waiter fussed with the pepper mill, I thought of my initial impression—that my dinner partner had appeared to be able to see me outside, in the dark. Could he have the kind of sensitivity I had? Did he really recognize it in me? We both remained silent even after the waiter left, and I realized the ball was in my court.

"You don't like coloring inside the lines either." The steak was delicious, and the first bite had brought me back to a more realistic conclusion.

It also gave Benazi an excuse to not respond, although he did nod slightly as he chewed.

"You're some kind of middleman, aren't you?" It wasn't exactly what I was thinking. It was, however, more polite.

Benazi didn't look like he agreed with my assessment. "Oh, Ms. Marlowe." His voice was pained. "You shouldn't try to reduce everything to some kind of…" He waved his fork, before spearing the bloody meat once more. "Some kind of transaction. It cheapens everything."

"I'll bet." Nothing about Benazi was cheap. Not that jacket, not the wine. Not our steak dinners, either, and so I took another bite. I had no idea how this evening was going to turn out, and I was not going to leave any of this dry-aged grass-fed treat uneaten. "But you do provide something—maybe a service?—for some of my more upscale clients."

I was fishing. He looked up, pausing as he cut into the steak. I'd hit close to something.

"For the Haigens?" I met his eye. "This wouldn't have something to do with Richard's car, would it?"

He addressed his steak once again. I'd missed something, though I didn't know what.

"As I was saying, Ms. Marlowe, we both share certain…skills." The pause, as well as his delicate choice of word, made me look up. He didn't stop. "For my part, I have found it most congenial to share your company, when our paths intersect. So many live in…" He paused. I was waiting: *cages*, I thought he'd say. Though why that and not something less animal, I couldn't have said. "…within preordained boundaries," he corrected himself. "It can be hard to find colleagues, much less peers."

So he thought we were both outside the law? Despite my iffy past, I did my best to sound offended. "I don't provide any shady services, Bill. Or any—" I thought again of that fancy gun— "goods. I train people's animals. I solve their behavior problems. I'm good at it."

One eyebrow came up, and I wondered again just how much he knew. How much he sensed. When he started talking again, however, it was as if he hadn't listened to me at all.

"What we do can be exhilarating." He was making good progress on the steak, and I wondered if he too was keeping track of the time. "Exciting even." He cut into the beef with care, looking for all the world as if that was all he was concentrating on. "Particularly to one who trusts in her own peculiar sensitivities." He took a bite, chewed, and then swallowed.

He attacked the remaining bit of meat without looking up. "But it can also be dangerous." His tone was gentle, almost warm. Listening to him, I heard the concerned tone of an older relative. Someone who knew me, and knew my capabilities. A caution, cloaked as a gentle admonition. An elderly gentleman's advice to a newcomer, at the very least. I'd not finished my steak by then, but I put down my knife and fork. My mouth had gone dry, but I'd lost the taste for the bloody meat, for the good red wine, and I waited. Finally, his own steak done, Benazi looked up at me, his dark eyes as cold and deep as I'd remembered. I looked into those eyes, neither of us speaking, and his last words took on another meaning. I knew them as a threat.

NINETEEN

I DIDN'T STAY for dessert. And while Wallis would be peeved when she learned of it, I rejected the waiter's offer to box up the rest of that good, aged meat. What I had swallowed would stay down. I'm tough that way. I was angry, rather than scared. Furious at the bait-and-switch the grizzled gangster had pulled to get me out here. But I had no desire to bring anything from that meal home with me.

Benazi got the message loud and clear. "I gather you wouldn't care for a brandy?" He sounded a bit regretful, as if threatening me had been an unpleasant task that he'd hoped could be skimmed over, quickly forgotten. "A café filtre?"

"I believe you've said what you called me here to say." I'd folded my napkin and replaced it on the table. If the waiter had any sense, he'd be bringing my coat. "And I've had more than my fill."

"Please, Ms. Marlowe." He raised his hand, as if to wave off my concerns. As if, even empty-handed, he wasn't dangerous. "I didn't mean to offend. I'm sorry if I did."

I didn't respond. I had to admit, I was still curious. Plus, I don't like to be chased off. "Well, then." I relaxed back in my seat and tried to figure out how to phrase my questions. "Tell me what you're doing in town," I said finally. I was too pissed to be polite. "Why were you watching me? And what's your connection with the Haigens?" I wanted to ask why he was threatening me. What I had gotten too close to—or who. I didn't think he'd answer those questions, though.

"And why do you think I know the Haigens?" That smile. As jolly as the grave.

"Come on." It was my turn to growl. That was the easy one. To his credit, he chuckled, and I found myself relaxing.

"You really do have a sense for such things," he said. "And, yes, you are right. I am acquainted with the Haigens. As you so astutely noted, I, like yourself, am particularly equipped to provide certain specialized services."

He paused. I waited. The waiter hovered. He might be afraid to drop off the check, but I had no compunction about leaving whenever I wanted. This was Benazi's party, and if he wanted to keep me here, he had to talk.

He came to the same conclusion. "The wealthy enjoy a different class of entertainment, at times," he said, brushing off the poor server with another eloquent gesture. "A touch of the, shall we say, exotic?"

I nodded, as if I understood. I didn't, not exactly. Don't let it be girls, I found myself wishing. Or, hell, boys. I thought of Dierdre, buttoned up so tight, and it seemed possible. Richard was an enigma to me. I didn't care about them, but I realized with a start that I didn't want to think worse of Benazi either. For some reason, I still felt some kind of link to him. Some connection. At any rate, I was curious.

"So what new toy have you brought them recently?"

I leaned in now, waiting for the big reveal. "And why are you warning me about it?"

"Because of what you do, Ms. Marlowe." He smiled, his eyes as wide and innocent as they could ever be. "Because of who you are. And because, Ms. Marlowe, I care."

TWENTY

CATS CAN'T LAUGH, not without producing a fur ball anyway. And Wallis was way too dignified for an involuntary barf. She did, however, manage to convey an amused skepticism as I related the tale of my evening.

"And then you ate?" She put her ears back a little with that, and I realized the obvious: she hadn't been fed.

"It's not just that." She watched as I shredded a chicken leg onto a plate. Her ears had righted themselves, and she'd begun kneading the floor. I smiled, but averted my eyes. She wanted to be taken seriously, I could tell. *"It's that you fed...willingly."*

I paused, a piece of skin in my hand, and thought about that. A small chirp, the feline equivalent of her clearing her throat, brought me back to the task at hand, and only after I had placed the plate on the floor did I finish thinking through what she had said.

She was right, in a way. I hadn't finished my steak, and now that I was home, I was regretting that I hadn't taken the leftovers with me. However, I had gone willingly with Benazi.

"It was a public place." I looked down at the back of her head. Wallis was digging into the chicken, and I found my own mouth watering as she savored the roasted meat. "Besides, I was curious."

"So you don't..." A pause as Wallis savored a particularly toothsome bit. *"You don't fear him. Not really."*

"I don't know." I leaned back on the counter to consider. "I didn't going in, but…" As best I could, I let her know my mixed emotions, replaying in my mind what had happened as I approached the restaurant. That strange sense that he could see me, out in the dark.

"Rather feline, don't you think?" She was looking up at me now and licking her chops.

"You just like him because he likes cats." Wallis had been much more comfortable with Benazi's adoption of the white Persian than I had been. Then again, I suspected him in the death of a human witness. He'd always been kind to animals.

Which brought me back to my original question: What had Benazi been telling me? If he wasn't a threat to me—and I rather respected Wallis' take on that, if for no other reason than that his demeanor had continued courtly, even as I grumbled off into the night—then what? He could have been warning me. Something was definitely off in the Haigen household—something besides a problem with the help, and now more than ever I was convinced that Mariela's death had its roots in the big house.

I had tried to get him to tell me more, to explain what he had been doing there, and what he meant by the Haigens' taste for the exotic. Standing in my own kitchen, with Wallis' eyes on me, the answer came to me. Mariela. When she'd first donned that silk blouse, she would have been beautiful. With her thick black hair and café au lait skin, she could qualify as exotic, as well. Richard Haigen might be going blind, but that didn't mean he wouldn't want his last sights to be of a woman noticeably younger than his beleaguered wife, and, of course, sight would be the least of the senses he might indulge. Was murder the exotic thrill he now craved? Or was her death an accident, and her mutilation an attempt to cover up some horrible game gone wrong?

It was possible. Add in his anger—at his wife, at the world—and the idea gained credence.

With a sigh of relief, I realized another thing. No matter what I thought of Benazi, I doubted he had been involved with obtaining Mariela for the Haigens. I'd seen the young woman both times I'd been out at the house, and her duties—at that point—had seemed fairly standard, if somewhat demeaning. Benazi was strictly high-end. So what had brought him out to that sterile house?

By this point, Wallis had left the room. I followed her into the living room, to find her staring pointedly at the fireplace. It was cold enough and I still had logs left, and so I built a fire and poured myself a bourbon. Maker's Mark was my only other company as the evening wore on, however, and I let the logs burn down to embers, watching the shadows fade into the night as the room grew dark.

There really was no need for comment, and for once, Wallis didn't intrude into my thoughts. We sat there in a companionable silence, and I found myself watching the glow turn to ash, contemplating how little any of us—two- or four-legged—really understood each other.

TWENTY-ONE

"YOU'RE UP BRIGHT and early." With so many questions rattling around my head and no Creighton to distract me, I'd slept badly. Wallis picked up on my snarky tone as I walked into the kitchen and acknowledged it—barely—with a flick of her tail. "Want some breakfast?"

It was a peace offering, but she took it, jumping down from the sill to brush ever so slightly against my bare legs. I waited a moment to enjoy the soft touch of her fur, before fetching the eggs and butter. Once the pan was warming up, I started my coffee. I knew I'd been out of line.

"I miss him, too." Her voice reached me as I fetched my mug, but by the time I turned, she was facing away from me again. Wallis puts a premium on dignity. All cats do.

"Thanks." It couldn't hurt to acknowledge the courtesy. There really wasn't anything else to say.

"Not to say, perhaps." She'd come back over as I gave the eggs one last scramble. *"Doesn't mean you just have to roll over."*

I placed her plate on the floor. "We've had this discussion, Wallis."

"More than one way to dispose of a rival..." Her thought trailed off into a reverie of butter.

"You're thinking of Mariela, aren't you?" No answer. She didn't need to. I'd wondered that myself, though in the light of day the idea that the young woman had been murdered by the overbearing millionaire seemed increasingly slim. For starters, he would have to have intended—from the start—to make it look like an animal attack. The mutilation I had seen had been the cause of death, Creighton had said. Not postmortem. That ruled out a sudden act of passion. Although I didn't have any reason to trust our county coroner—he was basically a country GP—I figured he had the basics right. But how could it have been done? And why?

"Rival." Wallis' word stuck with me. If I was looking for a motive for the young woman's death, I could see Dierdre Haigen having one. I didn't doubt that her husband could be cruel. He may have cheated on her. He seemed the type. But he was also rapidly growing more dependent and, if anything would give her the upper hand, his blindness would. Why would she kill a rival when in a few months, the younger woman's youth and beauty would be worth a lot less than her committed caring? When, soon, he would be essentially in her control?

Unless, of course, she didn't want to become her husband's caretaker. Maybe she and Raul... No, none of it added up to a mauled body in the woods.

"Are you going to eat those?" Wallis was staring at me, but her thoughts were on my breakfast.

"Yes, I am." Last night's steak had been interrupted, just as my exploration of the Haigen grounds had been. Laurel Kroft had been out there, though, and she knew more than she'd said. Creighton had seen it, too. He'd be questioning her, I had no doubt. I didn't want to think about what means he might resort to to get the truth out of her. Better to think of my own methods.

Pouring my coffee into a travel mug, I scraped the last of my eggs onto Wallis' dish. Thoughts of Laurel with Creighton had soured my stomach, and Wallis likes her food. It's the only appetite she has left to indulge. I don't think that was why she was purring, though, as I got ready to start my day.

First, there was Growler. In the year since I'd been walking him, his person—if old lady Horlick counted as human—had started using me more often. That wasn't out of concern for the bichon's health, I was pretty sure. More likely, she was hoping to put me on a leash. Gossip was like oxygen to her. Or, more likely, nicotine. And while I never gave her anything intentionally, the fact that I had been in the middle of some small-town scrimmages made her want to hang onto me. At least, that's what I figured her interest was. Until Growler had made that comment about the old bag losing her man, I'd not given any thought to any other possible desires.

"Hey, Growler." I broached the subject once I had freed my charge from his noxious human. "What's the story with old smoke-teeth?" I used the name he'd given her with a certain relish. After all, she'd been the one to saddle him with the cutsey-poo Bitsy.

"The story?" He looked up at me, a bit peeved. I should have waited. He'd just gotten to the birch on the corner, and the thaw had released a winter's worth of scents.

"Sorry." I didn't think he heard that often enough. "I was wondering about what you'd said, that she'd 'lost him.'" I paused, unable to tell if he was ignoring me or if I wasn't getting through. "Did she have a relationship with someone? A man?"

A short bark let me know he'd heard. And that he

was amused. *"If you can call it that!"* For a tiny, neutered animal, Growler was very conscious of his masculinity. *"Yes. They sit together."*

I pondered that as we walked on. If we think the ways of our domestic animals are strange, imagine how they feel about us. Sitting could mean almost anything. Did they dine together? Did she babysit some old codger, maybe someone who didn't have the wherewithal to escape her tar-stained clutches?

"Yes, that's it. They hold things." Of course, Growler had been monitoring my thoughts. He'd also stopped walking and was staring up at me. And so I tried to blank out my mind and simply accept what he wanted to show me. I looked into his black button eyes and got an image of...

Feet. Well, yes, to Growler, most human activity was too high up to observe in detail. But another sharp bark brought me out of myself, and I realized I was getting more. There were feet, four pairs of them. But they weren't holding weight; the people were seated. Close together, at a small table.

"They play *cards* together?" It was my tone. It was all wrong. Scornful and a little amused. I knew it as soon as the words were out of my mouth, but by then it was too late. Growler was walking again, tugging on the leash as he made the rest of his rounds. Even as I apologized, he pulled me forward, exerting just enough pressure to remind me that I was, after all, the servant here, the one hired to do his bidding. By the time he squatted to crap in the middle of the sidewalk, I was as repentant as I'd ever been. I cleaned up his mess without a word of reproach, and let him set the pace the rest of the way back.

Before we turned up the Horlick walk, however, I had to try again.

"Growler, I'm sorry. You know I am." An appeal to his pride couldn't hurt, I figured. Acknowledging that he could read me better than I could him was the kind of admission he'd usually get a kick out of. "I simply don't understand."

He trotted ahead of me, looking for all the world like a happy pet. When the door opened ahead of us, I realized what he already knew: Tracy Horlick had been peeking out her window. Whether she was simply waiting for our return or had been hoping to catch me in some bizarre behavior was immaterial. She was sharp enough to recognize that I didn't quite fit into our small town. I didn't need her guessing at anything else.

"It's about time." She stood in the door, ignoring the lead I held out to her. "I thought, maybe, since you've been spending so much time alone, you'd tried to steal my dog."

I'm taller than she is, but she was in the doorway, while I was standing two steps down. It was a power play, expressing dominance. I smiled back up at her, refusing to answer even as she let out a cloud of smoke and took Growler's lead. I forced myself not to blink as it hit me full-on and Growler, still silent, walked past her into the house. It was a petty victory, and she'd probably make me pay for it later. I didn't care. I have my limits.

"I hear we're both spending some more time on our own." I couldn't resist.

She blinked and drew back. I'd scored.

"I don't know where you get your information." Her

eyes, already heavy lidded, narrowed like a snake's, and she hissed. "Or maybe I do, considering…"

I held my smile and waited.

"You are a cold one." She stepped back, unwilling to give me more. It didn't matter. Something about her response, watching me. Studying my face. She had clued me in: The feet? They were seated around a card table. The "he" who had gone missing? Probably just a bridge partner. Knowing what I did of the old lady, I doubted there was anything more tender going on. Maybe they had signals arranged. I could easily see her cheating. That had to be it, though. Some old man had changed his seat, sick of her domineering ways or the stale scent of unfiltered Marlboros.

I could take some satisfaction in knowing that I'd gotten to her, but that was it. I was musing on her final comment as the door closed, and had turned to walk away when I heard a sharp yelp.

That shook me. Tracy Horlick was a horror. She certainly wasn't above taking out her frustrations on her dog, and if I'd made her mood worse, I was just as responsible for his pain.

"No! No! No!" I almost stormed the door, some latent instinct fighting with my common sense. Anything I did now to intervene would only make things worse for the little guy. *"Stupid lady!"*

I paused, frozen in place. Yes, Growler was barking, but he wasn't addressing Tracy Horlick. He was talking to me, the one who could understand him, only his voice—as well as those clipped cries—were fading. I heard the old lady muttering to herself, and could easily imagine the scene inside as she dragged him by his lead down the hall.

"Growler?" I put everything I had into the question, leaning my head against Tracy Horlick's front door. If anyone passed by, they'd have something to talk about. I didn't care. *"What is it? Are you okay?"*

"Stupid lady, getting her angry." The answer came with the scrabble of claws as an inside door closed. *"Look at the shoes, walker lady! The shoes! Shoes! Shoes."*

TWENTY-TWO

THE SHOES? GOD, I was dense. Growler would know that I lacked his sensitive nose. That any scents that he'd tried to convey with that one image would be lost on me. Still, there was something that he thought I would see—that I could have seen, if I'd only had half my wits about me.

I'd driven around the corner and parked. Sitting there, I tried to reconstruct the image the bichon had presented. Yes, I'd seen Tracy Horlick's shoes—faded aerobics shoes, the kind that allowed plenty of room for her bunions. I'd never seen her in anything other than scuffed-up slippers, but something about those feet was familiar. Maybe I wasn't as hopeless as I'd thought. She was partnered with someone similar: tan walking shoes, the orthopedic kind. The third belonged to a man, a big man and one who still had it together enough to go outside. Topsiders, a bit worn, but paired with socks, I was glad to see. The fourth pair had been clad in leather. Old leather, to be sure, but surprisingly nice, now that I thought of it. Soft-looking, and evenly worn, as if they'd been crafted particularly for this wearer.

I saw tassels, the kind of detail an Italian shoemaker might...

No, I blinked to clear my mind. Clearly I was conflating memories. Putting my own thoughts on the picture Growler had given me. My imagination was getting away with me, much like that fifth pair that I now saw, walking up behind the old man. Those weren't old lady shoes. Nor did they belong to a nurse or a servant. Unable to stop myself from watching the movie playing out in my head, I saw the glow of buffed leather. The pointed toe of a boot and, when they turned, a stylish heel. Not too high for Beauville. Outdoorsy, though still sexy. The kind of heel that elongated legs that were already long and lean. The kind that went with a four hundred-dollar pair of boots. Provided, of course, you were one of the better paid professionals in the area. Though what Laurel Kroft had to do with Gregor Benazi or Tracy Horlick, outside of the fevered imaginings of my sleep-deprived mind, was totally beyond me.

TWENTY-THREE

THAT WAS IT. I needed to sit down with Laurel Kroft and find out what the hell was going on. She could dally with Creighton. He was fair game. She could even fool around with Benazi, if she wanted. It would be her funeral. Or not. In reality, I found myself thinking as I drove across town, the sly old coot was much too suave to do violence to a woman he had a personal relationship with. Business, well, that was a different matter.

And it hit me, with a force that made me pull over to the side of the road. Maybe she had been in that scene on business. A quartet of oldsters, playing bridge—or poker—around a card table. That scene could have taken place at the retirement community where Laurel consulted. Hey, for all I knew, her high-priced services involved monitoring their card games. That would also explain some of Tracy Horlick's latest gossip. Maybe Creighton had visited the good shrink while she was making her rounds. Nothing untoward needed to have happened. Horlick had a nose as keen as Spot's for that kind of thing. And Benazi? I didn't see him as a resident, not even if he did fit the demographic. Visiting a friend…or a client. Yeah, that was possible, too.

Was that what he'd been trying to talk to me about? Was he warning me about Laurel Kroft?

Pulling back onto the road with an urgency that left rubber, I headed into town. Laurel Kroft was going to answer some questions. And if she wasn't willing, her dog would. But first, I needed some background. Doc Sharpe had originally referred me to her. At the time, I'd been grateful enough not to ask any questions. Part of my charge was to find a suitable foster for Spot, the first dog in my care. The fact that she was a single woman, with the means to feed and house an animal and without any kids to grow overly attached to the temporary pet made her seem perfect. Talk about gift horses.

That didn't mean I couldn't prime the pump. As I drove, I called. The call went straight to voice mail.

"Laurel? Pru Marlowe here." I paused. I hadn't totally thought this out. "I wanted to talk with you today before I take Spot out. I'm wondering if he may have some issues interacting with other animals, and if that's something we need to work on." It was a reach, but if I wanted to link Laurel with Tracy Horlick—and maybe Gregor Benazi, too—I would use what Growler had showed me. I hadn't seen Spot in the bichon's vision, but I could fake that. I could ask what other animals she'd come in contact with. Maybe even facilitate a meeting, see what came of it.

My mind was wandering over the possibilities as I drove. Yesterday, I'd acted hastily. I should've taken Spot over to the Haigens' house. Could I do that today without arousing suspicion? Was there any other way to get more info about the dead girl?

Another call. Another direct to voice mail beep. "Hey, Laurel. Pru again." It hit me as I spoke. "Do you know if there's going to be a funeral or any kind of memorial for Mariela? I might want to take Spot to it, if so. Animals can really benefit from closure." I managed the shrink word without choking. Jargon aside, I was telling the truth, although I doubted that any service devised by a human would do the trick. Besides, I'd just about reached County by then.

Pammy wasn't who I wanted to see. But like some ponytailed Cerberus, she sat at the front desk of the animal hospital, popping her gum with a ferocity no guard dog could emulate. I didn't think it was stupidity that made her gaze so blank, though. No, as she looked up at me, slowly blinking, I felt something else going on behind those pink-shadowed lids.

"Pammy." I nodded. That was as much acknowledgment as I could muster. The waiting area was full, and to my ears the usual animal cacophony had an added dimension, as hurt and frightened animals called out for help or for their people. "Doc Sharpe in?"

Another pop, as she took a sudden interest in a stray lock of hair. I'd been through this with her before. The silent treatment, a la Pammy. Usually, it was because I worked directly with Doc Sharpe if not quite as a behaviorist, then at least as an actual vet assistant, rather than a part-time receptionist. Last time, it had been worse. I'd not only refused to help her with the rudimentary crowd control, I'd spoken roughly to some young hunk. He might have been a football player, but he had no understanding of the terrier mix he'd adopted, and I'd needed to break through his jockish preconceptions.

"If this is about Igor, you've got to get over it." He was big, but I'm considerably tougher. I had him near tears by the time he left. I'd probably saved his dog's life, though, so all in all, it had seemed a good tradeoff to me. Not to Pammy, obviously. "Think of it this way. I was the bitch, so you got to be nice girl."

That registered. I could tell because she closed her

mouth. When she looked up, there was something like recognition in her wide blue eyes. "His name's Ivan," she said. "And he does think you're a, you know…the B word."

"Good for Ivan." If this was her victory, she could have it. "Doc Sharpe?"

"In the back." With a flourish, she pressed the buzzer releasing the door. The gesture showed off her newly lacquered nails and the kind of ring that probably counted as an all-access pass. I decided to ignore it, but as I walked past, she waved it in the air.

"You catch more flies with sugar, you know." I smiled, tight-lipped, to keep from responding. If I wanted flies, I'd trade Wallis in for a toad.

"Pru! Good to see you." Doc Sharpe stepped into the hallway, emerging from one of the examining rooms. "I hear you've had a little excitement."

This time the smile was real. Doc Sharpe might sound like a refugee from another century, but his heart was in the right place. "You could say that," I said. "Spot came through like a trooper, though."

"Good." He nodded, satisfied. "I've always known you've had an affinity for certain animals, Pru. And, given your predilection for fieldwork, as opposed to, say, an academic discipline, I believe the service-dog program is proving to be the right track for you."

As I said, he talks like that. He had also nudged me into the training program, and as clearly as a Labrador pup was begging for a reward. "It is. Thanks again, Doc." I gave it to him. "It was a great idea."

His smile couldn't have been more doglike, and I wouldn't have a better opportunity. "Speaking of which,

Doc, I was wondering if we could talk a bit about Laurel Kroft?"

"Oh?" I'd followed him down the hallway. He'd just unlocked the large closet that serves as the hospital's drug dispensary, and looked back at me, a note of caution on his face.

"Sorry." I stepped back. He trusted me with the drugs, I knew that. It was training. Well, training and a recent scare we'd had in town with prescription abuse. I leaned back on the door frame, arms crossed, as he opened a refrigerator and counted out some vials. "Busy?"

He made a noncommittal noise, and started counting again. When he was done, he looked up. "Must be the change in seasons. I'm seeing a lot of stressed animals. I don't like to rely solely on psychopharmaceuticals, even when indicated, but sometimes…"

I nodded, waiting while he closed the fridge and placed the vials on a small tray. Medicating animals is as much an art as a science.

"I've been seeing it, too." This was the line I'd taken with Laurel. "In fact, I'm wondering about some interactions that Laurel may have brought Spot into. That's why I wanted to talk with you."

His white eyebrows went up. "You don't think… the cougar?"

For a moment, I didn't understand. I had a few years on Creighton. Laurel might have had a few more. But, no, he meant the cat. "I don't think she exposed the animal to danger." I wanted to interrogate her, not get her arrested on animal cruelty charges. "I do have some questions, though."

"Pru, I don't like to get involved in personal matters.

You know that." Those eyebrows had begun bunching in distress. "And I know you tend to get involved with, well…" His voice trailed off. Maybe he had meant the other type of cougar.

"I don't care who she's dating. Jim Creighton is his own man." There, I'd said it. I almost believed it.

"Jim, who? You mean Detective Creighton?" I'd spilled my guts for no reason. Doc Sharpe looked as puzzled as a Pekingese, and I felt the color flood my face. God, I was getting as bad as Pammy.

"I—never mind. You were saying?" I waved my confusion away like an annoying fly.

Yankees aren't comfortable around emotions. Or women, most of them. Doc Sharpe was happy to recount his little vials and step back into the hall. "What I, uh, meant, Pru, is that, well, I feel I know you by now."

Not that well, clearly, I wanted to say, but I waited. He was having enough trouble getting this out.

"I'm happy to discuss options for your charge. For Spot, that is." He seemed to be having trouble with the keys. "And, of course, any legitimate questions about his care, and the fostering and care of any future service animals you may be chosen to—you may choose to work with."

He got the door locked to his satisfaction at last. As he looked up at me, I saw a deep sadness in his tired eyes. "You will have to learn to distance yourself, however, Pru. Part of this program, perhaps the hardest part, is training these beautiful creatures and then handing them over to others. That's what you're doing. That's why you're doing it. If you're going to get so attached that you feel a false sense of competition with Spot's foster parent, well, then, perhaps I was wrong, and this field isn't right for you."

TWENTY-FOUR

NOT MUCH CAN leave me at a loss for words, but Doc Sharpe had done it.

"I'm not—" It wasn't that I didn't try to explain. "I'm…" It's that each time I started to stutter out a response, I realized I was about to get myself into more trouble. No, I'm not overly bonded with the dog. It's just that another dog showed me something? Doc Sharpe already had enough weird ideas about me, I didn't need to give him another.

I was settling on something noncommittal that neither of us believed. But as I turned to make my escape, I heard another voice—a sheltie, I think—calling out in pain and fear. *"Ow! Ow! Ow!"* It was horrible—an almost-human cry of distress, more like a hoarse wail than a canine howl. The sound came from one of the examining rooms, but it was loud enough to reverberate through the hall. I could hear the voice as clearly as I'd heard Doc Sharpe. To the white-haired vet, it was probably just so much barking.

Still, he paused, raising a hand to stop what he figured would be my continued protestations. And in that moment, I marveled again at the forbearance of the man. He thought he knew how odd I was. He didn't know the half of it, but he not only put up with me, he tried to help me, steering work my way. And while he might not understand animals in the way I did, he did what he could. He tried.

"Doc, want some help?" It was the least I could do, and when he nodded, distracted, I followed behind.

Pammy, of course, was there already. Not that this was a good thing. She'd taken what looked like a mother and young son into the examining room, and was trying to calm down the shaking sheltie that she had placed on the cold steel examining table. Now that we were in the room, the source of some of the dog's distress seemed obvious: his person, the boy, was near tears. And Pammy wasn't helping. Between rolling her eyes and popping her gum, she'd also managed to insert herself between the boy and his mother—and, more to the point, the agitated dog, all the while holding the dog so that he couldn't turn away from the flustered mother and toward his primary concern, the boy.

It was a little thing, but it was the worst move possible. Shetlands are sheep dogs. They herd; it's what they do. To a dog in pain, reasserting some kind of order on the universe was essential, and Doc Sharpe's blonde catastrophe was making that impossible.

"Why don't you let me help you?" I kept my voice low and even as I moved in. No point in trying to train this one, no matter what Doc Sharpe might think. Resisting the urge to elbow her out of the way, I slid between her and the table, so she had to step back. Released, the little collie turned and I felt something like a warm pulse as he and his boy saw each other again. Before the dog could jump into his arms, however, I put my hands on his small, warm torso. It's protocol for a reason: Doc Sharpe didn't need to have an injured animal sliding off a table.

But this time, I was the one who nearly hit the floor.

"Pru, are you alright?" I blinked. Doc Sharpe was staring at me. The sheltie, luckily, was back in his boy's arms, the pair being held by a mother in full-on tiger mode.

"I'm sorry." I shook my head to clear it. I was back against the counter, as if the dog had thrown me off. I had no idea how I'd gotten there. No idea. "It must have been static electricity."

It was the best I could come up with, that's what it was. And although Mama Bear didn't look at all convinced, Doc Sharpe nodded as if what I'd said made sense.

"Why don't you go lie down?" He had a practice to protect, after all. "In my office."

I nodded, trying to salvage a smile for the mother and her boy, and staggered out. The dog would be fine, I was sure of that. He had a cut on his paw, and something— a sliver of glass, it seemed—was still stuck deep in the pad. Doc Sharpe would excise it, clean it, and put some antibiotic salve on the wound before wrapping it. He'd apply some balm to the sheltie's people, too, laying on the gruff charm that was as responsible as his actual expertise for his popularity.

What got me was that he shouldn't have had to do any of it. This was a minor injury. The equivalent of a canine splinter. Ordinarily, he could have greeted the people, and nominally overseen my diagnosis. Then he could have moved on to more urgent cases, leaving me to irrigate the wound and apply the dressing. Even Pammy could have done it, if it weren't for her execrable bedside manner and complete disregard for the feelings of those around her.

Feelings. That's what had gotten me in trouble. And now they had made additional work for Doc Sharpe, not to mention adding to his suspicions of me. I couldn't help it, and as I made my slow way down that hallway, I tried to piece together what I'd felt. What I'd seen. It didn't make sense.

"Pru?" The whine in her voice broke through my stupor. Pammy, pouting. "Is Doc Sharpe still in there with those people?"

I nodded. At least her dimness was predictable.

"Because we're piled up ten-deep out front. And if you're not going to take some of the work from *him*..." She had crossed her arms, but the way she was tapping her fingers let me know she was jonesing for a butt. Besides, she had a point. If I couldn't help out the vet, I should be willing to handle the front desk.

"Sorry, Pammy." I shook my head. Doc Sharpe was right. I should lie down. His consulting room had a small couch. "I can't."

"Are you sick?" Her voice ratcheted up half an octave. "You look awful!"

"Yeah, well..." I couldn't do it. I knew what she was waiting for. The barbed comeback that would reestablish our equilibrium. The snark that would send her flouncing down the hall. If I wouldn't cover for her during her break, she at least wanted a good grudge.

I wasn't up to it, however. I had no fight in me. I had lost the focus. I had made it as far as Doc Sharpe's door, and was reaching for the doorknob. His sofa and the oblivion of sleep seemed like heaven. If I could sleep, that is. But I was strangely exhausted, and I wanted to try. What I didn't want was to think about what I'd just seen. What I had just heard.

I had worked through my own fears, early on, about what this supposed gift meant. I had some theories, and I'd had Wallis' unsentimental attitude to pull me out of what could have been a major funk. The sensitivity had even given out on me once or twice, when I needed it, making me value it all the more when it came back. Unless, of course, it had never been a special sense. Unless it had never been more than my behaviorist training leaching somehow into the slow erosion of my sanity. Because it had been a long winter, and a cold one. I knew that, knew it with every sensible New England fiber in my being. But what I also knew was that—although that poor little sheltie couldn't identify his nemesis—the animal that had scared him so much, that had caused him to panic so badly that he had run without any hesitation over shattered glass, was not possible.

There was no way that Beauville was being stalked by a snow leopard.

TWENTY-FIVE

I'M NOT THE fainting sort. Far from it, but just then, the idea of lying down for a bit was very attractive. Trouble is, I've given in before. Got myself hospitalized, back when my sensitivity first manifested itself, when all those voices seemed to be coming out of nowhere. And while my stay in the bin was voluntary and I was able to leave under my own power three days later, it wasn't an experience I wanted to repeat. And so, just as I turned the knob to Doc Sharpe's consulting room, it hit me that I had to leave. Other people's problems might be solved for them while they reclined with an ice pack or a beer. Me? I'm on my own.

County has a back door—fire regulations being what they are—and I took advantage of it, striding out as quickly and purposefully as I could, a don't-mess-with-me look on my face. No human dared stand in my way, although I did hear a startled squawk from the bird room. Smaller animals are the most attuned to this kind of determination. They have to be to survive.

My motivation wasn't that different, I realized as I cut up the alley toward my car. Sure, it presented as ferocity, but that's my own form of protective coloration. In reality, I was as shaken as I've ever been, save for that one time. And my instinct was to run to the one creature who had been able to reach me then: Wallis. She'd been pissed when I'd checked myself into the hospital, not to mention hungry by the time I'd gotten home. But she'd taken care of me, in her way, alternately cajoling and chiding me into something akin to acceptance. I owed her my life, although neither of us likes to speak of it. I was going home to her now. Lunch, and a consult with my cat. That's what I needed to set me right.

I pulled onto the highway, my mind racing. The thaw had left damp patches on the pavement, and now I was seeing them as leopard spots. The shadows, too. Trees casting dark blotches against the tawny ground. Taking a deep breath, I made myself lift my foot from the accelerator. Just because my breathing was fast didn't mean my reaction time was. Not right now. Until I was sure, I needed to be careful.

Sure of… What? I could tell my speed was inching back up, but for a moment there, I felt like normal. I was regarding this as a problem, as Wallis would. Well, if Wallis could drive and worried about things like her sanity. Because it really came down to two options. One, I was losing it. Perhaps temporarily through some combination of low-level alcohol poisoning, stress, and hunger. Perhaps not. Or two, there really was a snow leopard, a majestic beast more customarily found in the mountains of Central Asia, loose in the woods around Beauville.

Suddenly, I started laughing out loud. If I was losing anything, it was my edge. Wallis would have a heyday with this. *"You trusted a dog?"* I could hear her voice, but I no longer doubted my sanity. Because it hit me: I believed what I had seen. I had seen—in that scared little sheltie's eyes—the big paws and beautifully mottled coat. Even more, I believed what I had heard: snow leopards don't roar. They chuff. They growl, and, yes, they wail. But there clearly had been some mix-up. I didn't know how a New England dog would have a mental image of a Himalayan cat, but stranger things had happened. Maybe it had seen one on TV and freaked out when confronted by a bobcat. Maybe the little dog was delusional.

Or, maybe, it was me. The funk returned as I raced down the road, trying not to see lurking beasts in every shade and pothole. Maybe that was why I reached for my phone when it rang. That, and the sneaking feeling that maybe I still had other problems that needed solving.

"Laurel?" In this state, I needed to keep my eyes on the road. As I spoke, though, I tried to remember just how I had been planning on tackling the shrink.

"You tell me." It was Creighton, though his greeting had me momentarily speechless. "Pru, you there?"

"Yeah, Jim." I snuck a glance at the phone. Sure enough, he was calling from her phone. "But I'm sure you can understand my confusion." My words dripped acid. I could hear it myself, and I knew my mood—my current vulnerability—wasn't helping. Well, what did he expect? "I'm here, and you're…"

My mouth suddenly so dry I just couldn't say it.

"I'm at Laurel Kroft's house." He did. "And you were the last person she called."

"That's impossible." I shook my head, not that he could see me. "I've been trying to reach her, but I've just been getting her voice mail."

"And why were you calling her?" His voice was cool. His cop voice. Mine wasn't. If he was waiting for me to erupt into jealous mode, he had another think coming.

"Why do you think, Jim?" I pitched my voice low,

working to keep it even. "Don't you have a murder to investigate? You talked to us both. You could see it as well as I could. Laurel was pretending. Holding something back. She knows something about Mariela—or about the Haigens, that's for sure. Maybe they were into something together." Benazi. One thing I'd learned from him was that wealthy people like their toys. They also like to think they're above the law. "Maybe it was some kind of a scam."

I was on a roll. "Or maybe it wasn't the Haigens. Maybe she and this Mariela had something going." I heard the intake of breath, a warning I'd gone too far. "Or maybe not."

"Or maybe you two were brewing up something, and now she's lying low." His voice was even, smooth, like a fishing line cast perfectly into the pool. "Or maybe you were working together, and you didn't trust her."

"Me?" He had to be joking. I laughed. He didn't join me. "Jim, you're not serious. Are you?"

"We know you called her, several times. We know you talked at least once—the call lasted close to a minute."

"What? No." My exit was coming up, and I let myself drift to the right. "I never reached her."

"Why do you think I'm calling you from Ms. Kroft's house, Pru?" I didn't answer. I hadn't thought. "I wanted to see who she had spoken to last. We have your messages, and it's clear she called you back."

I had slowed down enough to check. "Maybe she left me a message. I have one." I'd let the car stop on the shoulder. Things were complicated enough without an accident. "I didn't speak to her, Jim."

"Your phone's on."

No arguing with that. "I was at County." Doc Sharpe could back me on that. Not that it would help his opinion of me. "I guess I didn't hear. But, wait…" Something really strange was going on. "What is she saying? Why are you tracking her calls?"

He didn't say anything. In that silence, I heard enough. "She's saying something about me, right? That there's something going on with me…"

I didn't know what she had picked up. I flashed back over all my interactions with Spot, wondering what she had seen. What she had been able to deduce.

Creighton, meanwhile, wasn't helping. The silence was getting to me. "Jim, I swear, I don't know anything. But I do know her." That's when it hit me: "More important, I know Spot. I've been working with him for weeks now, and he's been living with her. He's a good dog, and he's not some little toy. If somebody threatened her… If something…"

I flashed back to our walk. The shadow in the brush. Except that Laurel would have had no reason to take the dog out to the preservation land. Would she?

"Jim, did Laurel go out to the woods?" My mind was racing. Could have been out of curiosity. Could have been for another reason, especially if she had had some idea of what had happened to Mariela. "Could she have taken Spot out to where Mariela was found?"

Spot wouldn't have willingly tracked whatever was out there. But I'd just spent several weeks training him to put aside his own preferences. Teaching him that his desires, even his instincts, were to be subjugated to the commands of his person. If Laurel had gone out there and sought to hunt down whatever had killed Mariela, he could have done it. Hell, at this point, I was kicking myself for not having thought of it.

"She didn't take the dog." That stopped me. "The dog's here, Pru."

This wasn't making sense. "Creighton, I don't know what you're saying. You're at Laurel's house. Her dog is there, and she's not, apparently. And you say she called me, which makes sense because I've been trying to reach her. None of that is odd. I mean, it's the middle of the day. She could be off seeing clients. Or, hell, maybe she had a personal errand." I paused, my original beef coming back to me. "Some of us do have private lives, Jim."

"And some of us have real jobs, Pru." He'd heard my snark and lobbed it back. "In this case, Laurel was part of it. She had been holding something back, when the three of us spoke. She wanted to talk to me. In private. Only she never showed, and so I came here to find a dog stuck in his crate and crying like he'd just been whipped. And there's no sign of Laurel. Only two messages, each saying there's something important. Something that has to be dealt with. And both of them are from you."

TWENTY-SIX

"I KNEW I hated her." I was fuming, pacing back and forth between the refrigerator and the door. "With that faux-country look and that frosted hair. Like that color comes from anything besides Clairol."

Wallis didn't comment. Didn't have to, really. I knew she thought I should have taken Laurel Kroft out of the running weeks before, by any means necessary. She knew I hadn't, that I didn't have it in me. Now, as she enjoyed the roast turkey that should have served as both our lunches, I was paying the price.

"I'm going to have to get that dog, you know," I said, although putting it this way to Wallis might have been a mistake. From what Creighton had told me, Spot sounded distressed, but not frantic. That could mean something as simple as he needed to be walked. It could also mean that he knew something had happened with Laurel, or that she was upset by something before she, presumably, stormed off, forgetting her appointment with the hunky detective. It didn't sound like he'd witnessed an abduction, or worse. Creighton may not have my sensitivity, but he's not a complete jerk when it comes to animals. Hell, if he were, he wouldn't have been so good with women.

"And?" Wallis twined around my ankles, leaning in to let me feel her warm soft body.

"I am not bringing Creighton back here." I paused.

"Not now." I'd said I'd meet him at Laurel's, but I had no intention of turning our meet-up into a tryst. For one thing, I was furious at him. He might not believe the worst of me, but he was following his own particular rulebook, and that meant he had to consider what role I was playing in the sudden disappearance of someone who was about to confide in the cops. For another, as much as Wallis might dismiss the notion, I did have a job to do—and a duty to Spot, at least until his primary caregiver returned. And finally, and if I was going to be honest, I might as well admit this reason trumped all the others: I was intrigued. As Creighton had noted, Laurel had called me. Her message, however, had raised more questions than it had answered. Before I would share them with our mutual boyfriend, I wanted a stab at figuring out what my shrink rival had meant.

"Pru, Laurel Kroft here." Like I could confuse that fake-smooth voice with anyone else I spoke with regularly. "I think I know what you're getting at, I really do." There was a pause so long, I was checking to see if the voice mail had cut out, when her voice came back again. "But the hypothesis I'm working with is that it was an accident." Another pause, in which I could almost hear her constructing her excuses. "A horrible, horrible accident. I'm seeing what I can do about it."

Well, that was lame. And while I couldn't see smooth-as-silk Laurel Kroft involved in anything bloody, it didn't put her in the best light. She was involved, one way or another, and already trying to dig her way out.

That message had made clear she knew I was onto her. And that meant I should step back. I might not like her, but she was smart enough to have read my actions correctly as a threat. If she were that desperately trying to cover something up—an "accident?"—she'd damn herself. And as far as Creighton was involved, it would be better if I weren't involved. I only had to wait. Didn't mean I couldn't wait over at her place, though.

"Suit yourself." Wallis had clearly followed all of my convoluted reasoning. Not that she agreed with it. *"Me, I'd say 'carpe diem.' But I'm just a hunter. A simple predator. You're the one with the...brain."* Before I could retort, she had left the room.

The combination of aggravation, coffee, and last night's whiskey had left me with a sour stomach and no appetite. I needed my wits, however. Plus, I liked the idea of making Creighton wait, at least a few more minutes. So I made myself a sandwich of what was left of the turkey. As I ate, I thought about going after Wallis. Because of the Kroft situation, I hadn't had a chance to tell her about the sheltie's bombshell, if that was indeed what it was. I had a feeling she'd get a kick out of my vision of a big cat. Then again, she might just confirm that I was losing it. Start speaking in tongues, or something.

Whatever. I might want to annoy Creighton. I couldn't afford to really piss him off. And so as I wiped the crumbs off my hands into the sink, I switched my thoughts to what I needed to do—and how I could slip my own agenda into Jim's.

For starters, it only made sense that I would take the dog. My sometime-beau wanted to question me. He'd made that clear. But if Spot needed to go out, that would buy me at least a temporary reprieve, and maybe help me get to the bottom of the situation. Then…yes, I had it.

"Bye, Wallis!" I called, grabbing for my keys. "Back later!"

"Jealous…" I felt rather than heard her voice, accompanied by a low throb of emotion, more growl than purr. *"Doesn't recognize human nature. Doesn't recognize anyone's…*

"Jealous and she doesn't see it."

"I see it all right," I muttered to myself as I donned my coat. Let Wallis pick that up, if she wanted. I wasn't going to let anyone's snide comments stop me now, not even my cat's.

"You're not thinking of every possibility, you know." Wallis' voice reached me, even as I locked the door behind me. *"She could be there, when you get there. Then what would you do?"*

Count on a cat to have the last word.

TWENTY-SEVEN

SHE WASN'T, AND I took that as good news. I'm not above
a little primping, and I'll confess, I had fluffed my hair
a bit, tucked in my shirt, as I made my way up to Laurel Kroft's door. If she'd been there, I'd already have
an edge—our friendly neighborhood detective doesn't
like to be stood up, especially when he's on the job.
I'd already decided that I'd be gracious. A nod and a
smile to Creighton. A soft aside about trust. Then I'd
take Spot, as if for our regular training session. Maybe
I'd even throw in something about how I'd changed my
schedule, because of the circumstances. That might be
pushing it though. Jim knew I was reliable. Predictable?
No, that I never wanted.

But there was no sign of her fancy SUV when I'd
parked, and when I rang the bell it was Jim who answered, looking a little red in the face and ruffled.

"Hoping for someone else, Jim?" I only brushed him
slightly as I walked past. Wallis couldn't have done it
better. "I did tell you I'd come by."

"You did." He wasn't going to thank me, so I let it
go. Instead, I walked over to where Spot sat on his rug.
He'd looked up with more longing than my sometime-
lover, and so he got the caress as I knelt by his side.

"Want to go out?" I cradled his heavy jaw in my hands.
Silently, as I stared into those dark eyes, other questions
formed: *"What's going on here? What happened?"*

"I don't think you should leave, Pru." Creighton was standing behind me. I stood and turned toward him.

"Don't worry, Jim. I'm not leaving." He hadn't backed away, and we were close. I'm tall, almost as tall as he is, but I made myself focus on his eyes. "Not while you want me here."

He looked down then, and took a step back. Pity.

"I'm on a case, Pru." He rubbed his hand over his face, and I realized then how tired he was. "That girl was dumped."

"I know." I did. "I'm sorry." I slumped against one of Laurel Kroft's uncomfortable-looking chairs, no longer on the attack. But something was bothering me. Something Wallis had said. "Jim, how sure are you really that the cause of death was an animal mauling?"

He looked up, eyes tired. "I thought you were the one saying that the whole thing might have been an animal attack? That a wild cat must have moved her?"

I shook my head. "Something about the wounds." It was hard to think. Creighton's presence didn't make it easier. "Cougars don't—" I stopped, unsure of what exactly was bothering me. "Just seems wrong somehow." It was the best I could manage, but I could feel Creighton's eyes on me. He'd heard me stop myself.

"Hey," I said, after a moment's pause, "I really should take this dog out. Just for a minute." I was trying to change the subject. It was also true.

Creighton waited a split second before he nodded, and Spot thumped his tail on his mat. I was back in a moment with his lead. At my nod, he stood, and I snapped it on. Creighton was watching us, but his mind was elsewhere, I could tell.

"Jim, I'll be back as soon as Spot has relieved himself." He nodded. "We'll talk, okay?"

I needed to work fast, but it was hard to stop thinking about the man inside the house as I walked Spot down to the street. On one level, I believed him: I had a too vivid memory of what had happened to Mariela Gomez to wish her forgotten. At the same time, I didn't understand why Creighton was so distressed about Laurel Kroft. Well, I had some ideas, but not ones that I liked. As far as I was concerned, the pretty shrink could take care of herself.

"She thought so." The voice came so strong and so clear, I stopped short.

"Spot?" I looked down. He was sniffing a tree trunk, which he proceeded to water. "Are you talking about Lauren?"

I pictured my rival, focusing on her honey-blonde hair, on that golden shearling coat. I tried to keep my own mixed emotions out of my mind, but some of them must have leached through. What I got back was confused and a little frightened.

"I'm sorry, Spot." I knelt by his side, putting my hand on the velvety spot right behind his ears. "Let's try again." I closed my eyes. Creighton, if he were watching us, wouldn't likely see that. He'd only see me, the trainer, kneeling beside the dog. Something normal, in other words.

"My job." He pushed his head against my hand. *"Let me work."*

"I'm sorry." This was a dog who wanted to be exercised. Who needed to keep occupied. Laurel had clearly been leaving him alone too long. At least, she had today. "When did she leave?" I visualized that blonde hair, again. This time, from the back, walking out. Walking through the front door.

"My job. I wanted to do my job." Yes, of course, he had wanted to go with her. Unless…

"Are you saying she needed you?" A soft whimper. I wasn't being clear. "Laurel needed you to do your job…with her?"

A little more pressure on my hand, the canine equivalent of a head butt. I cursed Laurel Kroft silently. She'd not only left this dog alone, but she'd gone off to do something that he felt he should be doing with her.

Had she gone to the Haigens? Spot was smart enough to pick up Richard Haigen's increasing disability. It was possible. It also fit with what I had suspected—that Laurel knew something more than she'd told me or Jim.

"She doesn't… She wants out." The words I was hearing were making no sense. Whatever Spot was trying to communicate was beyond his ability to translate. I leaned forward, putting my forehead against Spot's warm fur.

The improved contact paid off. I saw the gold of Laurel's hair, or maybe her coat—that sheepskin must have made quite an impression on the shepherd mix. I sensed urgency. Well, she'd blown off Creighton. Me as well, so something had been pressing.

I closed my eyes, waiting for the rest. A visual. Some sense of who else was involved, but all I got was that need to push, to break out. Something had to happen. Something was waiting. And that's when I felt it, like a wave breaking over a seawall, as golden and lush as Laurel's blonde locks. Only it wasn't warm. It wasn't comforting. There was something wild in the rush and the charge. And something very like fear.

"Pru?" Creighton was standing in the door. I'd been squatting here for several minutes, my thighs as well as the tone of his voice let me know.

"Hold your horses," I barked back. I'd been locked into something with Spot, and I hadn't yet plumbed the depths. "We're coming."

I looked down at the dog. He looked up, eyes wide and trusting. He'd been scared, scared and strangely exhilarated. He'd also been worried about Laurel; that was a big part of his fear. But the anger? The jealousy? There was too much I didn't understand, but maybe my attempt had done some good. His big tail swiped a few happy wags as I signaled him to stand and follow me. A burden shared is a burden halved, they say. The fact that I had no idea what the service dog had laid on me didn't make me feel any better, though. With a shrug and a smile, one for me, one for Spot, I led him back inside.

TWENTY-EIGHT

"I ERASED IT," I told Creighton for what had to be the third time. "I'm sorry, Jim. I just wasn't thinking." I hadn't been, although in retrospect it had been a smart move. "I did call Laurel a few times, and I gather she called me back while I was with Doc Sharpe in County. She left me a message, but there wasn't anything of substance in it, and I erased it. I don't know what else I can tell you."

Jim Creighton has the bluest eyes. Light. Clear. More true than a robin's egg. More blue, even, than the newish paint job on my GTO. Yet, despite their cool color, they can be surprisingly warm—the blue spark revealing the heat inside the cop exterior. I'm a dark girl, in more ways than one, but I'd grown fond of those eyes. Susceptible, even, when they looked at me a certain way, the skin crinkling around them in a wicked smile.

They weren't smiling now, and I was reminded just how cold blue can be. Cold and maybe a little sad. Jim Creighton was disappointed in me, and I felt a twinge of something that might be called regret.

"What?" I heard the snark in my voice. I don't like feeling vulnerable. "You think if you stare at me long enough, I'll change my story?" He opened his mouth to speak. I felt a wave of dread. This was it. Something final. Something bad. "So your new girl stood you up, is that it? And you've got to blame someone, so you're looking at me."

It wasn't pretty, and it wasn't smart. Wallis could have told me that I'd lose it at some point. From the look on Creighton's face, I just had.

"You think that's what this is about, Pru? Really?" There was no softness in his voice. No sympathy. "You think that everything I do revolves around…" He closed his mouth, the muscles in his jaw working. Usually, I see that, I want to get close. Not right now. "This side of you worries me," he said finally. "Professionally."

"Wait, what?" This wasn't what I'd expected. "You think I did something out of—what—jealousy?" I could hear my voice ramping up, the pitch climbing. "You think I've got her tied up in my attic? Wanna check it out?"

For a moment, there, I saw a flash of a smile. Jim knew my shambling old house well by now. He knew my attic, too. A hot flush climbed to my face as I remembered the day he'd helped me reshingle a north-side eave, and how we'd celebrated in an impromptu manner while waiting for the plaster inside to dry. That was back when we still talked and laughed during our nights together. Before our trysts became both silent and single-minded.

"I'm not trying to drag you back." Now it was my pride that was hurt, as much as anything. I've never been good at talking, and I seemed to have lost whatever knack I'd once had. "I didn't mean…" It was hopeless. I waved off the rest of the sentence.

His face softened. "I don't believe you've intended harm to Laurel. To Dr. Kroft." I kept my face neutral as he corrected himself. That slip said it all. "I do know you well enough to know you're hiding something from me, Pru. Trust me on that."

We were standing, back in the blond-on-blond living room. He'd had me crate Spot, which wasn't necessary. Then again, maybe it was just as well. I was still getting those strange signals from Spot, and I could sense his intense curiosity about our little drama. Neither of us needed the distraction.

"I'm not hiding anything." My voice broke as I said it, and I looked to Spot.

"Go?" Yeah, well, I'd have loved to. He must have caught some of that, because he whined, ever so softly. Jim, meanwhile, was picking up on other signals.

"Pru." He'd stepped closer to me, took my arm. Spot whined again, a little louder, and I felt my eyes begin to sting. "Come on."

It was pity. Pity or—I had a flash of Wallis, her green eyes glittering—tactics. I couldn't let myself forget: Creighton was a cop. I was a suspect. I stepped back.

"Forget it, Jim." I pushed my hair back from my face. Blinked to clear my sight. "Look, if you want to charge me or anything, you know where to find me. Otherwise, I should take Spot here." The dog stood at the mention of his name. "Letting him out to pee is not the same as giving him exercise. And I've got a job to do, too."

Laurel Kroft would come back at some point, and I had no desire to witness their reunion. I didn't even want to question her anymore, but I'd make myself go through with that, as soon as she surfaced. Right now, I just wanted out.

TWENTY-NINE

"WHAT THE HELL…" I was driving too fast, and I knew it. Spot, seated beside me, was looking at me instead of the scenery, and I could tell he was trying to make sense of the confused jumble of emotions in my head.

I hit a curve and leaned into it. Second nature for me, but when I heard his claws scrambling for traction on the leather I made myself slow down. No sense in taking out my mood on the one creature innocent of sparking it. Besides, I should be using the drive for some prep work.

"Sorry, Spot." I glanced over. Those dark doggy eyes had so much soul. "I know, you didn't ask for this." He settled in, and I kept talking. I'd been the one to bring him to Laurel. I'd gotten him involved in all of this. Some of the confusion I had picked up had to be from his divided loyalty. Here I was, training him to devote himself solely to one person. And now I was battling with his caregiver in one of the most basic competitions there could be. "You've never fought over a mate, have you?"

Nothing. He'd been neutered as a puppy. I knew that. Still, both Growler and Wallis had taught me not to confuse desire with the ability to procreate. Besides, he had already referenced what I was feeling once before.

"You know 'jealousy,'" I said now. If I could get it all

out, I'd feel better. On top of everything else, I didn't need to screw up this pooch, too. "You told me…"

I went back to what Wallis had said after Spot and I had found Mariela. "She's jealous," Wallis had noted, once I was home. I had assumed my tabby was referring to the killer, that she had been channeling Spot's impressions, translating them into something easier for me to understand. She had done that for me before, and it seemed to fit the scenario. Mariela had been young and pretty, especially dressed in something other than her maid's outfit. In retrospect, though, maybe I had it wrong. Maybe Wallis had been talking about Laurel, picking up her negative feelings about the command I had over Spot—or over Creighton. Or maybe she'd been talking about me. Wallis loves me, as much as she is able. She's also pretty unsentimental about how she views the world, quite capable of referring to me in the third person by saying, "she's jealous." That would be her way of softening the blow.

Poor Spot. No wonder he had no idea what was going on. Only, of course, that Laurel was missing.

"What happened?" I had come full circle. "What can you tell me, Spot? Where did she go?"

I reached over to give his broad back a companionable pet and felt him adjust in the seat in response. I left my hand there, and asked again. It didn't matter. I got the same mix of urgency and confusion, a rising tension. We were driving past the preservation land now, and the air had to be redolent of wildlife—not to mention memories. I didn't need Spot to remind me of Mariela, or to make me believe that the pretty girl's death had sparked Laurel's disappearance. The question remained—where did she go?

We, at any rate, were headed to the Haigens. I wanted to get back to those outbuildings, and I wanted Spot's good nose with me. If Laurel had been back around there, he would pick up on it. Hell, if anything else was going on there, his strong hound instincts would probably let me know. Because, let's be honest, Mariela worked in the house of a wealthy man and his beleaguered wife. If anyone was going to be jealous, it very well might be Dierdre Haigen. Though what Laurel Kroft had to do with the brittle brunette, I didn't know.

I was nearing the turnoff now for the Haigens. I'd let my speed creep back up, more from pleasure in the open road than from anger at this point. The drive had relaxed me, Spot's quiet company the balm I needed. Therefore, it was a jolt when I saw him, pulling out and speeding by me. The red Maserati. I didn't know why I'd thought he'd have left town. I still didn't really know why he was here. But Gregor—excuse me, "Bill"—Benazi had just pulled out of the exit that lead from the Haigens' estate. He'd passed me going fifty, at least, accelerating fast as he turned onto the highway.

I didn't know if he'd seen me. I'd only been alerted by the fire-engine color of his car. I'd seen his face as he raced past though, and it stuck with me as I watched him disappear into my rearview. He was, as I'd noted before, a handsome man, the cragginess of age only adding to his character. Just now, though, he didn't look suave and he certainly didn't look kind. The snapshot in my mind showed a mouth set in a tight, thin line. A furrowed brow that bore down like thunder, and eyes that could have sparked lightning. He was the one accelerating, and I pitied the trooper who tried to pull him over. What had driven the dapper gangster into a rage?

THIRTY

DIERDRE HAIGEN DIDN'T look happy to see me. From the way she leaned on the door, she didn't want to let me in. That's when I was glad I had Spot. She didn't look happy to see him, either, but she couldn't argue with the fact that he was soon going to be an indispensable part of her life.

"Hi, Dierdre." I pretended not to notice the furrow in her forehead—or her lack of any verbal greeting—and gave her my biggest smile. "I remembered to bring Spot this time."

She opened the door. Positive reinforcement works that way. "We weren't expecting you."

"Is Richard available?" Ignore the negative behavior, and it goes away. "I'd really like to see how they get around together."

"Richard? I really don't know if he's up to this."

Too late, I'd heard a deeper voice, male, back in the house, rumbling. "Who is it now?"

"Hello, Richard," I called back, announcing myself.

I walked right by the lady of the house, wondering if I'd see another visitor in that sterile sitting room. If Nick was a fixture. But instead of finding her husband sitting beside anyone in those uncomfortable-looking chairs, I found him standing alone in the doorway, one arm on the wall.

"Pru, is it?" Behind his coke-bottle glasses, watery eyes blinked.

"It is indeed, Mr. Haigen." I used the more formal mode of address. I needed him on my side. "I've brought Spot with me. I was hoping we could try walking on the grounds."

"On the grounds?" He seemed amused by the suggestion.

"Well, now that we've had a thaw. And besides, you can't be as familiar with every step out there, so it's a better test of your abilities—and of Spot's." There was some truth to this, though I had my own reasons.

"Let's see if this animal can keep up." I'd hit the right note. Haigen was responding as if to a challenge.

I was dying to know what Benazi had been doing out here. And I was hoping that if I got Richard Haigen alone, I could bring it up. Dierdre tagged after us, however, first trying to fuss over her husband as he pulled a butter-soft suede jacket on and then wanting to take his arm as Spot led them both down the slate path.

"I can do this." He shook her off, a little more roughly than necessary, I thought. Maybe he couldn't see the hurt in her face.

"It's better if he relies on the dog," I added, trying to soften the blow. "Let them go ahead."

I took her arm, then, to bodily restrain her as the big man and the dog walked on. Spot was on his best behavior. Even from a few feet back, I could feel his focus, the way he was eying every dip in the path, keeping just close enough so that he could guide Richard around any obstacles. It was beautiful to watch, and a tonic for Spot after all the confusion. But I had other goals to pursue.

"I'm glad your husband is keeping up his social contacts." It was lame. It was also the best I could come up with by way of making an opening.

"Huh." She held her head up so high, I was afraid she'd trip. So much for girl talk.

"Having a disability can be isolating." I tried again. "If you can encourage him to keep up his friendships, it would be good for him." For her, too, I was thinking. Then again, maybe she liked being his doormat.

"Richard has no *friends*." She spat out the final word with such vehemence that I saw Spot's ear flick back. She wasn't a threat, not yet, but he was on guard. "He has people who serve him. People he uses."

This was interesting. Mariela, in the most basic sense, was a servant. But Gregor Benazi? Still, I needed to tread carefully.

"Losing a faculty, like he is, can bring out the best in people—or the worst." Silence. I guess I had my answer. "Does he have any kind of support system? Old friends, people his own age who he has known for a while?" It was a blatant attempt at flattery. Dierdre was probably no more than ten years younger than her husband. Then again, I was aiming to find out why I'd seen that Maserati racing away only minutes before.

"I'm his *support system*." The emphasis she put on the last words spoke volumes. She must have known it, because she pulled away from me. I caught up with her as Richard and Spot reached the turn in the path. Good, we were headed for those outbuildings. Or we would have been, had Dierdre not taken Richard's arm.

"Don't you think that's enough for the day?"

He turned on her, his tone peevish. "What has gotten into you? Can't I have any fun?"

I made myself drop back in the hope that they'd forget I was there.

"I think you've had enough *fun*." Dierdre lowered her voice. Not enough. Part of it was that she had turned, as if to drag her husband off the path.

He pulled back, his bulk causing her to stumble, and I felt Spot go on the alert. "You and—" Richard's scowl said it all, and my ears pricked up, too, though he didn't bother finishing the sentence. "Ruining my fun."

"Richard's tired." Dierdre had righted herself and turned to me, her voice overloud. "We should go back."

"Richard?" I kept my voice neutral. I'd wanted this fight to continue. As I waited, I reached out to Spot. He was still on guard, every muscle stiff. Sensing...what? Was Dierdre that much of a threat?

It didn't take Spot's hound nose to pick up the conflict in the man. Mouth pulling in on itself, tight with words unsaid. Anger at his growing disability, obviously. At his wife, too. And who else? I flashed to Benazi, driving away, furious. Had his wife found a more sympathetic partner in the dashing gangster? He probably wasn't much older than her husband. He certainly had more charm than Nick. In which case, poor Mariela's role in this domestic drama might have been a bit more understandable.

"Let's go back." Richard barked, as surly as Growler could be. I was disappointed. We'd still not checked out those outbuildings. But even Spot relaxed as we turned and headed toward the house.

"Hey, is your gardener around?" It was a reach. I didn't want to miss the opportunity.

"Who?" Two blank faces looked up at me.

"Raul? Maybe he's the handyman." Richard and

Dierdre turned toward each other. Neither spoke. "I'd like to take Spot over to him, let them get acquainted."

Another look I couldn't read. "Is there a problem with that?" I was getting a little tired of this.

"Raul is no longer with us." Richard said the words, but it was Dierdre who was looking at me. "He didn't react well to the changes around here, and we were forced to let him go."

As if on cue, they started walking faster after that, and while Spot was happy to follow their pace—happy, I thought, to lead his charge away from those outbuild-ings—I was less than content.

What had Raul done? Yes, he'd seemed erratic, even violent, to me, and that would certainly be grounds for dismissal. But people are at heart animals. We do things for a reason, even if the reason might not fit the response. I thought back to my encounter with the man. I'd wondered, at the time, what his relationship with Mariela had been. Now, I had to wonder how his two employers fit the bill, and whether the anger I had witnessed had in fact been provoked by one of them.

"I'm tired," Richard Haigen announced as we mounted the front stairs. It was a dismissal, and I ig-nored it, following Dierdre into the entranceway. She turned, as if she'd block me bodily if she had to. Rich-ard, meanwhile, had dropped Spot's lead, leaving the dog like some discarded cap. I swallowed what I wanted to say, and instead picked up the lead myself. There were still opportunities here.

"I'd like to take Spot through the house again." Rich-ard had shuffled off, comfortable back on known turf, and I addressed Dierdre.

"Richard needs quiet in order to rest." She puffed herself up like a little pouter pigeon.

"I understand." No need to challenge her. "I'll just do a walk-through."

"I can't have you here." She turned from me to hang up her coat. "I've got things to do."

I bet. "Do your plans involve a drive in a red Maserati?" It was a long shot. Also, a cheap one. She'd pissed me off.

It worked. "You don't know what you're talking about." That hiss again. Dierdre Haigen wasn't a pigeon. She was a snake. "Richard is the one who likes expensive toys. Richard who—" She tossed her head back as if she'd felt the reins pulled. "But that's over now, and it's nothing you need to worry about."

"Maybe you could tell me?" This was getting weird. And Spot, at my side, was getting anxious. He wouldn't say anything—he was too well trained to bark. But I felt him move a little closer to my side. Did he see Dierdre Haigen as a threat?

"Like I said, that's all my husband's territory. And he's taking a nap." She slipped by me and opened the door. "Good-bye."

For lack of a comeback, I stepped out the door. "What was that about, Spot? Do you know?"

"Jealous?" One word, that was all. Whether the dog was talking about Dierdre, about Richard, or about me, I had no idea. What I did know was that Spot had picked up that word from me, and that it didn't begin to cover the complex array of emotions we'd both picked up on. Jealousy? Sure, why not? But something else—something beside anger. If I didn't know better, I'd have thought it was fear.

For Spot, the pitch of the emotion was key, and I felt him focusing hard to figure out his role in all of this. It's what I was training him to do: to anticipate and to act. Right now, however, I needed us both to sit back. While it went against our discipline for me to remove Spot from an area where, clearly, some guidance was needed, he was a good dog and he followed me back to the car. To make it more interesting, I let him lead me, making a point of not looking back. That was also because the lady of the house might be watching us. Despite the announcement of her plans, I thought she might want to make sure that one nosy female had left the premises. So we walked to the car and I drove us to the street. There, to Spot's confusion, I parked. If Dierdre Haigen thought she'd won the field, she'd let her guard down sooner or later.

It wasn't easy. Spot was restless. We were right next door to the preservation land with its wealth of local wildlife. But I didn't think it was a deer or coyote that had him so riled up. Whatever he had smelled out back, behind the Haigens', was getting to him, and I could feel him trying hard to resist the basic hound instincts to track something down. I also kept getting that sense of fear, of something almost akin to panic. I'd thought it came from Dierdre, but now I wondered once again if I'd been training him too hard. Was this agitation coming from a conflict in his desires? Every fiber of his hound being would want to follow a scent, track it to its source. Everything I'd been training him to do, however, was to ignore that urge to act independently. To subjugate that drive in order to place himself at his person's beck and call. Maybe it was too much too soon for this dog.

Or maybe there was something out there that confused and intrigued him, just as it did me.

"Are you curious about something, Spot?" I asked, as he turned his face up to mine. "Are you picking up on my feelings?" Anything was possible. And if I could only sneak us both back onto the Haigen property, I might get a few answers.

The afternoon shadows had extended over the Haigen drive, and I was just about convinced that it would be safe for us to venture back, when my phone rang. I looked at the number before answering. It was Creighton. I let it go. Either he was still angry and suspicious. Or the beautiful Laurel Kroft had surfaced, with some fine reason for her disappearance. Either way, I didn't want to hear it.

"Shall we go, Spot?" His doggy face was in shadow now, too. He whined softly. Dinnertime was getting close, probably. "Don't worry. She'll be there for you." I couldn't get jealous of a dog, too.

I let myself out and walked around to get Spot, locking the doors behind us. I'd given up that city habit since returning to Beauville, but too many things were going on now to risk it. Sensing Spot's reticence, I gave him the command to heel, and let him follow me as I sidled past the Haigen's house. Sure enough, the gardens were deep in twilight now. I hugged the trees, hurrying from shade to shade as we walked past those oversized windows.

"Go?" One word again, accompanied by a faint whine.

"Soon." I looked down at my companion. "I promise." Poor guy. He missed his home. It wasn't his fault that his temporary caretaker had taken off. Or that his trainer was leading him on a mission that even he could tell was off. Animals don't know guilt the way we do. They can sense skulking, though. I was acting like prey, rather than like an alpha dog. It was enough to make any stouthearted canine nervous.

"Gone?" That was it. I'd misheard the question. No wonder he was upset.

"I think so." I looked up at the windows. Now that the light was fading, I could see inside. If she wasn't around to draw the curtains, then maybe she wasn't...

As I watched, someone closed the shades. Well, that was information. I knew that Richard was home. I didn't think he was the type to care about such niceties, though, even if his sight was still perfect. That meant Dierdre, and maybe others, were still at home. Could Nick have been there all along? Closeted with his friend—or waiting for his mistress? Either way, the windows being covered meant that I could move more freely. Spot seemed encouraged by the darkness as well, and I watched him sniff the ground as we moved from behind the oak.

"What is it, boy?" I knew I was encouraging the wrong instincts. Right now, I didn't much care.

The response I got was strong enough to throw me. Something wild, a rich scent like I would associate with wine or mushrooms. Spot was letting me in, letting me experience the world as he did. It was heady, but with an edge of danger.

"Cat?" His voice broke through, perhaps sensing my confusion at the flood of sensation.

"I don't know." I pictured Wallis, and got a strong sense of a negative. A bobcat, maybe? We had those, and although they were smaller—more of a threat to a rabbit than a person—they would register as wild. I tried to picture one: the tufted ears, the distinctive facial markings. Instead, the image of a puma—long, lean, and nearly invisible in these shadows—passed through my mind. I dismissed it, forcing myself to see stripes instead of tawny fur. What I got were spots, large, mottled spots, and I shook my head hard. I had a hard enough time translating what animals gave me. If I started to let my own fancy seep in, then I wouldn't be able to trust anything I got.

"Let's go." I gave the signal to proceed, and Spot responded. Not all of my training was being subverted here, and in the dark, I was grateful for his superior senses as he led me steadily down a path I could no longer clearly see. This might be better training for his seeing-eye duties than our brief outing earlier in the afternoon, even if that wasn't what I had intended.

"Over here." The outlines of the trees, and the buildings behind them, were still visible in the dusk. I turned toward them, and suddenly felt Spot in front of me. It was a protective move, like he would one day use to stop his person from stepping into traffic or off a cliff. Why he'd stopped me now was a puzzle.

"What is it, Spot?" I held still, trusting his instinct, but I peered into the shadows as I waited, hoping for some kind of comprehensible response. "Is someone there? A person?"

I was thinking of that gardener. Yes, the Haigens had said he was gone, but I'd seen the look they'd given each other when I'd asked about him. Either they were lying, or there was some other kind of story there. I had no more desire to meet an angry ex-employee than I did someone who was in hiding for whatever reason, especially when one of his colleagues had turned up dead.

"Spot?" He was sniffing, reading the air as I would skim the paper, and I didn't want to rush him. While I waited, I thought about the missing man—and what his relationship might have been to the slaughtered woman. Mariela. I needed to stop thinking of her as an abstract, and to ground myself, I pictured her not as I had last seen her, but as she had been when I'd first met her. Young and quiet, with the large dark eyes that poets rhapsodize about—eyes that could be seen as mysterious, or as haunted. At the time, I'd thought her shy, reticent to talk to a guest with her employer present. Now, I wondered if there had been other secrets, secrets that she veiled every time she lowered her head, and those long lashes, submissively.

Had Raul loved her? Had they been family? Were the Haigens the sort to cover for a faithful handyman? Or had they been involved in some way?

These questions would have to wait. Spot was on the move again, leading me down the path. He hadn't answered my query.

"Safe now?" I'd trained him to make decisions, to act for his person when his person couldn't. That didn't mean I didn't want feedback.

"Safe." I got back. Well, at least he was doing his job. Heading downhill into deeper shadow, I let myself close my eyes, imagining how it would feel for a blind person to be guided in this way by the solid little dog.

That was why I almost tripped when he stopped again, blocking my legs with his body.

"What?" I confess, my tone wasn't the friendliest. Spot could have toppled someone less sure-footed to the ground with that move, and he'd startled me. "Slow down." I pictured a more gradual stop as I gave the command. We were not at a cliff's edge or a highway median now.

"Wait..." One word, if I could call it that, shut me up. A command, in its way, from Spot in his new role, the one in which he was in charge. It was an unusual response, and one that an ordinary person wouldn't understand. In part because I was intrigued, I did.

Scent. That was it. I got a feel of it again, that same fierce, wild flavor. And, again, I wondered at Spot's fitness for this job. If he was going to be distracted by every bit of game that wandered across his path, he'd be a better hunting dog than a service companion. For a moment, I thought of Albert's request for a dog. Our bearded animal-control officer was no hunter, but Spot would be a great scent hound—that nose, his blood were all made for such work. And there were legitimate uses for hunting animals out here. Even the state police used trackers.

Would Creighton? Spot had proven his worth the day Mariela had been found. Maybe he could combine his skills working for our local force. Maybe I could train Creighton...

"Come." Spot started moving again, nipping that fantasy in the bud. Just as well, I thought, as I let him lead me to where I'd been confronted by Raul. Right now, I tried to keep that memory from my mind. No sense in adulterating whatever Spot was getting.

"Danger?" Too late. I cursed myself silently.

"No, no danger," I said out loud, trying to silently stress the peacefulness of the scene. "Nothing here. All is quiet."

It was. I took a step forward, toward the closest building. Spot, most strangely, did not.

"Spot?" He could have been glued to the walk, and so I stepped closer to the barnlike building. The door, I could now see, was ajar. I couldn't resist. I opened it and peered inside.

I saw…nothing. The interior was too dark to make out, and even if I'd had a flashlight, I wasn't sure I'd risk it, so near the house. Still I stepped in and felt the air. I'm no bloodhound. My meager senses don't even match up to Wallis' on her worst day. But I've learned something from the animals I work with. Something about vibrations and the way air can feel. This building was empty. An oversized work shed. Maybe it had once held gardening equipment; it was large enough for a tractor. Maybe in a few months it would be filled with potting supplies. Now the air was still and slightly sour, like an animal had been here. Not a horse, though. I paused, thinking suddenly of rats.

"Cat?" I turned to Spot with a smile. Would he react this way to a barn cat, or a clowder of them? "Is that it, Spot? A lot of cats?"

But if I was expecting a rational answer, or even an image I would have to struggle to decipher, I was mistaken. Instead, at my words—or maybe it was that strange, stale scent—Spot started to bay. Loud and long, each emphatic cry as resonant as a bell, his voice rang out. "Wow, wow, wow!" That distinctive hound voice, and underneath, I heard the words: *"Cat! Cat! Cat!"*

It made no sense. His reaction was wildly out of proportion. More to the point, it was blaring. Hideously so, and I ran out of the doorway to put my hands on his muzzle. "Hush!" I used every command I knew.

It was too late. Already the alarm had been raised by someone in the house and a switch had been flipped, flooding the garden area with stark white light. I was trespassing, we both were. And even if I could brazen it out, I had Spot's reputation to consider.

Whether or not he'd be a good service dog, he didn't need to get in trouble on my account. With his lead in my hand, I ran to the side of the building, listening for the footsteps that were sure to come. When they didn't, I looked around: Those bright lights also cast deep shadows, and I made for the nearest, determined to work my way back past the house to my car.

"Who is it?" Richard Haigen. In this light, he wouldn't be able to see me. "Who's out there?"

Surely he had other servants. Rich people always did.

"Who's out there?" He called again. "We'll find you."

Maybe his security team was arming itself. Maybe it was coming up the side. I didn't wait to find out. Urging Spot to a run, I made a dash for it. For one bad moment, I fumbled with the keys—cursing the urge that had made me lock the car doors—but then we were in. I saw more floodlights go on, illuminating the side and the front of the house. I didn't wait for the flashlights that were sure to follow. Without turning my own lights on, I sped off down the road, Spot now silent beside me.

THIRTY-ONE

I'M NOT SENTIMENTAL. Neither is Wallis. If prodded, I'd probably admit to loving her. How else to explain my continued acceptance of her verbal abuse? If poked, she'd undoubtedly lash out. But I believe she loves me, too. How else to explain the way she nestled into me predawn, as I lay awake, staring into the gloom and waiting for the ceiling to appear? It wasn't so much dawn I was counting on. I'm a night person, always have been, and I don't mind getting up before sunrise if that's what's needed. It was more what that first light would mean. And as I lay there, waiting for the moldings to appear, I knew I was looking at my future. My near future, anyway. I'm not a fatalist, nor that kind of a psychic. Emptiness slowly turning to gray, the cold, clear light of the early spring morning bringing definition to my room. My empty room. Jim Creighton had not come by.

It wasn't a surprise. As I lay there, struggling to make out the place in the corner where the paint was peeling, I let my mind wander. We'd had some fun, and that fun had extended beyond this room to take in some good dinners and a fair amount of laughter. Our recent meet-ups, however, had been more constrained. That last time? We hadn't even spoken, not unless you count the few words necessary to place and position as conversation. The writing had been on the wall for

weeks. Maybe it would have been even if Laurel Kroft
had not come to town. And I knew it was as much my
choice as anything—Jim was, at heart, conventional.
He'd wanted more. And I, well, even excusing my ambivalence, I didn't know how to do more. More than
affection. More than a regular playmate. Not with who
I am, with what I can do. Not if I wanted to stay out of
the loony bin. That was the price of freedom for me,
and that's what I could never explain to Jim. He couldn't
know me, not the way he wanted. I didn't dare let him.

Still, it stung. I hadn't thought it would come like
this. I'd called him, once I'd calmed down a bit after
leaving the Haigens. Laurel still hadn't shown up, but
he'd agreed to meet me at her place so I could bring
Spot in and bed him down for the night. Jim had been
agitated, and I'd played it cool—no more teasing when
he seemed genuinely worried.

Spot at least had calmed down. He had gotten a
snootful of something back at the Haigens and kept
playing it over in his mind. I kept getting that wild
scent, that mix of thrill and fear. Even back in his own
place, he wouldn't let it go, and I found myself confused
by the mix of Laurel scents and that strange aroma.
With Creighton hanging over us, I couldn't ask Spot,
not in any real way. And so after feeding him and refill-
ing his water, I put him in his crate with barely a hug.

"Gone." That was all. "Yes," I'd said back, murmur-
ing into one plush ear. "For now.

"I'll be back in the morning," I said to counter the
rising anxiety I felt as I retreated. "If Dr. Kroft hasn't
shown up by then," I'd added for Creighton's benefit.
While it did seem out of character for the long-legged
shrink to disappear for the better part of a day, the pos-

sible explanations were legion. As to why she hadn't called our mutual beau, I didn't want to speculate. I refuse to play those games. Doesn't mean I'm in the majority.

"I'll call first thing, Jim." I'd paused by the door before leaving. "I'd like to take the dog out for a long session anyway. But if she hasn't surfaced..." I left it at that, watching my words sink in. He didn't respond.

I'm not a sadist. Besides, this was hurting me, too. "I can see myself out." I turned and started down the steps. Behind me, I got a sense of loss, of pleading. It came from Spot.

"Pru?" I paused and turned. Creighton was following me, and I waited as he locked Laurel's door and joined me. "Can we talk?"

"Sure, Jim." I'm good at deadpan, usually. Now I just stared at my car. "What's up?"

"Look, I know things have been less than great between us." He stopped, but if he was waiting for me to chime in, he'd have to wait longer than he did. "I know you think we're really different, at heart. That we want different things."

This was it. I'd had this talk before, and I didn't want to again. "Is this the part where you tell me I really do want to settle down? To have kids and learn to cook?"

I was interrupted by a burst of laughter. "No, Pru. I'm not fool enough to do that. It's just—" A burst of radio chatter stopped him short. Carol, back at the headquarters, was calling for him—listing numbers like they made sense. He held up his hand, listening.

"Jim?" I didn't like how this was going, but that laugh... I toyed with the unlikely possibility that I had been wrong about him.

"Hang on." He walked over to his car, and I stood there like a fool as he traded numbers and fiddled with a GPS. "Right away," I heard.

"Pru?" He didn't even get out of his car, just turned those baby blues up at me. "Can we pick this up later? Maybe tonight?"

"Sure, Jim." I nodded. "You know where I live." He was closing the door as I said it, reaching for the ignition. Just as well, I figured. I was having trouble keeping the stupid grin off my face.

That had been hours before. Hours during which I had bathed and scented myself, opened a bottle of wine, and then followed it with a water glass of bourbon. I was drunk by two. By three, I should have been asleep. But by five, I'd given up, and that's when Wallis had made her presence felt, landing on the bed like an animate bean bag, and kneading my arm till I moved it from its place rigidly by my side. She cuddled into the crook of my arm, then, purring like an engine.

"You don't have to do this, you know." I didn't have to explain further.

"Doesn't have the sense of a kitten." She was talking to herself. *"Gets herself mixed up with dogs and all that..."*

"At least it's almost spring." I rolled onto my side and pressed my face against her fur. She smelled like baby powder.

"Not the sense of a kitten." The rhythm of her purr subsided somewhat. The warmth grew more steady. *"Never listens, never learns."*

Her tone was scolding, but she didn't move, not even when my hot tears must have soaked through her fur and I stopped looking for the light.

I WOKE WITH a start, alone, the phone buzzing like a beetle on its back.

"Hello?" I croaked, once I had finally landed the little bugger. "Who's this?"

I was too late. The call had gone to voice mail, and I fell back on the pillows, trying to marshal my thoughts.

The bourbon had been a bad idea. Coffee, that's what I needed. Coffee and about a gallon of water. Then I should hit the road. This particular brand of craziness had to be nipped in the bud.

"Morning, sunshine." Wallis sauntered into the kitchen like she owned it. *"Well?"*

"Hang on." I got the coffee started and began cracking eggs. She sat there, tail curled around her front paws, waiting for service. I obliged, as grateful for her silence now as I was for her comfort last night. "Here you go," I said finally. I'd made the eggs with extra butter. My way of saying thanks.

"Mmm…" She acknowledged the treat with a purr. *"And perhaps we needn't have worried after all, hmmm?"* Her face was buried in the plate, not that her expression would have given anything away. I poured myself a mug and sipped. Too hot. Finally, I couldn't help asking.

"Wallis? Do you know something?"

"Mmmm…bird…" The warmth of the egg was overlaid with an image of a nest. Fantasy or something from Wallis' hunting days, I didn't know. *"We all have our hungers."*

"Wallis?" Silence. I looked at the coffee and back at the cat. *"She's gone."* Spot's words came back to me. Inexplicable, unless…

Wallis looked up, licking her chops. I ran back to the bedroom for my phone.

Sure enough, the call I'd missed had been from Jim Creighton. With a sinking feeling, I replayed the message.

"Pru? I need you to come in, as soon as possible. There's been a development."

This wasn't an apology or an explanation. And at that moment, I didn't want one. His tone said it all. The call was official. From now on, any need for me would be purely business.

THIRTY-TWO

I TRIED FOR the same cool tone when I returned Creighton's call. Voice mail made it easier, and I left the simple message that I'd be by as soon as I finished my morning rounds. Steeling myself to face Tracy Horlick would be good practice.

Not that she made it easy. In fact, the old harridan seemed to know already that something was amiss. Standing in her doorway of her house, she made no move to fetch her little dog and instead fixed me with a basilisk stare.

"Good morning, Mrs. Horlick." I did my best.

"Hm," she responded. "Must be nice to be rich." She picked a stray bit of tobacco off her lip and looked at me as if her pronouncement was supposed to mean something.

"Excuse me?" I knew I wasn't at my wittiest, but this sounded like a complete non sequitur to me.

"To be rich." She clearly savored the word. "If I'd known they'd let that car go for a song, maybe I'd have made my move. Or maybe you should have."

"I don't know what you're talking about." I peered behind her, looking for Growler. "But I've got an appointment, Mrs. Horlick, so—"

"I hear you're going to have some time on your hands." Her lipstick cracked in a smile that looked more like a leer. "Now that you're not the new game in town."

Unable to conjure any kind of response, I ignored her and looked past her into the dark hallway. Growler had to be in there somewhere. What I was doing was good training, but she was as tuned into body language as any predator, and she must have picked up something in the way I was peering past her, looking for the little white dog. "Or the freshest." She licked her lips, and I flashed on what I hated about her. And what Growler had told me.

"You should know." It was childish. I was tired. Hungover. And right then I didn't care. Her eyes narrowed, though that could have been from the smoke. I should have left it. I didn't. "Your bridge partner?"

A laugh, more like a bark than anything Growler ever made. "I'm not some girl to get all moony over nothing." She took another drag, appraising me. Had I been wrong in my interpretation of Growler's memory? "But that car had to be worth fifty grand."

"You said it yourself, it's good to be rich." I doubled down. She had to be talking about the Haigen's Benz, though I'd be damned if I could see the connection.

"Huh," she snorted, smoke coming from her nostrils. "Like he's even calling the shots."

For a moment I was stymied. I'd thought Nick was dealing with the sale of the SUV, but it had been Benazi I'd seen in Growler's vision. And if Benazi was working for someone else, I didn't think I wanted to know about it. Then I remembered: Laurel Kroft had been walking around the table. That made more sense.

"So was it Bill who told you about the SUV or Laurel?"

She shrugged, but her smug smile let me know I'd come close. I had to wonder why anyone would confide anything to Beauville's biggest gossip. Then again, some people need an audience, and cards could be awfully dull.

"I guess it just wasn't that important to them," she said at last. I'd thought the Haigens cared more for the big Benz than they had for Mariela. Maybe both were ultimately disposable. Maybe we all were. The thought didn't improve my mood.

"Yeah, well, I'm kind of in a rush." I caught myself: I wasn't the one who would suffer for my comments. The old witch would take it out on Growler. "I'm supposed to meet Detective Creighton," I gave her that with a smile, "and I wouldn't want to cheat Bitsy out of his exercise."

In the brief pause created by her intake of breath, I called out to the little dog. "Bitsy!" He hated the name, but he'd forgive me. And in response, old lady Horlick turned. Sure enough, she'd locked him in the basement. I heard the scramble of claws on the wood stairs and barely had time to clip the lead onto his collar as he pushed past me.

"Took you long enough." Rage came off him like heat.

"I'm sorry, Growler." I made a point of using his chosen name. "I was late, and she was…" I lacked the words.

"I get it." The waves of anger subsiding, he chuffed out his gruff acknowledgment. *"Come on."*

Still fighting the fog of my hangover, I let the bichon take the lead, and we made our way down to the corner with unusual speed.

"You okay, Growler?" This couldn't all be because

of my recent interaction with Tracy Horlick. "I'll make nice with her when we go back."

"Huh, she doesn't care." I felt him sniffing the damp earth around a birch. Felt, too, his relief as he watered it. *"She laps this up."*

Of course. I could have slapped myself: Tracy Horlick enjoyed seeing me react. It gave her something to talk about—with who? I remembered that table. Those feet.

"Growler, who does she gossip with?" I was wondering about those hand-sewn Italian shoes. "Can you give me more?"

"Huh." Onto the next tree. I wasn't sure if Growler didn't know any more, or if the subject was simply too painful to revisit.

"After that time? I wasn't invited." He'd read the question in my head, even before I'd decided how to word it. *"She went for him. For the man."* I couldn't help it. I pictured Benazi. No, it wasn't possible.

"Ha!" A short bark. Confirmation. *"No! The other one. The one with Sal's lady."*

"Jim?" No, that wasn't possible. This was getting confusing. "Sal's lady? Who is that, Growler?" Nothing, he'd moved on. "Is Mrs. Horlick—old smoke-teeth—going back?"

Another yap. This time, I took it for a no. *"Ha! Not there. Not with that lady. She smells too good."* Of course, Tracy Horlick wouldn't want to spend much time anyplace she couldn't smoke. I imagined what Benazi's woman would smell like. Something sophisticated from Paris or Milan.

"Good!" Growler was quite vocal today. *"Not like a city, walker lady. Good, like sheep."*

Like sheep? I pictured a shearling coat. Laurel? If

so, who was Sal? For a moment, I wondered if she had
another man—someone Creighton didn't know about—
and my traitorous heart leapt. Growler took care of that,
tugging at the lead with a look of scorn. A low growl
confirmed his annoyance, and I realized I was imagining caramel-color fur and a moist nose. Spot. Was
Spot's real name—his chosen name—Sal? If so, why
had he never told me?

"He doesn't care." Growler had moved onto a fence
post. *"Never did."* I looked down at the bichon. That
white fluff, the black button eyes: it was harder for
him to express his dignity than it would be for the big
shepherd-hound mix. Was that why Growler insisted on
being properly addressed, and Spot didn't?

"It's his job, silly." Those black button eyes were
looking up at me now. *"Spot's his work name."*

I nodded. What else was the service dog keeping
from me?

"Trying to protect you, most likely."

"From what?" Another glance, as Growler turned
around and started back to the house. "Hang on, Growler.
What are you saying to me? What is Spot trying to protect me from?"

"Dog help us." He was muttering, a low rumbling
growl too soft to be audible. *"She thinks she can hear.
But she doesn't listen."*

"Help me then, Growler." I was walking fast to keep
up with him. I couldn't imagine he wanted to go back to
Tracy Horlick. Only his annoyance with me was making those short legs move so quickly.

"All this time and she doesn't get it." More grumbling, and I had to fight the urge to scoop him up in my
arms and force him to talk.

Some of that must have gotten through, because the bichon stopped in his tracks, turned and looked up at me. *"Hey, walker lady. Are you deaf?"* I had a brief flash of an all-white cat, and shook my head. *"Then listen. Look around you. He likes toys. He collects…"* I got a confused image of something bright and big. Too big for our town.

"Spot? I mean, Sal?"

"No!" A short bark. *"Shoe!"*

"Benazi likes pricey toys, I get it." I did, at least I thought so. "And, what? He'll hurt anyone to keep them? What?"

"Sheesh." Growler had started on again, and we'd come to the edge of his walk. I could see Tracy Horlick scowling out the window, and before I could ask Growler to explain, the door opened. With another bark, Growler trotted up the walk, with me in tow. I didn't have a chance to make up with the old lady as I'd promised I'd do before one clawlike hand took the lead from me and the little dog slipped inside. I guess I just had to accept that Growler had made his peace with the human who had collected him. Either that, or straightforward animosity was preferable to the scorn he felt for me.

As I walked back to my car, I realized why. The other man at the table—the one Tracy Horlick had hoped to snag—must have been Richard Haigen. Laurel must have put a game together for local seniors, though the pairing of Tracy Horlick and Richard Haigen would be ludicrous to anyone who knew them. And Benazi? Well, he fit the demographic, though I didn't think his hawk eyes would need the extra large cards the retirement community dealt out. He must have been there for Hai-

gen, and Tracy Horlick must have been in hog heaven.
Everyone in town knew the old man had a roving eye.
Granted, both his latest wife and all his rumored par-
amours were younger—and better looking—than the
old shrew who had just slammed the door in my face.
But she didn't necessarily see herself that way.

Still, it was a reach. Not only was Haigen currently
married, his taste clearly ran to a different kind of
woman. *"Pretty toys."* Women like Dierdre or…yes,
it seemed clear now, Mariela. Plus, try as I might, I
couldn't see Tracy Horlick in any kind of romantic relationship. Birds do it, as I was becoming increasing
aware in these early spring days. Bees, too, though I'd
been spared their amorous buzzings. But Tracy Horlick?

There had to be some other explanation, I told myself as I unlocked my car. *"He's no longer calling the
shots."* Something was going on that led her to think
she could grab onto the man. Manipulate him. His eyesight? I imagined her nicotine-stained fingers closing
over his on Spot's harness, and I shuddered. No wonder Spot—Sal, whatever—didn't want me to get too
close. Unless it wasn't old lady Horlick… Could this
have been what Laurel was hiding?

Despite my distaste for the shrink, I'd have to pursue
it. Later. Although he'd been trying not to let anything
show, Creighton had not sounded happy, and I knew
that his mood would not be improved by the wait. I had
fifteen, maybe twenty minutes of peace left. I wasn't
going to waste them on Laurel Kroft.

It's not easy for me to turn off the things I hear from
animals. My own thoughts, though. That is a little simpler. Driving, for me, is hypnotic. Not that I'm ever not
fully engaged, but the act relaxes me. Takes the edge

off and lets my mind run free. The road was my own this early, and the light flashing through the bare trees dappled the road with shadows. There were no tourists. Wouldn't be till May, probably, but this season had its beauty, too. Wilder and less compromising. It was almost enough to take my mind off the pretty shrink and my upcoming confrontation with Creighton. Still, my head felt heavy, and I rolled down the window for some air.

"Flee! Flee! Flee!" Well, beauty came at a price. I was moving fast enough so that I didn't hear what had alarmed that crow.

"Danger!" Something on the ground: an opossum? Again, gone before I could follow it. So much for spring's rebirth. Besides, I was coming up on the turnoff for Beauville center. Time to face the music.

Just then my phone rang. Creighton must be getting impatient. Well, I hadn't lingered. And I'd be there in five minutes anyway. I ignored it as it rang two more times, then reached for it. No sense in antagonizing my former beau.

"What?" I wasn't in the mood to be friendly. "I'm almost there."

"Pru?" It was Albert.

"Sorry, Al." I thought of that possum, and what silent cry our poor old animal-control officer would be sending off right now. "I thought you were, well, someone else. What can I do for you?"

"Oh, uh…" My offer probably frightened him more than my bark. I smiled while he gathered his wits, fighting the temptation to ask him to put Frank on the phone. "Are you coming down here?"

"I can." I didn't know how I'd feel after meeting with

Creighton. But now that he mentioned it, I thought of Spot. If Laurel were still missing, I would need a place for the dog to board. My place—I didn't need to check with Wallis to make sure—was not an option. "Do you need me to bring something by?"

I envisioned Cheetos or maybe beer. If the former were for Frank, I might even comply.

"Yeah, maybe." He still sounded tentative. If it involved porn, I was not going to spare him. "Do you still have access to that dog?"

"That dog? You mean, the one I'm training?" I remembered his earlier request. I wasn't going to let him use Spot to track an errant raccoon or someone's lost schnauzer. Those weren't the instincts I needed to encourage. "Why, Albert? What do you want him for?"

"There's a bunch of us want to go out to the preservation land, Pru, and I thought we could use him." I knew what he was going to say before the words came out. That didn't make them any easier to hear. "We're going to track that cougar out there down. It's time we finally found that thing and killed it."

THIRTY-THREE

I WAS SEEING RED. Bloody red, but there was no point in shredding Albert a new one. He might be a jerk, but he was a timid one at heart. This was someone else's bad idea, and he was merely the messenger.

"Are you insane?" That didn't mean I had to like it. "Albert, tell me you're not really going along with this."

"We've got to do something, Pru." If you didn't know him, he might have sounded reasonable. "It's a—uh—a public safety issue. There's been another incident, and once they get the taste for human blood…"

"Right." I shut him down. Someone saw a shadow, I was betting. Someone's pet went missing. I did feel a twinge of guilt—I'd been the one complaining about poor Mariela. How nobody took her death seriously, and no one seemed to care. I'd been gassing on about her employers, though. I didn't buy the idea of a cougar stalking humans, but I'd have to push a little harder to get to the bottom of this. What I needed now were the details of the meet-up.

"At the entrance to the state road," Albert told me, apparently convinced that I would be joining them. "Everyone's supposed to be there by noon."

Whoever was behind this had some sense. If the posse would be gathering at Albert's office, I'd have been able to drop by with Creighton in tow and put a stop to this nonsense.

He might never use them, but I knew Albert had a folder of the latest Fish and Wildlife postings, as well as the guidelines issued by the state. Short of cuffing him about the ears, invoking some of those laws—and pointing out that the Beauville police were headquartered next door—might nip this thing in the bud, or at least dissuade some of the participants from trekking out to the woods. But meeting at the preservation land made sense. The good old boys, and I just knew they'd all be boys, would have already made the drive. They'd probably be liquored up, too, which would make getting them to give this fool's hunt up even harder.

I had reached police headquarters. I made a noncommittal noise to Albert, stopping just short of a promise to help, and got him to agree not to start anything without me. I turned off the phone as I pulled up to the building the cop shop shares with the town shelter. I sat there, looking at the door. It would be so tempting to blow Creighton off. This was an animal emergency, after all. Something that required my particular expertise. And something that would be better tackled now, here, while Albert—and, I hoped, Frank—were in the office, rather than off in the woods.

Albert wasn't a threat, but I doubted he was the ringleader behind this particular circus. Albert might not be too scrupulous or too knowledgeable about his legal duties as the animal-control officer of our fair town, but he knew enough to know that hunting an endangered animal was a federal offense. Sure, there was the chance that a stray puma this close to human habitation could be labeled a "nuisance animal," one of those tags that drove me nutty, but hunting it with a dog would violate too many laws to name. Besides which, I'd rather have a cougar in the woods than most of the idiots Albert hung out with. The cat probably had its own good reasons to be there, and it sure was more aesthetically pleasing.

It also, I realized with a sigh, had a better chance of surviving if I got the law on my side. And that meant keeping my appointment with Creighton. So be it. I wasn't going to let this get personal. I wasn't going to show anything, and I sure as hell wasn't going to touch him. In and out, surgically, like a knife.

Tossing back my hair with a little more vehemence than usual, I started the long walk toward the front door—and the end of my sometime-romance.

THIRTY-FOUR

"Pru, what do you know about cougars?"

It wasn't the question I expected, and for a moment I wondered what he meant. I wasn't that much older than my blue-eyed beau. Of course, Laurel might have had a year or two on me.

Creighton must have seen something on my face, because he clarified. "The wild cat, Pru. Mountain lions, pumas. What do you know about them?"

Christ, not Creighton, too. "What do you want to know, Jim? Family *felidae*, meaning they're cats. Latin name, *puma concolor*, which means they're pretty much one color—dun or tan. They're big, they're carnivores. They've pretty much come back in the West, but the ones around here? The Eastern cougar? They were considered extinct. And, yes, there have been some sightings, but nobody seriously believes they're back. Most of those were probably frightened hikers. City folk who saw a bobcat or—who knows?—a coyote in the wrong light. The last confirmed case, where there was a carcass, turned out to be an adventurer. DNA showed it had come all the way from South Dakota, only to be hit by an SUV in Connecticut. Which means, realistically, that we're a lot more dangerous to them than they are to us. At least, our cars are."

That was more than he wanted, and I knew it. But if he was getting pressure to join Albert and his buddies on their wild-cat chase, I wanted him to know the whole story.

"So there *are* cougars here?" He was looking at me funny. "In the woods, here?"

"No, Jim." Something was going on I didn't understand. "There were, like, a hundred years ago. Probably our own subspecies. These days, sometimes a Western cougar might show up here. But it's a really long way for a cat to walk on its own."

"I don't care if it's a native or if someone flew them in from Wisconsin." Creighton was getting heated now. "There very well could be some kind of wild animal loose out there that we know nothing about. That we—"

"Hang on, Jim." His mounting anger was distracting me. Something he had said…a memory… "Just— hold on."

"What? So you can tell me that we're invading its space? That we should let people get killed. That we…"

He broke off and turned away, shaking his head.

"Jim?" I couldn't help it. I'd never seen him so vulnerable, and I went over to him. He was staring at the window, but I doubted he was seeing anything, and the way his jaw was working, I could have sworn he was trying not to cry.

This was wreaking havoc on my plans. Despite my best intentions, I reached for him. When he didn't move—didn't even acknowledge—my hand on his arm, I stepped closer and wrapped one arm around him as I looked up at the side of his face. "What is it, Jim? You can tell me."

He swallowed. The line of his jaw kept moving. Whatever it was, it was sticking in his craw. "Jim?" I reached up to his face, to turn him toward me.

He jerked away and turned toward me, his eyes dry. "This is serious, Pru."

Whatever emotion had threatened to overcome him was gone now, replaced by cold steel.

"I need to know the full extent of your last conversation with Laurel Kroft." He had walked around behind his desk, but instead of sitting he leaned forward on it, the muscles in his arms standing out with the tension. "If you told her you'd meet her someplace, if you told her to go someplace, get it out now. I am not going to accept any more excuses."

"What? I told you. She left a message…" I stopped. What had she said? Something not very specific. "She said she had an idea about what had happened. That it had all been some kind of horrible accident. I thought…" I stopped. I wasn't sure what I could say.

"You thought what?" Creighton's voice was as cold as his eyes.

I took a breath. "Look, you don't know everything about me, Jim. And there are some things…some things you'll just have to take on faith. But I have reason to believe Laurel Kroft is involved with a shady character."

Those eyes were slits now. I kept talking. "Do you remember Benazi? Gregor 'Bill' Benazi? The slick older dude who was involved with that gun case? Well, I've seen him around again."

"And you're saying you saw him and Laurel together?"

"After a fashion." Well, I had.

"I need to know where and when, Pru." He saw my hesitation. "This isn't a game. God help me, if you're lying about this."

"I'm not lying, Jim." How to explain that I got my info from a dog? "It's just that I didn't see it per se."

"Who did? I'll need to question him or her."

"You can't." I slumped against the wall. This was hopeless.

"Who are you protecting, Pru? It's not that ex of yours…"

"Which one?" I didn't know what had gotten into him. I did know I didn't deserve to be talked to this way. It made me punchy. Punchy and reckless. "You seem to think my past is littered with every bad boy east of the Mississippi."

"Maybe because it is." He leaned forward over the desk. For a moment, I thought of a puma, ready to pounce. "Tell me about Benazi."

"I don't have anything to say." He was pissing me off.

"How do you know he's in town?"

"I saw him. Saw his car." I remembered the red Maserati. "He must have seen mine. He called me."

"Because of your car?" Now his voice was frosty.

"Yeah, Jim." I thought back. "I thought at the time it was about the Haigens' SUV. Dierdre was trying to unload it—Richard's car. I mean, he can't really drive it anymore. It's a stupid car, totally overloaded. I thought she'd want an arm and leg for it." I thought of what old lady Horlick had said. How the packed Benz had gone for a song. "It wasn't my style anyway."

"Benazi was selling her car?"

"No." I shook my head. It was confusing, even to me. "He just knew about it. She wasn't advertising it locally. I mean, a diesel Benz? In Beauville?" I laughed. He just looked at me. "It's a car thing, Jim."

"And you met to talk about the car?"

Time to 'fess up, at least as much as I was able. "No, Jim. I thought that maybe that's what he wanted. And I was curious what he was doing back in town. He took that white Persian, you know." It sounded lame, even to me. "We had dinner." I thought back. "It was creepy."

I saw Creighton take in a deep breath. Watched him let it out again. When he spoke, his voice was more calm than it had been in a while. "Pru," he said, finally. "I am going to ask you a question, and I want you to think carefully before you answer it. I don't want you to try to second guess me. What I want is the truth. Can you do that, Pru?"

I think I nodded. Something about his manner. At any rate, he seemed satisfied enough to continue.

"Would this man have any reason to hurt Mariela Cruz or Laurel Kroft?"

"What? No." That jerked me upright. Then it hit me. "Jim, what are you talking about? Laurel—I thought…" The tears, the tension. Even, maybe, his unexplained absence last night. "Jim, has something happened to Laurel?"

He pulled out his desk chair and sat, heavily, like a much older man. "We got the call last night. Some kids saw the car, out in that parking area. The preservation land… Probably were going to break into it, but then they saw her."

"She was…in the car?" I didn't know where this was headed, but it didn't sound good.

"Only a few feet away. Dragged." He stopped, as if the word had choked him. "It looks like another animal attack, Pru. Laurel Kroft is dead."

THIRTY-FIVE

I WAS LUCKY Creighton's office had another chair, the way this hit me.

"But, this doesn't make sense. Mariela wasn't even—" The facts weren't adding up. "She didn't even die out there."

He was shaking his head. "*She* did, though. Laurel did. Forensics has her car. I haven't seen it, but I was told there was blood all over, signs of a struggle. We don't know if she tried to get back in, to get to safety. It'll be a few days, before…"

He couldn't do it. He put his face in his hands, and I was beside him, holding him. Talking nonsense I didn't know I knew.

"Oh, baby, I'm so sorry." This wasn't me. "It's okay, Jim, just let it go." Wallis would have a field day. But she wasn't there, and for a minute or two, it was me and Jim again. Not like I'd ever wanted it to be, but there it was. And then he pulled back and pushed himself upright in his seat. I dug a crumpled Kleenex out of my pocket and he blew his nose. And we were back to business.

"So." He motioned for me to sit again, and I did. "You can see why I need to know about this phone exchange you two had."

I nodded, I did. That didn't make my dilemma any easier. "And I'll help you, Jim, the best I can. Only, you don't really think I had anything to do with her—

with what happened to Laurel, do you?" I'd changed my wording out of deference for his feelings. Only after I'd spoken did I realize what my phrasing implied, and before he could answer, I followed up. "What do you think happened anyway, Jim? I mean, what you're saying is this sounds like an animal attack. But you're looking for a person?"

"I don't know, Pru." I didn't think I'd ever heard him say those words. "Forensics won't be back for a while. But we do know that Mariela was moved after she was killed. And Laurel? I don't know what happened, but if she was out there... If she was looking for something..." He swallowed hard. I could see him straining, willing the cop part of his mind to take over. "It can't be a coincidence."

"Could it be a copy cat?"

He looked up. "What?"

"Something about this doesn't feel right." I was running through everything I knew about wild cats. Everything I'd read. "Maybe," I was winging it, hoping that talking it out would help me make sense of my unease. "Say someone knows how Mariela died...hell, everyone knows how she died. So someone killed Laurel and made it look the same, at least at first glance."

But I had thought something was off with Mariela's death, too, I remembered. Besides, Creighton was shaking his head.

"Occam's razor, Pru," he was saying. "If it looks like a cougar killed one person, and another is killed, then it makes sense that a cougar killed them both. What I need to do is figure out why Laurel was out there. What she was looking for. Which means..."

In the pause as he gathered his thoughts, I remembered Albert's call. "So that's why Albert has a posse."

I was relieved by Jim's blank response. He had no idea that our animal-control officer was part of an illegal hunt and, to his credit, he immediately announced his intention to put a stop to it.

"This can't happen." He pulled himself out of his chair, looking as if the day had already been too much for him. "For one thing, somebody could get hurt. Somebody else."

I bit my tongue on my retort: that any crew Albert was a part of was more likely to injure itself than get anywhere near a wild animal. Creighton was doing his job. For once, it coincided with my interests.

"I'll join you." I stood as he moved toward the door.

"No, Pru." He was back in cop mode. "I'll handle this."

"I need to be there, Jim." This wasn't about Mariela's death, or not only. I couldn't forget that strange vision I had had—what I had seen through that panicked sheltie's eyes. Besides, my particular sensitivity might save another life. Not that I could tell that to Jim. "You know I'm more of an animal expert than Albert is. Besides, I told Albert I would go. He wants me to bring the dog."

He didn't look convinced.

"Look, I've got to pick up Spot anyway, Jim. We can't leave him alone. After that… I'm a private citizen."

He didn't argue.

"Do you want to give me the key?" I wanted to spare him. I felt for him, I really did. I also wanted a chance to look through her place.

"You won't need one. I've got people over there now."

So much for that idea. "I'll call them and tell them you're on your way."

He turned away and started down the hall. I had the feeling that he wanted some privacy, but I had another question.

"Jim?" He paused, then looked back toward me. "Did you get any more information about Mariela?"

Now he turned. "What do you mean?"

"Do you know if it was in fact a cougar that killed her?" I swallowed. If only I could tell him.

"The results were inconclusive." He shook his head. "Why?"

Some tech was covering his ass. "I was just wondering." And now I was covering mine. "Maybe we're looking for the wrong kind of animal."

"It's not the cat we're looking for, Pru." His voice was cold now. Determined. "We're looking for who dumped Mariela there. Who lured Laurel out to the woods. A person's much more dangerous than any wild animal, if he—or she—wants to be."

THIRTY-SIX

I WAS GLAD to be alone, driving back to Laurel's. Too much was going through my mind, and Creighton knew me too well for me to be easy about it. Unlike Doc Sharpe, he never seemed concerned about my strange connection with animals. He did note it, however, and he'd spent enough time at my place to see how Wallis and I interacted.

As I drove, I went over what I knew: Laurel had been looking into something when she'd been killed. Had that something gotten her killed? It seemed likely. It also seemed like my buddy Gregor Benazi was somehow involved. The Haigens, too, though I still didn't understand how. I tried to remember everything Tracy Horlick had said about them. About him. Growler seemed to think that his person was angling to become Haigen's next wife, but Richard would have to be deaf and dumb as well as blind before he traded Dierdre in for the old coot.

Laurel, however, might have been tempting. Was the late shrink flirting with the moneyed old man? Personally, I couldn't see trading in lively, young Jim Creighton for a half-blind billionaire. Then again, he might be easier to train. Unless he wasn't. As I sped down the highway, a scenario played out in my head: Creighton and Laurel were getting serious. She'd made her choice and gone to tell Richard Haigen it was over, stalling me with some nonsense about an "accident." And he, what? Kills her? And Mariela, too? Because…she knew about Mariela? Or was it something else entirely—was I looking at the wrong Haigen? Had both women died because someone else had been there first?

Dierdre seemed too self-possessed to go into a jealous rage. But maybe it had been a practical, rather than emotional, move. If her security were on the line, she would have had more reason to lash out. But if Laurel Kroft had been moving on—leaving Haigen for Creighton, Dierdre would have had no reason to get rid of her.

None of it was making sense. And none of it had anything to do with a cougar. This was all about rich people, one rich man, in particular—Richard Haigen— and the women who may or may not have been part of his life. Could that have been what Benazi was trying to warn me about?

If so, the old man was going to have to be clearer. At any rate, I'd arrived at Laurel Kroft's house. Sure enough, the county van was parked out front, and the door was open. I let myself in and shouted a greeting. No sense getting law enforcement mad at me.

"Oh, it's you." The white-coated tech didn't even look up. I don't usually get ignored by men. Then again, lab techs are a special breed. "Jefferson has been looking for you."

I didn't know any Jefferson, but I walked gingerly through the house, staying on the clear plastic that had been rolled out over the floor.

"There you are." I'd just entered the living room when I heard the voice behind me. It had spooked me, and I turned quickly, a little annoyed at the lanky tech who had crept up so quietly.

"Do you mind?" I nodded over to Spot. He was whining, his tail between his legs. Between Laurel's absence and these strangers, he was clearly in distress.

"By all means, take him." He made a gesture with his gloved hand as if he were bestowing a blessing. "I need to check his cage, anyway."

"It's a crate," I corrected him, reaching for the lead. On top of everything else, Spot really needed to go. "What are you looking for, anyway?"

"I don't know if I can tell you." He looked quite happy that I'd asked.

"Fine." I let Spot lead me past. It did him good to take back a familiar role, and I was happy to be away from this jerk.

"But since you're such good friends with Detective Creighton," he continued, as he bent over the crate, "it probably wouldn't do any harm."

This is what I hate about small towns. Not only did Mr. Smarmy know my business, I couldn't cut him down to size. Whatever happened next between me and Jim, Jim would have to work with him. And I'd probably run into him again, too.

"Yeah?" I couldn't say it nicely.

He didn't care. "Drugs," he said, looking up, a self-satisfied smirk on his face. "Just got the call, or I'm sure Detective Creighton would have told you. We're looking for sedatives, sleeping pills. Roofies. Anything that could have been used on a woman her size that would keep her still long enough to cut to shreds."

"To cut?" Spot was tugging gently. I begged him, silently, to wait.

"Stab. You know…" He made an obscene slicing motion over his throat and belly.

Surprise left me momentarily speechless.

"I thought…" I stopped. This was what I'd suggested to Creighton. I struggled to remember why. "So, she wasn't killed by a wild cat?"

"Depends on how you define 'wild cat.'" He had a truly unpleasant smile. "Drugging someone and then slashing them? Seems like a woman's way to kill, doesn't it?"

He shrugged, not waiting for an answer, and began scraping something off the door of the crate. "Besides, she wasn't attacked out in those woods. The blood in the car? Hers—and mainly on the passenger side. Someone did their best to make it look like she was mauled and then drove her out there."

"And left her." My mouth was dry. I was trying to make sense of this. I was failing. "So she wouldn't have felt much pain, right?"

"Who knows?" Even with his back toward me, I could see him shrug. "It wasn't like she could yell for help or anything."

THIRTY-SEVEN

It must have been his choice of words. That or seeing him kneeling on Laurel's blond wood floor. The reality was sinking in, and I felt a wave of nausea. I also felt the increasing desperation of the dog by my side.

"I'll be back in a few," I said to the tech, as I made my escape. "Come on, Spot. Let's go."

Spot relieved himself on the first tree we came to, but even as he moved on, watering another and finally squatting out by the road, he remained agitated.

"Is it Laurel?" I asked. A leading question, but the poor dog had been through so much, I wanted to give him an easy one.

"Gone, gone, gone." A silent wail, as heartbreaking as a bay, broke through. I knelt on the ground beside him, to take him in my arms.

"I know, Spot. Or is it Sal?" He looked up as I leaned into his warm neck. Growler was right; this dog didn't care. "And, yes, she's gone."

"I told her. Warned her. She's gone, gone, gone!" He was still trembling, with some combination of fear and—could it be, anger?

"Are you angry at her? Is that it?" I tried to put myself in his place. Your person is taken, hurt by someone. "Are you angry at her attacker?" Dogs have been known to act heroically, facing off against much larger animals when their people are threatened. I drew on that knowledge now, hoping to calm the shepherd mix. "You would have fought for her. I know you would have. You're a good dog."

"Bad, bad, bad." I hugged him closer. If he let his loyalty eat him up, I wasn't sure how to get him back. *"Bad."*

"Not bad. You did what you could, Sal. I mean, Spot." Now didn't seem the time to mess with what we'd become accustomed to. "You did what you could."

"She didn't listen. Told her, told her, told her." His thoughts were breaking out now into vocalizations. Soft at first, but growing louder. A howl of grief and of regret. I held him close, wondering what the techs inside must be thinking. For them, it was a case. It was evidence. Science.

"Not your fault, Spot. Not at all."

"I told her, told her. Told!" His voice had silenced all the birds in the area. Even the squirrels had quit their chattering. And as I leaned in, I felt the full force of his sadness and, yes, that anger again. But not at whoever had mauled the beautiful Laurel Kroft. No, underneath the bristling rage, I felt the same sense of something wild. Something big and lethal. And feline.

"I told her," Spot was saying.

"It wasn't a cougar." I kept my voice calm, my tone even. I visualized the words as I spoke them. Anything rather than picture a large tan cat. Or, worse, a spotted one. "It was a person, Spot. A person."

He wasn't listening. *"Told her she was gone!"* The baying continued. *"Gone, gone, gone!"*

Spot was upset; there was no other explanation. And while I didn't want to confuse him further, I also saw no good coming out of his being put back in his crate. Besides, I had told Albert I would meet him—and Creighton as well, for that matter. I looked back at the house and made my decision. That tech didn't have to know how long a walk we were talking. I was going to the preservation land. Laurel had died there. With the cougar no longer being blamed for her death, Creighton would have to call the hunt off. But that didn't mean there wouldn't be some answers to be found. For me and for my bereft beau. Not to mention, for Spot.

STILL, I WAS uneasy as I drove us both back over to the preservation land, my mood as gloomy as the gray clouds that had begun to gather overhead. I'd had problems understanding animals before. Every now and then, I couldn't hear them at all. More often, it was that I misunderstood what I was getting. Trying to interpret their animal expressions in human terms. Wallis was the only creature I could really communicate with. More so, I realized with a bitter laugh, than Jim Creighton, at any rate. If she were here, she might be able to help translate for me. If she were willing to take on a dog. With Spot finally falling silent beside me, I mused about the possibility of making that happen. Making that happen without one of us getting scratched to bloody shreds, that is. Over twenty minutes of highway driving, I couldn't come up with a way to get it to work.

One look at Spot, as I pulled into the parking area, and I knew something was up. He had shifted as I parked, becoming both more alert and—for lack of a better word—apprehensive. I saw him lift his head, and he gave me a brief glimpse of his concentration as he took in the air for scent. That air was damp, rain was coming, and I didn't need him to make out the stale beer and testosterone. Several cars, in various stages of rusting out, were already there, and two pickups, both with gun racks. Neither belonged to Albert, and I sat in my car for a moment, wanting to see what kind of pack had gathered before I left its safe confines.

"What's up, Spot?" I put my hand on his back. To anyone outside, it would look like I was giving my pet a pat. "What do you smell?"

"She's here." The thought almost had a whine in it. The big eyes that looked up into mine were filled with sadness—sadness and fear. *"She's here."*

Poor guy. Animals, although some humans deny it, feel grief just as we do. Maybe more acutely, because they don't fool around with abstract notions of an after-life. Unlike us, they make no distinction between our physical selves and any ethereal essence. They know death better than we do. But they also, and I didn't want to think too much about this, know when something— blood, gore, bits of flesh—remain.

"Yes, she is here. *Was* here." He smelled her. Smelled some remnant of her, that much was clear. I thought he must know that she had died here, too—either from the lingering metallic scent of blood or from some other essence emitted in panic and pain, the scent heavy in the thick and humid air. So, yes, part of her was here, no doubt. More vivid to Spot than it would be to even our best forensics experts. But, no, she was not coming back. "Do you understand?" I'd kept eye contact as my thoughts rambled, hoping that something would make sense to the bereaved animal.

"She's gone." I felt a tremor go through him and then, to my surprise, his tail wagged, hitting the leather seat with a thud. Well, maybe he had been caught up

in Laurel's pain, in her last moments. Animals understand relief, too.

Just then, another pickup pulled up. Albert. And so I got out and let Spot out, snapping on his lead. That was more for show than anything, but I figured it couldn't hurt to maintain some kind of physical contact with the dog. For whatever reason, I had a hard enough time reading him, and if he picked up anything out here, I wanted as clear a picture as possible.

"Hey, Pru." Albert was holding a brown paper bag but not, as far as I could see, a ferret. "Uh, glad you could come."

I nodded in response and looked around. Creighton should have been here by now. He should be the one to break the news. Albert misread my look and gestured to the milling pack. About a dozen men had assembled; I seemed to be the only female willing or foolish enough to come out. "I'll introduce you to the guys."

"Great." I tightened up on Spot's lead. I recognized some of the men from Happy's. The rest looked like they did their drinking at home. I didn't think they'd put much stock in anything I had to say, and I was glad to have a dog by my side.

I joined Albert as he walked up to the knot of men, standing by his side as the grunts of greeting were exchanged. With a crowd like this, I wanted to make clear from the start that I was an equal—or, at least, Albert's equal—and that I could meet them on their terms.

"Pru, Pru Marlowe," I said with a nod to the biggest of the bunch. "And you are?"

"Butch," he said, predictably. "What's this?" He nodded at Spot.

"He's part hound," I interpreted. "We found Mariela's body together."

"Oh yeah, I heard about you." A light went on under his bushy brows, and I wondered if this was the ringleader.

"Pru, over here." I turned. Albert was motioning me to come to him. He was talking with a dirty-blond man in dirty jeans. Not too tall, and wiry rather than muscular, he had the look of a street fighter. I nodded in recognition and stood my ground.

"Albert." The street fighter's mouth twitched. Could have been a smile, could also have been that his teeth were bad. Whatever, he started walking, towing Albert behind him.

"Stu." He held out a grimy hand. I took it. He'd recognized my immobility for what it was, and he was giving me my due.

"Pru," I replied. Albert, meanwhile, was getting all puppyish, bouncing around us. "Stu-Pru, it rhymes," he said.

This, then, was the boss. "So Stu, what makes you think you can find a cougar in a hundred acres of forest?"

He accepted my question with a nod. "I know a little something about animals." That closed-mouth smile again. "And Albert here told me you'd be bringing the dog."

"Hey, Stu." A big guy, bushy beard and a beer belly, yelled from near one of the pickups. "When we gonna start?"

"The natives are getting restless." I was watching his face, looking for an opening. He was waiting for something, but I didn't know what.

"They've got beer. They're happy." He was watching me, too. It wasn't a comfortable feeling.

"What are you waiting for?" Sometimes a direct approach can shake something loose.

It didn't. He smiled for real. To my surprise, his teeth weren't bad. No meth then, and not the kind of poverty you often see out here. "I was wondering when you'd spring your surprise."

My eyebrows asked the question.

"You don't want this hunt to go on," he answered. "I know about you."

"Do you know that the Laurel—the second woman— wasn't killed by a cougar?" He was watching me, and I couldn't read his eyes. "By a wild cat?" That wasn't it, or not entirely. "And that the first victim had been moved?"

"I've got a job to do, too." It was an odd statement. "And, as I've said, I've worked with animals before."

"Then you know there's probably nothing out there. Nothing hanging around, anyway." He didn't look like a fool. Then again, maybe he was taking some fool's money. "I mean, this is as much a wild goose chase as it is a cougar hunt."

He shrugged. "You don't have to hang around."

That had to be it. Haigen, I was betting. Paying by the day. "No way am I leaving." If this crowd cornered any animal, I wanted to be there to intercede. At least until Creighton showed up.

"Suit yourself." With that, he turned. "I guess we're good to go."

He raised his hand, and the assembly gathered like bears around a garbage can. "I'm glad you all came out. Thanks for spreading the word." He nodded at several of the men, turning to acknowledge them. "This is important work." It was funny. He was a head shorter than most of them, easily fifty pounds lighter than most. Didn't matter, he was clearly the boss, and each time he nodded, the recipient pulled himself up, pulled his belly in, at least temporarily.

"Look, the way we're going to do this is simple." He was speaking their language, but I got a sense that he actually had a more thought-out plan. "Pru and I are going to go ahead, with the dog. We're going to see if we can get the cat's scent. You all stay back a bit."

A little grumbling. None of them wanted to take second place to a girl.

Stu scanned the crowd, making eye contact with each man in turn. "We don't want to frighten the kitty cat away, do we?" Mumbled assent, a little confused. "When we've got the cougar's trail, that's when you'll all come in." A low roar. This was more like it. "We're going game hunting today, boys. We've got to be smart about it."

That little speech led to enough hooting to scare almost anything away. But something about Stu's approach made me think he wasn't worried. Before I could ask him any other questions, however, he waved the big beard over.

"Pete, I want you to do something for me." The big guy nodded. "Keep these fellows back, will you? I want at least a hundred yards between them and me. I need to do some tracking."

Another nod, and he turned to me. Clearly, he did know something about me—and about animals. "Shall we?"

I didn't dare turn around. He'd have known I was

looking for Creighton—my "surprise," as he'd called it—and I didn't have any other tricks up my sleeve. What I did have was a dog who was quivering with eagerness, and a man who was not what he seemed. And so I signaled to Spot, who stood at attention, and nodded to the man to take the lead. In for a penny, in for a pound. We were going on a hunt for a cougar.

THIRTY-EIGHT

WE SET OUT in silence, letting Spot take the lead. Once we were well away from the parking area, Stu stopped. Reaching inside his jacket, he took out a bunched-up cloth and knelt on the ground. "Come here," he offered it to Spot.

Spot hesitated for a moment, until I gave him the okay. Then he reached over, burying his nose in the cloth. Stu didn't offer it to me, and when Spot withdrew, he shoved it back inside his jacket.

"The cougar's scent?" I was asking the obvious. What I wanted to know was what that cloth was, and where Stu had gotten it.

"From the girl. The first one." He answered my unspoken question. "I know one of the deputies."

It was a good answer, but it was a lie. For one thing, the cloth was white. Mariela had been wearing that colorful blouse. I hadn't seen a sweater or a scarf near her, and the loose fabric Stu had now secreted away didn't look like an undergarment.

Whatever it was, the scent it held was potent. I was trying to focus on Stu, to figure out what was going on with this strange man. But my mind was being flooded by impressions. Not images—Spot took things in through scent—but more three-dimensional than anything we could describe as smell. Stronger than whiskey, this was like moonshine—raw and intoxicating, heady in a way that edged into dangerous and yet had a kind of crazy appeal. In this damp weather, scents were amplified, exaggerated. The image of the snow leopard came into my mind again—the big spots, the lush tufts of fur. It was the wrong image, a picture my mind was putting on the scents Spot was getting, and I pushed it from my mind. Ordinary people anthropomorphize their companion animals. That's what gets them in trouble. What I do is overinterpret. It's just as bad.

I turned from Spot to the man by my side. I wanted to push Stu, find out what he had held out to the dog, but with Spot's impressions still flowing through me, it was all I could do to stand upright. Something incredibly captivating was out there. Something fierce.

"You okay?" His question pulled me back to reality.

"Of course," I snapped. Being caught off guard makes me cranky. "Why?"

"You just…" He looked away. "It's nothing."

It wasn't. He either knew something or sensed something, and I didn't know how to get it out of him. Maybe it didn't matter: Spot was trembling with anticipation, that wild and heady perfume filling his mind. "You ready?" I turned to the dog. *"Please,"* he responded with every fiber of his being, and so I unhooked the lead. "Hunt," I said.

He didn't take off. I didn't expect him to. The hound part of his makeup was a tracker, not a chaser. What he wanted was to find that scent—that tantalizing brew—and follow up on it. And so for all the drama of letting him off the lead, we basically were doing nothing except watching him sniff the ground.

"You said you had experience with animals?" I tried to make it sound casual. I already knew that what he'd said was true because of the way he waited, watching Spot for any sign that he'd picked up the trail.

"Yeah," he said. I've met Maltese that were easier to read.

"Around here?" Subtlety wasn't working, and Spot was still searching for a lead.

Stu only shrugged. Just then, Spot got it. I felt it like a jolt of adrenaline, and only after the briefest of pauses realized that the scent was old, stale. The same scent, though, and we both turned to it. Turned, I realized after a moment, back to the parking area—and back toward the men who still waited, looking at us.

"Get back," Stu called. He might not have picked up the same signals as I did, but he could read a dog. Sure enough, Spot retraced our steps, weaving through the men. He'd come to the spot where we'd parked the other day, right by the wall of brush. For a moment, I panicked, waiting for the bay that would announce a trapped animal. But although Spot raised his big head and sniffed the air, the message was clear. Whatever had been there was gone. The trail was dead.

I knew it. I thought Stu did, too. But before I could ask, we heard the sound of tires on gravel. Creighton's unmarked had finally arrived.

THIRTY-NINE

"Hi, Jim. What brings you out here?" I nearly batted my eyelashes, only I thought Creighton might laugh.

"Pru." His nod was his non-answer, and he looked around until he saw Albert, skulking toward the back of the pack. "Albert. May I have a word?"

Albert blanched, at least the part of him that wasn't covered in beard did. But he took a few toddling steps forward, and Creighton did him the courtesy of escorting him around the back of his cruiser. The rain that had been threatening all morning had started, a thin mist that was beginning to bead on the car.

"Albert, what's going on here?" Creighton asked. I, of course, tagged along, just close enough to hear.

"Nothing." Albert couldn't have looked guiltier if he'd tried. Being damp didn't help.

"Doesn't look like nothing." Creighton had his cop look on. Even from where I was, I could tell.

"Jim, we went out already," I broke in. "Spot led us back here." I couldn't believe I felt bad for Albert, but I did. "The trail was cold."

Albert looked from me to Jim and back again, then started edging away. "We'll be talking," Jim called to his retreating back. Then he turned toward me.

"You took your time." I felt bad for him. I did. But I didn't like that he'd left me there alone for so long—or that he hadn't bothered to tell me the news about Laurel.

"I had someone else to talk to." The cop look again. I stared. Waited. It was pointless. He wasn't saying anything more, and I was getting chilled. When he finally broke the silence, it was with a question of his own: "So?"

I filled him in, at least as much as I could without getting myself locked up. I didn't care about getting that tech in trouble, and it didn't make sense to hold out what I knew. Besides, it added to the strangeness about the hunt—and about its leader, Stu.

"He knows about Laurel. Knows she wasn't killed by a cougar. Knows that Mariela was moved, too." I concluded. "When I told him, he didn't blink an eye. There's something else about him, Jim."

"Oh?"

I bit my lip. I wanted to say, "He knows about me, too. About my sensitivity." I couldn't, of course, but I shared what felt safe. "I have a feeling someone's talked to him about me. Told him to look out for me—in both senses. And I think maybe someone's paying him to be here. To hunt for a cougar that nobody has seen."

"Interesting." If I hadn't just seen Creighton break down over Laurel, I would have thought he was feeling a bit possessive. I shook the idea off: Laurel was dead. Someone had tried to make her murder look like an animal attack. This was part of the case. Creighton's interest was in the evidence, not me.

"Which of these clowns are you talking about?"

I nodded toward Stu. Now that Creighton was here, he looked smaller, somehow. It could have been the rain. Some of the crew had sweatshirts on, but most were just kind of ducking down, as if they could dodge the drops. In Stu's case, I had a feeling the posture was intentional, like he wanted to melt away into the crowd of soggy good ol' boys.

"Why him?" Creighton knew me better than to doubt me. He wanted my reasons.

"He was leading the hunt. He knows about animals." I paused, unsure how much to reveal. "He knows I do, too."

Creighton didn't comment on that. He did take a few steps toward the shorter man. "Excuse me."

Stu looked up and blinked. Except for the lack of a beard, it was a dead-on impersonation of Albert, blank face and all. "Who, me?"

"Yeah." Jim's eyes narrowed, trying to see what I had. "You were leading the hunt."

A shrug. "I wanted to help the lady with her dog."

"He had a scent rag." I hadn't wanted to show my hand. I also didn't want him to get away without answering our questions. "Something from Mariela, he said."

"What, this?" Stu reached into his pocket and pulled out a scrap of blue towel. "I just use this on my own dogs to get 'em started," he said. "It's got a mix of my own on it. Fox urine, basically."

"He—" I stopped myself. It was pointless. In the few minutes since Jim's arrival, he'd had a chance to ditch the white cloth, and the smile he now turned on me looked less ingenuous than smug. This round went to the mysterious stranger.

Creighton knew it as well as I and dismissed the crowd with a general warning about "taking matters into your own hands." When I started to protest, he raised one hand, ever so slightly. It was a gesture I recognized from my own training, and I shut up. No sense in getting reprimanded in front of this crew; my status was tenuous as it was. Besides, they hadn't planned on the weather. As far as they were concerned, it could have been a hurricane. It was definitely Miller time.

Using Spot as an excuse, I wandered over to the edge of the clearing. Spot's nose was on alert as we approached the hedge, but all I got as he sniffed the ground was the usual local fauna: squirrels, a raccoon. Two opossum, half asleep and stumbling. Spot was interested, but only reflexively. We were both hoping for something more. I was about to take Spot off the lead again, to let him go into that hedge, when Creighton called to me.

"Pru, a word?" The last of the hunters were dispersed. I waited, standing to the side. He watched, hands on hips, as they got into their vehicles. When they were gone, he moved closer. "I'm sorry I wasn't here earlier."

It wasn't what I'd expected. "You've got your hands full," I said. I didn't add the obvious—that he was also grieving the most recent murder victim. "You don't owe me any explanations."

"I think I do." He was looking down the lane, as if he expected one of the hunters to drive back. Could be he was just avoiding my eyes. "You see, about me and Laurel…"

I didn't wait for a pause. "Jim, you and I never had any agreement. We were what we were."

"No, Pru, wait." He looked down at the mud, where a puddle was forming. No help was coming from there, either. "Laurel and I, it wasn't what you think."

"Oh?" I couldn't help the ice that dripped from that

one syllable. I knew he was in mourning. I needed him to know I'm not an idiot.

He laughed. That was a good sound to hear. "Pru, I'd give good money to know what makes you tick sometimes." He stopped himself. Motioned to his cruiser. "Want to come in out of the rain?"

Without answering, I walked around to the other side and got in the passenger side, letting Spot in the back. It wasn't cozy, exactly. But, well, any shelter in a storm. After a moment, he started talking again, answering the question I hadn't asked.

"Yeah." He stared straight ahead at the windshield. "Laurel and I went out a few times. You're a—You can be a maddening woman, Pru. Sometimes a man wants something simpler."

"And Laurel Kroft was simpler?" I couldn't help the smile that was making the side of my mouth twitch. I hadn't realized that Jim Creighton was so clueless about women.

"No." He sounded quite clear on that point. "But what she wanted was. And I…"

"You thought it might be nice to be housebroken?" I visualized Creighton in that sunny sitting room. His sandy hair would go so well with the white sofa and all that blond wood. The ultimate fashion accessory.

"Laurel didn't want a serious relationship either." Even in profile, I could see his own grin had twisted, acknowledging the irony of the situation. "Not with a small-town cop, anyway. And I realized, well…"

"Yes?" I drew it out. A girl's allowed.

"I guess I realized that if I'm not going to be taken seriously, then I'd rather be not taken seriously by you."

"Better a pizza delivery man than a rich lady's boy toy, is that it?"

"That's one way to put it." He turned toward me now and had the decency to look a little ashamed.

"Well, I'm glad that's settled." A girl doesn't want to think she's only won by default. "But last night, I assume…"

He nodded. "We were over. She and I had talked, oh, a few days ago." I thought back to his last nocturnal visit, only two days before. He hadn't spoken much, driven more, I thought, by straight-up desire rather than a longing for any kind of emotional connection. At the time, I'd thought he was cooling on me, indulging a generalized hunger with a willing partner. Now I saw his silence in a different light: he'd come to me out of need. Knowing him, he'd felt bad, and that had prompted him to end it with Laurel. Well, I'd give him his little fiction about the date.

"When she called," he was still talking, "she said she suspected something. Something that I should hear. She didn't say anything about Mariela, but I had a feeling—and it wasn't good. I pushed her to tell me what she had, what she thought, and to let me do the follow-up, but she wouldn't. Said she needed to check it out herself. Then, when she didn't show, I checked her calls. That's why I confronted you. Not because…" His voice trailed off.

I got it. It was reasonable that he'd be worried about her. After all, Creighton is a decent guy. And, yeah, he's also a cop. On occasion interests overlap.

Sometimes not. He was looking down at his hands now. We were sitting side by side, and I thought he was as aware of me as I was of him. Thought he was wondering if he should take my hand. Reach over and touch me. The parking lot had emptied out. The rain was likely to keep any other adventurers away.

But I am who I am, too. And I had information to share.

"I think I may know who she was checking in with." He sat up straight again, which reminded me to tread carefully. "Look, Jim, I told you about Benazi. That I think she was meeting with him?" I hadn't told him why. He didn't ask again, however. He only nodded. "I'm pretty sure Benazi is doing some kind of deal with the Haigens. That's his circle, and I'm wondering if Laurel was trying to get some information out of him."

"You're thinking he killed her?" He was watching me, gauging my reaction. "Is he capable of that?"

I shook my head, more because I didn't want to answer than because I didn't know.

"Is he capable of mutilating a body to try to disguise the cause of death?"

That was a harder one, as Creighton well knew.

"I don't know." I did know I didn't stand a chance of finding out what Jim thought, so I took his question at face value. The silver-haired gangster was capable of murder—and he wasn't squeamish about gender. I was pretty sure that one woman had already disappeared because of him. True, she had deserved it, but then, I didn't know Laurel that well.

"Could Laurel have been involved in anything shifty?" Maybe I was falling prey to my own prejudices, but I thought the old man probably had a code of honor, and that Laurel would have to have fallen afoul of it to meet her end at his hands. "You know, a black market deal or some kind of financial scheme?"

He did me the courtesy of considering it. After a

few moments, however, he shook his head. "No, I don't think so. She was honest. More than that, she thought she was smarter than everyone, and that she'd come out on top because of her intellect and education. You know, the rest of us were just animals."

I nodded and held my tongue. I'd already won, and besides, my rival was dead.

"I'm going to bring this guy in, though. As soon as—" He didn't have to finish. He held out his hand. "Your phone, Pru?"

With a twinge that felt suspiciously like disloyalty, I handed it over. Benazi had done nothing but scare me. Then again, he did so in the most courtly manner. I watched as Creighton scrolled through my calls.

"You did call Laurel several times." I nodded. He looked up from the phone.

"About the dog, Jim. About Spot." At the sound of his name, Spot wagged his tail, making a thumping sound against the car seat. He'd been very good, sitting silent while we spoke, but now I found myself looking back at him and wondering. *"What are you thinking?"* The question was formed almost before I realized.

"She's gone." The phrase I'd heard before. Only this time I noticed something strange. Spot wasn't sniffing at the air. He wasn't looking for the potent traces of Laurel's blood—or her car or any other trace of the fallen women. He was staring back at that hedge. And the sadness I felt, the regret? It was more akin to longing than the grief that an animal can feel.

"What is it, boy?" I twisted in my seat. I felt Creighton start slightly beside me. I didn't care. "What are you picking up?" It wasn't what I meant, not exactly. But it gave me an excuse. Just in time, too.

"Uh, Pru?"

"Wait a minute, Jim." I got out of the car and let Spot out, too. He was instantly on alert, and I put one hand on his back, my eyes on his quivering snout. "Spot's gotten a scent."

I heard him get out of the car. Heard him come up behind me, but I didn't turn, and he had brains enough to not ask me to. Let him think I was super sensitive in a normal way. Better he should believe that I'd picked up a normal signal, rather than the truth.

"What is it?" I left the question open, and breathed in, my mouth open. My own dull senses couldn't give me a quarter of what Spot received. Still, I was hoping to get something, thanks to our connection.

"She's...scared. Lost." The wet air tasted of leaves, of the last of the winter ice. A snowy landscape in the dark. Maybe I had it wrong. Maybe he was recapturing Laurel's last memories. *"She's gone."*

"She died here." I made the thought as simple as possible. As I've said, animals understand death better than most humans. It's more present, every day, and they don't sugarcoat it with any fables. I'd misunderstood animals before. Wallis would say I did so regularly. So maybe I was misinterpreting Spot's thoughts, putting nice-sounding human words to a more generalized canine grief. For sure, something wasn't right.

"She's gone." A low whine started in the back of his throat. *"Gone."*

"Laurel is dead, Spot." I spoke aloud, holding the dog's head. Let Creighton think I was a little nutty. I needed to be sure of what was happening.

"Yes, her warm is cold. Feeding lady is dead." Well, I didn't have to worry about Spot grieving overmuch,

if that was his reaction. So what? I waited. Took in the air—and got it: that heady aroma, wild and intoxicating, spiked with spices and something strong. Coming from the hedge.

"She was there, waiting. Watching. Scared." Now that I got it, too, Spot opened up. *"She was waiting there. Waiting to pounce. But she's gone."*

FORTY

"PRU?"

I looked up at Creighton. I didn't know what he could see on my face, but I did know that I had to fake something fast. "What is it?"

"Spot is responding as he would to recent markings by a large predator." It was true, all except for the slight ambivalence I'd inserted. *She's gone*, Spot had said. Now that I knew what he meant, his message was crystal clear. "Some animal, possibly whatever killed Mariela, was here."

Creighton shook his head. The rain had faded back to mist again, but his hair had darkened, gathering into little spikes of wet. "I don't know, Pru. Despite what Albert and his buddies are playing at, we have no proof that she was killed anywhere near here."

I looked up at that, wiping my own wet locks from my face. "What aren't you telling me, Jim?"

For a moment, he eyed me, tight-lipped and appraising. I could almost see the decision being made. "We know she was moved, Pru. You know that already. I have people on that, but now that we have another homicide—"

"Another?"

He looked confused. "I thought you knew. Laurel wasn't..." He paused.

I had no time for niceties. "Yes, I know she was

killed. That someone tried to make it look like a maul-ing. But you said 'another.'" He was silent. "Jim?"

"That's not an official ruling, Pru. Not yet." He ran his hand over his face, and I could see what this was costing him. Two deaths by any means—two women, one of whom he knew—it was a lot. "But I'm working on the assumption that there was a connection. That Laurel was following up on something."

That was it. He felt guilty. "What can I do, Jim?"

A hint of a smile. He had played me, a little, but right now I didn't mind. He held out my phone.

"You can make a call for me, Pru," he said. "Your Mr. Benazi is a bit of an elusive character. See if he wants to get together for lunch or a cocktail."

Now it was my turn to be taken aback. "You want me to set him up?"

"I want you to talk with him." Creighton eyed me, and I could almost see the gears moving behind those blue eyes. He thought I was weighing loyalties, consid-ering his decidedly irregular request.

I was, but not the way he thought. "I won't wear a wire." I licked my lips, which were suddenly dry. I couldn't explain what I suspected of Benazi's sensitiv-ity. I could let Creighton know I was afraid. "I don't know if he's involved with any of this, Jim. But he's not someone I want to mess with."

He got it. "I wouldn't ask you to," he said. "In fact, I was considering calling him in. Just for informational purposes. But he's not directly connected, at least not by anything substantial just yet. And if his residence is over in New York, and I have to reach across state lines, well…"

I nodded. It would mean a delay, as well as paperwork. And I could easily see someone as slick as Benazi managing to evade even the most polite invitation from an officer of the law. Meanwhile, Spot was getting agitated. Probably picking up the conflict between us.

"I'm not going to lie to him." It wasn't just respect for the older man. It was also respect for his potential for danger.

"You don't have to." Creighton knew he had me if I was arguing terms. "Look, Pru, things are more complicated than they seem, and, well, I could use your help right now. Just make a date. Who knows? Meet him in a public place, and I may just wander on by."

"Like you did here, today?" I still didn't know what had delayed him, and Spot's growing restlessness brought me back to the hunt.

"Maybe." He wasn't giving me anything but the phone. "Make the call, Pru."

I took it, in the process signaling Spot to be still.

"Hi, Bill?" The voice mail message was anonymous, the voice confirming the number warm and female. "Pru Marlowe here. We need to meet." It wasn't smooth, and it wasn't what I would have said if Creighton hadn't been watching me. However, it was done.

"Voice mail," I said, with a firm command of the obvious. "I'll let you know if he calls back."

"A public place." He reiterated. "And let me know before you go meet him?"

"Of course, Jim." I kept my eyes on his baby blues, but my thoughts went to the dog at my side. *"And you're coming, too."*

As I formed the words, I realized I had another challenge on my hands—and maybe another opportunity.

"Jim, have there been any provisions made for Spot

here?" I didn't know what legal bearing the dog could have on the case. None, I hoped.

He clearly hadn't considered any, and stood for close to a minute before shaking his head. "Doesn't the service group have people who can take a dog in?"

I shook my head. They did, of course. That wasn't what I was interested in. "There's no point, Jim. Spot here is nearly fully trained, and to re-house him when he's only going to go to his new gig would set him back." Mentally, I apologized to the canine for the slur. "What I'd like to do is see if I can keep working with him—only at the Haigens. I mean, if he's going to live there anyway."

It sounded true. It wasn't. What I wanted was an in. If what I feared were true, I'd do everything in my power to keep Spot from landing there permanently.

Creighton eyed me, sensing something, and I held my breath. To say any more would be out of character.

"You've been working with them anyway, right?" He asked finally. I nodded. "Well, you'll have to get their permission. And Pru? You're working with their dog. Nothing else."

"I don't know what you're talking about. Just because Mariela worked there…"

His eyes narrowed.

"Where were you anyway, Jim?" Going on the attack was good strategy. Besides, I wanted more. "You were late getting here, and that's not like you."

"That's none of your business, Pru Marlowe." He looked from me to Spot and back again. "Now, don't you have a dog to train or something?"

FORTY-ONE

I DID HAVE other clients, and rather than dump Spot I rushed through the rest of my rounds. The shepherd mix sat quietly while I checked in on the fish tank at the local Chinese restaurant. The tail rot was receding, and I promised Mrs. Han that I'd look into restocking her gouramis. Spot was equally calm when I left him tied to a tree outside the Paul place. Princess Ida, the Pauls' Siamese, was most intrigued by his scent, and I was taken aback by the flirtatious nature of her thoughts, not to mention her vocalizations, as I trimmed her claws.

By the time I got back out, the rain had stopped, and I took Spot for a walk around the block. I was hungry by then, and figured he must be, too. I'd been considering how to broach the subject with the Haigens, and had pretty much decided that showing up with the dog might be the way to go. It would make me look less professional, but it could be explained away by Laurel's death—and the ensuing crisis of Spot's care. Besides, it's a lot harder to refuse a dog who has already been delivered.

I'm no good on an empty stomach, though, and I needed something solid to chase the remainder of that hangover from my system. Going home was not an option. Wallis would undoubtedly love to interrogate Spot, but that would take hours. Besides, I didn't have anything appropriate for Spot to eat, and I was pretty sure Wallis would draw the line at sharing last night's chicken.

Laurel's house was the default option, and as I drove, I realized I was eager to return there. Now that I had a bit of distance on what had happened, I wanted to see if I could find out why. Creighton, after all, didn't have all the resources that I did. And I thought there might be more than kibble left behind in the shrink's showroom house.

Spot began whining softly as I turned into the drive. The crunch of the gravel under my tires made me aware again of how quiet this dog usually was. "Spot, do you ever let loose?" We were alone; the house was dark. "I mean, do you even want me to call you Spot?"

He turned to me, his large eyes liquid. *"Protect you."* I got that loud and clear, but I left him in the car anyway as I went out to forage. The house was dark under the still cloudy sky, but I'd assumed that Creighton would have left an officer on guard. It might, after all, be a crime scene. When nobody answered the door, I realized with relief that whatever had happened had probably happened elsewhere, and that I had to consider other options. No matter what Spot might think, I wasn't quite a helpless female. And as I wandered around to the back, I worked my knife out of my jeans. I was thinking of it as a tool; its blade is sturdy enough to shimmy most locks. Still, despite the absence of Creighton's techs, I couldn't help wondering where Laurel had been attacked, and the blade's weight, slight but balanced, put a little more strut in my step.

It also made quick work of the porch door. In fact, the only delay had been a momentary hesitation: a woman like Laurel Kroft, used to the city, might well have installed an alarm system, living alone in a big, old house like this. But the techies and the troopers I'd seen here before were unlikely to have bothered with it. Worst case, I told myself, I'd set it off. In which case, I could simply wait it out and tell whomever that I'd come back for the dog's provisions. It was simple and had the added benefit of being mostly true. Assuming that most of the local force also knew I had a thing with Creighton wouldn't hurt. I'd get yelled at, but I've been through worse.

I wiped my feet carefully before entering: if nobody knew I'd been here, I didn't want to make it muddily obvious. Once in, I found Spot's kibble easily enough. Everyone keeps their pet food in the same place: the low cabinets by the sink. Maybe that's natural when we stock the twenty-pound bags, but I think it's something else as well. It's as if we all expect our pet to get the food himself. I left it on the counter, though. If we were interrupted, that was my excuse, lame as it may be, and went to explore the rest of the house.

Bedroom first. I'll confess to a strange jolt of something as I looked through the top drawers of the dead woman's bureau. It wasn't her lacy underthings—I always considered La Perla overpriced—it was that this is where women hide their secrets. Still, when nothing more telling than a torn negligee came to light, I was happy to shove the drawer shut. Creighton had chosen me, the thought popped into my head. The rest was—like the woman—history.

The second bedroom—this house was as big as mine—had been turned into a home office, and I felt better about rummaging here. Partly, that was because someone else already had. Jefferson, I figured, or at least members of his crew, considering the smudges of print dust that marred the glossy cream windowsills. Vacant spaces showed where something had been taken. I was betting on a laptop, from the size. But Laurel was old school enough to have made printouts, and I was hoping that something in these would click for me.

I had no excuse for being in here, if anyone came in, and so at first I just stood there—one eye on the door, the other on the papers as I started casually rifling through them. The first few were obvious—spreadsheets of accounts and billing. I could see how she afforded this beautiful place, with those rates. Granted, most of the bills seemed to be going to corporate rather than private clients. The next few were household expenses and the like. Dull stuff, the kind of financial planning I'm too lazy—or just too scared—to do. Why tally up what you spend unless you know all the bills can be covered by month's end?

Five minutes later, I hadn't found out anything more incriminating than that she was addicted to eye cream. The pricey kind. This was turning into postmortem voyeurism, and I knew I should get out of there. On the odd chance that anyone was watching the house, I was spending way too long. Not to mention that Spot had spent most of the day in my car, and my own belly was rumbling now. Still, I might not have a chance like this again. I needed to see what was inside the desk.

Promising myself I would be quick, I pulled out the chair to sit and heard the slight crackle of paper. There was no way anyone would be able to tell I'd looked through the files on top of the desk, they had been left in such a mess. The drawers, however, proved to be a disappointment. The top had the usual pens and rubber bands, but the sides were largely empty. Any check-books or address books—assuming Laurel kept these in paper form—had been taken. The bottom drawer, deep enough to hold files, only held the paperwork on the house, including the bills for what were indeed pricey renovations and what looked like tax files that would put mine to shame for both intricacy and order.

I poked around some more. It wasn't likely that the good doctor had been done in by one of her patients. Most of them, according to what paperwork I had found, were in the old folks' home. If there were any others, their files weren't here. Creighton probably had them, I told myself. Still, my skin was tingling slightly as I pushed the chair back. I was ready to go, that was probably all that was getting to me. As I did, I heard that slight crackle again. The chair, I saw as I ducked down, had rolled over a stray page. I retrieved it and sat down again to read.

"Dear Valued Donor. Thank you for your recent donation." The heading—probably the top third of the folded page—had been torn off. Still, the page in my hand was clearly a letter, the kind that serves as a tax receipt. *"The Vision Institute of New England appreciates the generosity of your recent gift, valued at..."* Here the form letter ended and some poor slob had typed in $48,833. The uneven spacing might have been an error, but I saw it as a protest by some underpaid clerk. *"Such beneficence helps us see our way to a brighter future."*

Money. People who have it don't want to hear about it. That's why they use words like "generosity" and "beneficence."

"Thanks for the cash" would be considered crass.

At any rate, it was no concern of mine who received

the late doctor's bountiful gifts. Unless there was some strange payback going on, between this eye charity and Laurel Kroft's work, or some kind of a tax dodge, I couldn't see it being evidence of anything. I could see why Creighton's minions had overlooked this page. I was about to follow his lead and toss it onto the pile on the desk when something about it caught me: the amount.

Maybe it was the typing, that uneven spacing. It wasn't that I doubted Laurel Kroft made the kind of money to give nearly fifty K away. It was a lot, but I remember what city salaries were like. Hell, I now knew that the new floor downstairs had cost as much. Plus, Laurel had always seemed like the type who would donate in such large amounts—earnest, liberal, a little showy. Confident enough of her place in the world that she probably wouldn't even want to squirrel any extra funds away for herself.

But something about it made me stop, and in a moment, I had it. If you're writing a check for charity, you write it in whole numbers, right? This letter implied a different kind of donation. In its irregularity, if not its size, it reminded me of when I'd dragged a bunch of my mother's stuff to the Salvation Army. The hospital bed had been a rental, but the stool for the shower, the walker. The clothes. I'd still had my old hatchback then and I'd filled it to the brim with stuff I no longer wanted to look at. My receipt had said $186.38, though how they'd figured out those last few cents were beyond me.

In this case, I knew how the total had been arrived at. It was simple. What I was looking at was the Kelley

Blue Book value of a 2011 Mercedes Benz SUV. Assuming, of course, that it had been in good condition, and had been packed with all the trimmings.

FORTY-TWO

I HAD NO idea why Laurel Kroft would have a receipt that belonged to the Haigens in her office. I also had no idea why the Haigens would have donated those fancy wheels. Just because I didn't like them didn't mean they wouldn't have found a buyer, especially if they were willing to knock a bit off the price. But I was pretty sure that that's what I was looking at: a receipt for Richard Haigen's SUV.

As I sat there, another thought came to me. Forty-eight thousand. That was probably more than they paid Mariela in a year. Well, I had chided them for not caring about her, about a human being who lived with them. Maybe they didn't care about money either, except as a means of obtaining those pretty toys of which Richard was so fond.

That seemed unlikely, and I found myself re-reading the words on the page. *Donation*. That much was clear. Dierdre had said that they were selling the Benz, and Tracy Horlick had indicated that the sale had been at a loss. But maybe neither woman knew the whole truth. I briefly played with a scenario in which Richard gave the wheels to Laurel and maybe told his wife that he had sold it short, to explain why he didn't have any extra cash on hand to show for the deal. Nick had been the one handling the so-called sale, but that part didn't surprise me. Wingmen have been covering for their friends' affairs since long before SUVs had hit our little town.

That left Laurel's role in the little charade open. Or maybe not: I didn't see her as one of his pretty toys, but from what Creighton had said, she enjoyed playing the field. Personally, I found Richard Haigen repugnant. Then again, I wasn't so crazy about Laurel, and women have been swayed by money before. Especially women with expensive taste.

If she had been more involved with Richard Haigen than she had let on, then her reticence in talking to Creighton made sense, too. She wouldn't want to tell him that she and Haigen had been lovers. Wouldn't have wanted a payoff, either, and might have—out of guilt or remorse—donated the pricey car. In that light, the choice of charity seemed almost like a kiss-off. I liked that scenario. It had style.

It also didn't fit. Why, exactly, I wasn't sure. At first, I told myself that it wouldn't be on the floor. Laurel was too neat to have left this letter lying about. I was sure her taxes were a lot higher than mine, but I'd also have bet they were a lot better organized. On a whim, I went through her drawers again. Yes, there they were. Deductions, office. Deductions, home. Both folders were empty, the contents undoubtedly off with some forensic accountant. Creighton might know who—and for the span of a breath, I thought about telling him. About giving him this receipt and asking if, in fact, it was being deducted from the estate.

Of course, it could be that this receipt simply hadn't been filed yet. This one page could have been neatly stacked with the other bills and papers on her desktop. Probably had been, before the techs got here. But no.

That tech—Jefferson?—he'd been rude, but I'd bet he was neat. They all were.

Still, that wasn't it. This had been dropped, and then left in situ. Someone had deemed it unimportant without the context. Even the charity sounded innocuous. I shook my head and stood up. I was tired. Hungry. Spot was waiting.

I nearly sat back down, it hit me so hard. The charity was wrong. Granted, Laurel Kroft hadn't been under oath at the time, but I could still hear her going on about service animals. "People underestimate the range of a living creature," she had said. "What these animals do is priceless, and if I'm ever in a position to really help them, that's what I'd do."

Laurel wouldn't have given a car to research on eyesight. She'd have given it to help service animals. The only person who cared so much about vision research was Richard Haigen. It was his car. This letter had come from his house.

It was a leap; I knew it. And I had no idea what it meant. Just the same, I was sure I was right. And that I'd been in Laurel's place long enough. Folding the letter into my pocket, I went downstairs and grabbed the sack of dry food and Spot's dish. For a moment, I considered exiting through the front door. It would serve Creighton right if I left the big house's main entrance unlocked. It might also get a tech in trouble, and so I slipped out the back, the same way I had come in. Besides, I might need egress again, and it would be better if nobody had known I was there.

Spot smelled the kibble as soon as I opened the car door. He was too well behaved, however, to beg, and all I got was an echo of my own rumbling innards.

"Let's get you over to the Haigens," I said, giving him a pat. Maybe they'd have some answers. Maybe they'd feed me, too.

"DID WE HAVE an appointment?" Dierdre Haigen was looking better today, and as she eyed me up and down, I realized I, on the other hand, was probably the worse for wear. For one thing, I was still damp, as was Spot, and the smell of wet dog was stronger than the wood smoke I'd caught a whiff of as I'd walked up to the door. "Because Richard is taking a nap, and I would really prefer he not be bothered."

"Didn't Officer Creighton call you?" She shook her head, then caught herself. "He may have spoken to my husband. As I've said, he's now taking a nap. I assume it had something to do with that unfortunate woman?"

I nodded. That was one way to put it. "I'd say that you've acquired a service dog a bit earlier than scheduled."

She blinked at me and down at Spot, and it hit me. She didn't know about Laurel. She thought I'd been referring to Mariela, and my follow-up must have sounded like a non sequitur. Well, there would be time for that. Spot, looking up at her, remained quiet. In my head, however, I heard one word: *"Hungry?"*

That was enough of a cue for me. "Here," I said, holding out Spot's ceramic dish and making a big show of wiping my feet. "Why don't you take that into the kitchen?"

With little choice, she took the bowl and we followed her down a hall. While I'd been hoping for a cozy hearth with a spring fire roaring, I should have known better. With its white tile and stainless fixtures, the Haigen kitchen looked as sterile as the rest of the house and even less used. Two ovens, at least that I saw, would have made some women very happy, but Dierdre skirted these with distaste. I'm no homemaker, but it all seemed pretty nice to me. Nice enough so that when I spilled some of Spot's kibble, pouring it into his bowl, I felt compelled to pick it up.

"So, who will be in charge of Spot's care?" It was too much to hope that Raul might be back, but I certainly couldn't picture Dierdre doing anything in this room.

"Oh, we haven't yet figured things out." She giggled, a little nervous, I thought. "We'll be hiring somebody, I'm sure. But for now, well, we may have to cut back a bit."

"Huh," I said, trying not to sound curious. I had wondered about the lack of staff, but had put it down to the move—the self-imposed rustication—or to Richard's discomfort with his growing disability. If they were cutting back to economize, why donate a pricey car? Even if Dierdre hadn't been able to get the blue book value for the Benz, she could have made enough to pay a maid for a year, easily. Then again, if her husband had given it away behind her back, that could be a cause of the tension I had sensed. I wondered how long he'd be asleep and what I could do until he woke. In the meantime, I handed her the bag of dog food. She took it as if it were a sack of coal, holding it away from her body. I couldn't imagine her with anything less clean.

"I do offer my services as a dog walker." I didn't want to trek out here every day. Then again, that could be a useful entrée. And, yeah, I felt sorry for Spot. "For a fee," I hastened to add.

"I'm sure Richard and I will arrange something." She

made a vague gesture, like maybe the house would be able to run itself.

"Is Nick around?" I still didn't know his place in the scheme of things, but I was willing to bet he'd have one.

"Nick? Why, no." She was looking increasingly uncomfortable. "He's not been around for days."

That was curious and almost certainly untrue, but I couldn't think of a way to call her out. Meanwhile, Spot, always attuned to moods, had stopped eating and was looking up at us.

"Full," he said.

I almost replied out loud. *"You can eat."* I worked instead to project my thoughts. *"Be comfortable. Eat as much as you want."* I felt bad enough leaving this animal here. I wasn't going to have him make himself sick because Dierdre Haigen wasn't comfortable with animals.

"She's full." He looked up at me. I could sense frustration and something else: a sense of discomfort. *"Too much..."*

I got it. I nodded. Dierdre had her hands full. She wasn't the one who had my sympathy, though.

"Perhaps I could take him around now?" I really didn't want to encourage Dierdre to think of me as an on-call walker. I did, however, want an excuse to poke around.

"Oh, sure." Her pretty face would have been creased in concentration, if it weren't for the Botox.

"Do you have any questions?" I didn't care about her. Spot, however, was going to be here for a while. "About the dog's care?"

"No, no." She waved the idea away. "I just—we weren't prepared. It's been a shock."

There was no answer to that, so I signaled to Spot that he could lead me, thinking we'd go out back. The guide dog stopped before we reached the foyer and turned, sniffing the air, down a well-lit corridor.

"Walk." I gave him the command before Dierdre could say otherwise. Silently, I added to it. *"What's here, Spot? What are you smelling?"*

There was something, to be sure. Spot had stopped by an opened door. I looked in at what seemed to be an office. On the far wall, big windows opened onto the grounds. A low fog seemed to hang over the wooded area, dense and gray. "Oh, he won't be going in there," said Dierdre.

"But if Richard is working in there..." Spot, standing by my side, might have been staring out those windows. Now that the rain had stopped, the squirrels were getting frisky. I thought there might be something else going on that was attracting his interest, though.

"Richard no longer handles any paperwork. Not anymore." Dierdre had adopted a dismissive tone, and I wondered how long that would last once her husband was awake. The fog looked awfully thick. "He's retired."

"Retired, my ass." Richard Haigen announced himself with a growl, like a bear coming out of hibernation. I half expected to see him out in those woods, but when I turned, I found him rumbling down the hall, one hand out to the side in what had probably become a habit. "Who's there, Di?"

"It's Pru." I announced myself. At my side, Spot came to attention. "I'm here with Spot."

"And you didn't wake me?" That was directed toward

his wife. Neither of us responded, but I saw her pull herself up and waited for what was to come. "Dierdre?"

"You needed the sleep, dear." Even with the endearment, she didn't sound that affectionate. Still, I was surprised that she hadn't apologized. I got my second shock when he didn't respond, not even with a snarl. Maybe there had been a paradigm shift, as she assumed more of the day-to-day running of the Haigen household.

"Well, what's on the docket for today?" He seemed energized, perhaps by the nap. "Another training session?"

"We could do that, if you want." I still hadn't had lunch, but I'd trade a burger for a chance to get into that office. "I really came to bring Spot by, though. I know it's earlier than we had planned, but I thought, given everything, he should stay with you now."

He looked up, the confusion clear on his face. I guessed Dierdre had been wrong. Creighton hadn't called.

"You've not heard about Laurel Kroft?" I watched his face for any sign of response. "Have you?"

He stared at me, his mouth opening slightly, and I could have sworn his confusion was real. When he turned toward his wife, however, I thought I saw her shake her head, ever so slightly.

"Dierdre, what's going on?" Macular degeneration or not, he'd seen it too—or sensed some change in her.

"Now, Richard, don't start getting excited." She walked up to him and put her hand on his arm. But if she thought she was going to lead him out of the room, she didn't know her husband.

"Don't treat me like a child." He shook her off. "I'm going blind, not deaf. What *happened*?"

"Laurel had an accident, dear." She stayed by his side. "A tragic accident."

I opened my mouth and then shut it. So Dierdre *had* known about Laurel. Curious to hear what she knew—and how she was going to peddle this to her irate spouse—I waited. Spot stiffened, anticipating a threat.

To my surprise, Richard didn't argue. If anything, her non-explanation seemed to take the edge off his anger. "An—accident?" His voice was softer, uncertain. "She—you mean?"

Dierdre nodded. Then, as if unsure whether her husband could see her, she elaborated. "We've lost her, Richard. It was tragic, but…it happened. She's gone."

It was the coolest rendering of a murder I'd ever heard. Odds were, Creighton wouldn't have shared everything, but the platitudes Dierdre were offering sounded like Laurel had died peaceably in her bed. Maybe she didn't know the details. It was possible that nobody had told her. Still, she had to know the pretty shrink had died violently and way too young.

What was more chilling was that he seemed to accept it. As I watched, he deflated, all that anger dissipating and leaving him so weak, he reached for the wall. Spot, by my side, stood up.

"Work." It was a simple statement. He, too, sensed Richard's vulnerability and sought to go to him. I held the dog back, though, wanting to see what would happen next.

What I saw was a complete turnaround from their usual routine. Dierdre came forward and took her husband's arm again. This time, he didn't shake her off. Instead, he seemed to lean on her as she turned and walked him down the hall. I was dying to follow, but the reason I'd silently given Spot held true for me as well. Better to watch and learn.

"Work?" Spot wasn't convinced. Seeing the man stumble, I could understand why. But Dierdre had him by the arm, and so I held back.

"So…she's gone?" His deep, low voice was soft, but it carried clearly. Dierdre stiffened slightly, probably aware of how close we were, and murmured something I couldn't catch. "What the hell happened?" He was still audible and, I was glad to hear, not taking her simple explanation at face value.

I still couldn't catch what she was saying, but they'd turned now into that sterile living room, so I took the chance of moving closer. Spot's nails were the only sound we made.

"What the hell is he playing at?" Richard Haigen was whispering, but in his agitation, his question was clearly audible. "I've got to call him."

"No." Dierdre's answer was clear. "I'll—I'll talk to Benazi."

I froze. I'd known there was a connection, but still. A million questions raced through my head: Who was "he"—was that Benazi or someone else? Had Richard wanted to call Benazi, and had his wife's response meant that she would contact the man for him? Or was she offering the silver-haired gangster as an alternative? Short of bringing the dead back to life, I failed to understand what one man could do, anyway. Slick as he was, Benazi was no miracle worker. As far as I knew, he was better at making people disappear than reappear.

Before I could even phrase a question, Dierdre reappeared, her eyes widening at the sight of me.

"I wasn't sure if I should take off." It was the best excuse I could manage. "But I didn't want to interrupt."

She tilted her head and eyed me. I smiled. "I've got other clients, but I didn't want to leave Spot without giving you a heads-up."

She nodded and, after a moment, reached for Spot's lead. "I don't think Richard will be up for much walking today." Her voice was cold. "Still, he might like the company."

"I'm sorry I broke the news." I was watching her. Hoping to see something that would give me a clue. "I thought Detective Creighton had called."

She shook me off. "He forgets things. It's the stress. You should go."

I was being dismissed.

I stalled as she walked me toward the door. "Spot should be walked before bed." I gave her a rundown on the dog's basic care, wondering all the while what was going on. "Or you can just let him out in the yard."

I felt a wave of guilt. Not for Richard, who had appeared honestly distraught, and certainly not for Dierdre. They were, as Tracy Horlick liked to point out, rich. That money would cushion a lot of blows. But Spot was not going to be cared for here. Not unless the Haigens hired some more help and fast.

"I'll check in tomorrow." I also hadn't found out anything about that donation. Or Richard's relation to Laurel. "In fact, I'll make a point of coming by."

From the way she was looking at Spot, I wondered what room she was going to lock him in. Dierdre Haigen might be better dressed than Tracy Horlick, but they had some traits in common. "May I have one more word with Richard?" When she wanted to, Dierdre could out-shepherd a sheltie.

"You saw how upset he was." She might as well be nipping at my heels. I stood firm. "It's important that I bring Spot to him." I was making this up as I went along. She waivered. "I'm transferring dominance, you see."

She paused for a moment and then nodded, as if she did. I took the lead from her and Spot, eager to be doing anything, sprang up.

"Work?"

"Work." I said. It would sound more like a command than a confirmation. Together we walked into the sitting room where Richard had collapsed into one of those low white chairs. Beyond him, out the window, the fog looked more contained, like a small cloud. Like...

"Richard? What happened out there?" It wasn't the question I'd meant to ask.

"What?" He looked up, his eyes unnaturally large behind those glasses.

"The smoke." It was a guess, but it sparked something in Dierdre.

"Nothing." She pushed between us, just like Spot would do if I were a threat. "A small fire. One of the outbuildings."

"One of the buildings?" Her husband blinked up at her.

"You know." She snapped. "I told you."

He nodded, and she turned her focus on me. "As you can see, he is tired."

I couldn't argue with that any longer. Whatever spirit he'd shown must have used up the last of his strength. It was time to assume my public role.

"I'm going to give you Spot's harness now," I spoke slowly and clearly. Richard Haigen didn't respond. If I hadn't known better, I'd have thought he was staring out at the yard. At the smoke. For a moment, I wondered if he was even hearing me. But he looked up at me—and then down at the dog.

"That's a good animal," he said. "I like animals, you know."

"I'm glad." I confess, I was touched. And in that moment, I let my opportunity slide. I'd meant to ask him about the car—and about Benazi. But I stood there like a sap as he reached out to place one heavy hand on the dog's head. And then Dierdre was on me, ushering me out the door. It was all I could do to pause and turn back, to see the man and the dog sitting there together.

"Spot?" I didn't even know how to phrase my questions. Get what you can. I'll be back. All those thoughts ran through my head.

"I know." The thought came as strong and sure as if he'd spoken out loud. *"But she's gone. She's gone."*

FORTY-THREE

I COULDN'T EXPLAIN it all to Wallis, and when I brought up the fire my tabby colleague was particularly unamused. Fire in the wild is a bad thing. Dangerous for all, even when we humans think we have it under control.

"They knew, Wallis. It must have been an accident." Even as I said it, I heard myself wondering. We'd had rain, but no lightning. And speaking of rain, I realized the fire must have been recent to generate that mix of steam and wood smoke after the earlier storm.

"They think they can tame it." Wallis was not amused. *"Such fools."* She did, however, deign to share my belated lunch, licking at the rotisserie chicken I'd grabbed on the way home. Beauville's gentrification had a few upsides; the gourmet mart was one of them. If Creighton and I managed to get together again, I might even try one of their overpriced wines.

For now, though, I washed the food down with tap water. It had been a very full day, and I wanted to sort it out with a clear head. Besides, Wallis had already made a few snide comments about my "so-called thirst."

"You snore when you drink, you know." She chimed in now, as she finished off a wing. *"It's not attractive in a bed partner."*

I wasn't sure if she was referring to herself or to any potential lovers. Before I could ask, however, my phone rang. Not Creighton—Wallis isn't psychic that way—but a blocked number that I didn't recognize.

"Ms. Marlowe." It was Benazi. I looked at the phone. "I'm sorry it took me so long to return your call." I had the sense he knew what I'd just done. It was a little unsettling. "You left a message at the charming inn where I'd been staying, and I'm afraid it took them till now to forward it to me."

Charming inn, my ass. However, I got his message: he wasn't traceable. Not by me, certainly not by the police.

"Thank you for calling me back." For all the steel in his words, there was velvet, too. It was easy to fall into his courtly ways. "I was hoping we could meet again?"

From the silence on the other end of the line, I wondered if I'd lost him. Wallis stared at me from her perch on the table. *That was subtle.* I could feel her scorn.

"You…suggested some things when we had dinner." I kept talking. I didn't want to mention Haigen, or what I'd overheard, but there was enough going on to give me cover. "As you may have heard, we've had an eventful time here in our little town. I'd like to know if there's anything you think that I should know."

"I would be honored to help you." His voice was soft as always. Smooth. But the way he accented the last word meant something.

"Just me?" Wallis lashed her tail. I shrugged. At least he was still on the line. "Look," I decided to chance it, "you know the cops want to talk with you. I'm not helping them. But another woman died, and if there's something you can tell me so I'm not next, I'd appreciate it."

I didn't expect the chuckle. Even Wallis' ears pricked up. "Ms. Marlowe, you always had a way with words."

I waited. "Of course, I'd love the pleasure of your company again. Shall we say dinner this evening?"

"The inn?" It was what I'd wanted—a place Creighton could easily stake out—but alarm bells were going off in my head.

"Oh, let's try something new." He sounded playful. Flirtatious even. "Why don't I pick you up at your place. Shall we say, seven?"

I nodded, my mouth suddenly dry.

He must have heard my faint croak. "An unseemly hour, I know. But out here, our options are limited, and so…"

"Seven's fine," I managed to say. "I'll be here."

"Lovely." He sounded like he hadn't heard anything out of the ordinary. "I look forward to it."

Wallis was watching me as I hung up, and I could feel her curiosity. "What?" I asked her. "It's dinner."

I knew it was more than that. Knew, too, that I had changed the rules Creighton had laid down. What were my options?

"You didn't have to tell him about Creighton." She wasn't blinking, and her green eyes were intense.

"He knew anyway. He has a sense about such things."

"He knows you," she said, flicking her tail once. *"All he had to do was apply the slightest pressure… It's really quite an effective technique."*

I didn't want to hear it, and I turned away. If Benazi was going to pick me up at seven, I had a lot to do to get ready. Ostensibly, the old gangster was doing me a favor. Looking out for me. But something about him was as cold as a lizard, and I had no doubt he'd eliminate anything or anyone he viewed as a threat. I had to prepare myself for any eventuality.

"Don't you think it's already too late?" Wallis jumped down from the table and had begun walking away. For a moment, I worried that she was leaving me. She must have sensed it, because she stopped, turning partway to fix me again with those green eyes. *"You're worried about going out with him."* The afternoon light caught the green, making them unnaturally bright against the doorway's shade. *"But he's coming here, Pru. He knows where you live."*

"We, Wallis. Where *we* live." With a swallow, I confessed. "He's known for a while."

Her look said it all, dismissive with scorn. *"And now he's coming over."*

FORTY-FOUR

IT WAS WITH mixed feelings that I drove back to the shelter. I didn't want to run into Creighton again. Didn't want to have to lie to him about Benazi calling me back or about that strange donation letter. And as much as I'd have liked to have found out what he'd been up to while I was traipsing through the woods with Albert's friends, I doubted he was going to volunteer that info. But I had about two hours before my dinner date, and there was still one loose end I could tug. The more I could unravel before Benazi picked me up, the better shape I'd be in to get information. Or, well, I didn't want to think about what else. So I kept my phone off and parked down the street, slipping into the shelter as quickly as a vole into its hole.

"Hey, Pru!" Albert had no such compunctions, and greeted me with a wave. "I was wondering if you were going to come back here. Hey, where's the dog?"

"He's a service dog, Albert." I cleared the space between the door and his desk in record time, hoping proximity would lower his voice. "I took him over to the Haigens' place, where he can do what he was trained for."

"Man, they have all the luck." I suppressed a snort of laughter. He looked up at me. "No, really. I mean, getting any animal they want."

"The man is losing his eyesight." I wanted to be

angry. Albert was just too clueless. "I know he's rich, but that's pretty bad."

He nodded. "Yeah, but—" I waited to hear what Albert would find an extenuating circumstance. "Well, he gets everything."

It was a lame answer, best ignored. And I'd come here for a reason. "That was a good turnout for the hunt." I'd pulled the guest chair over and leaned back in it. "A good crew."

As expected, Albert puffed himself up. "We know how to band together out here."

"Yeah, I'm sorry we couldn't do any better." I thought about throwing in a smile and decided against it. No use scaring the man. "Your pal, Stu, he really knows what he's doing."

If Albert were a cat he would have purred. Then again, if Albert were a cat he'd be cleaner. "Real woodsman," I added for good measure, though what I was really wondering about were his other talents, the kind that gave him control over people. And who, if anyone, had hired him. "Know how I can get in touch with him?"

Albert's bushy eyebrows went up at that, followed by a blush. Our animal-control officer might be afraid of the opposite sex, but that didn't mean he didn't like to speculate. Well, let him. I gave him that grin now to fuel the fire.

"Dunno. Maybe you can find him at Happy's?" I shook my head. If that man had been a regular at our local bar, I'd have seen him before. I'd have remembered him.

"Doesn't matter." A little misdirection is always good. "I'll catch him at the next hunt. I figure we'll be trying again, once the weather clears?" No use in mentioning Creighton's prohibition. Not with that crowd.

Albert's face knotted up. Maybe I'd been wrong about their respect for my detective beau. "We won't?"

For a big man, Albert has a small mouth. Now it gaped open like a dying fish, red visible through the tangle of his beard.

"Stu went back out already." I kicked myself for voicing the thought out loud. Albert didn't need to know he was so easy to read. I needed a cover—and a consult. "So, you got Frank around today?"

The color fading from the parts of his face I could see, Albert nodded enthusiastically and pulled open a desk drawer. A triangular head popped out and swiveled around, taking in the scene.

"Hey, Frank." I held out my hand for him to sniff. It was the polite thing to do. It was also my way of catching the little mustelid up on my day.

"It's not safe out there." His nose quivered, moist, but those dark eyes locked onto mine. *"The hunter... big hunter..."*

I nodded. "Big" to Frank didn't necessarily mean size, at least not size as I'd see it. "So, Al, what can you tell me about Stu?"

Let him think I was interested in the man. It wouldn't do my reputation any harm.

"What...what do you mean?" I kept my eyes on Frank, and we shared a moment of recognition. Albert was afraid of the other man, and I had to tread carefully.

"Well, he's not from around here. I was wondering if he just came in for the day. If he works around here." Not many of Albert's friends were gainfully employed.

I had a sense that this Stu was different, though. "I figure, to go out in this weather—"

"He... I don't know." Albert is a lousy liar. I pretended to believe him and nodded, smiling. To Frank, I directed the thought: *"Big hunter?"* I visualized the wiry little man. Something about him reminded me of Frank. Maybe it was the eyes. I reached over for him, to stroke his back. Physical contact can aid communication.

"Watch it." Albert sat up with a start, bringing me back. Frank, too, had stood up. Back arched and erect, he bounced from one foot to the next, like a boxer in the ring. It was a classic display—fear or aggression, something had gotten Frank riled up. "He'll bite you!"

"What is it?" I couldn't reach out, not with Albert watching. It was difficult to make eye contact as his head weaved and bobbed.

"Big hunter. Big! Take cover." With that, he turned and dove first into Albert's lap, startling a shout from the hairy man, before climbing into his vest.

"Well, that was intriguing." I felt the hair on my neck stand up at the voice, soft and yet cold. "And so educational to see you at work with animals, Ms. Marlowe."

I turned and rose. Greeted the man standing there in his mohair coat and city shoes. Italian loafers, complete with the little tassels. Gregor "Bill" Benazi had come to call.

"I'M EARLY, I KNOW." Benazi leaned toward me as if confiding a secret. "I thought it might be better if we met sooner. Especially if you had something urgent on your agenda."

I didn't even try to smile. I'd been outplayed, and I

knew it. I still hadn't decided whether to tell Creighton about my dinner date or not, but the old gangster wasn't taking any chances. He'd preempted any precautionary move I could have made, a fact he hadn't denied when I confronted him, my voice low and fierce.

"I care about you, Pru." He had all the warmth of a shark. "Why is that so hard for you to believe?"

"Define 'care.'" I was snarling. I don't like being ambushed. We were outside the shelter by then, both of us preferring to take our discussion away from Albert's ever-widening gaze.

The dapper man just laughed. I realized we'd walked over to his car, the red Maserati. His smile had a glint of humor in it now.

"Admit it, Ms. Marlowe. You're curious."

"You'd let me drive?" If this was his game…

"Maybe." He unlocked the passenger side. "Perhaps we should have a chat first. If it's not too early for you?"

I had the feeling he knew my schedule. Knew that I had finished my afternoon appointments. Probably knew, as well, that I hadn't parked in the lot. Creighton wouldn't be seeing my car when he left for the day. Might not notice it for a while. Wallis would, I thought. At least, she'd miss the regular meal service. Not that she'd be able to communicate any of this, if I were to go missing. Or worse, be found, bloodied and broken, like two other women already had, their bodies left out in the woods.

He was holding the door open. Waiting.

I got in.

FORTY-FIVE

WE DROVE FOR a while in silence, Benazi taking the curving back roads that climb out of town and up into the hills. It was lonely up here, no houses and no other cars. The snow had hung on here, too, turning the landscape into an etching of black on white.

I should have been nervous. This was very like another time I'd run into Benazi. That time, he may have just disposed of another inconvenient female. But as I looked out the window, I realized I wasn't. Maybe it was the car. Even though I wasn't driving, I enjoyed its smooth shifts, the feeling of power as it took on the steeper grades. He smiled over at me after one shift, and I felt a kinship. An understanding of power and machines.

Then again, maybe I was completely delusional.

When he abruptly pulled off the road and started driving up a rutted track, I began to panic. Forget my car, my body wouldn't be found here for months. But just as I was considering the viability of jumping out of a moving vehicle, the road turned again and I saw it. Perched among the birches and indisputably more modern than any house in the town below, still it seemed to fit. The gray wood, the windows reflecting the clouds. It was a perfect hideaway, and when Benazi pulled to a stop in front of the tall front steps, I no longer wanted to run.

"Please." He climbed the steps in front of me and opened the door with a key. "After you."

Stepping into the spacious room, I was vaguely aware of a stone fireplace, of low-slung chairs and rugs. What drew me in, though, was the panorama laid out before me, from those still-frosted peaks down to the rooftops of Beauville. I walked over to the floor-to-ceiling windows, barely aware of Benazi coming up behind me. If this were the last thing I saw, there were worse ways to go.

"Ms. Marlowe?" I turned. He was holding out a tumbler of something golden. I sniffed and got smoke. I sipped and got more, followed by a smooth heat that took the edge right off and reminded me that I'd been wet and chilled not that long ago. I'm not a Scotch drinker, but this tasted like the good stuff.

"Please, have a seat." He gestured to a low chair the color of wheat, and I sank into it. "I thought it best for both of us if we spoke privately."

I took another sip, enjoying a warmth that was as enveloping as the cushions. I was here, disarmed, and it was his show.

"Ms. Marlowe." He settled into a chair facing me and leaned forward, as if about to confide. "Thank you for coming with me today. I don't mean to pry into your life, but it has come to my attention that we share certain, well, shall we say characteristics."

I looked at him, waiting. This could be interesting. He looked at me, and I realized he was wondering if I was going to respond.

"The details aren't important." Once he saw that I wasn't, he brushed the idea away. "What does matter, what concerns me today is that we both tend to conduct our lives according to more personal compasses than others may."

"We break the law, is that what you mean?" I enjoyed the courtly talk up to a point. Besides, I was nearly done with my drink.

"We live independently." He corrected me and glanced at my glass.

I held onto it, and, I hoped, to my wits. "You don't want me looking into you—into what you do." I was going to have to venture something.

"I value my privacy." Those dark eyes were sharp. "As do you, I believe."

I didn't respond.

"We all have our secrets." The words were simple. Innocuous, but as I sat there, waiting for him to go on, I got the sense that he had made his statement. And that, however he managed it, he knew about me. About what I could do. As if responding to that thought, he smiled ever so slightly. I couldn't say the sight of his even, white teeth was reassuring. "But you helped me adopt my beloved pet, and I will always be grateful to you for that."

A chill ran through me. He did know. He had to. That white Persian had refused to let me in for the longest time, but she had taken to Benazi in a flash. They had understood each other. Had that white cat…well… ratted me out?

"How is Fluffy?" My voice sounded dead, even to me. He smiled as if I had given him the warmest of greetings.

"She's grand, thank you for asking."

I looked around, half expecting to be interrogated Wallis style.

"Oh, she's not here," his voice was light now. "I maintain more than one home. The weather…" His words trailed off, inconsequential.

"Well, give her my best." I breathed a little easier. He had let me know that he was well disposed toward me. Now we could get down to business. "So, I gather you do have some information to share?"

"You have become embroiled in an investigation." He stated it as fact, and so I felt no need to respond. "And while I don't see myself as actively helping…" Again, his voice trailed off. He must have thought I was wearing a wire.

"I'm not, you know." I was rewarded by an ever so slight widening of those hooded hawk eyes. "Wearing a wire or any kind of recording device. I told Creighton I wouldn't." It was a courtesy, one he understood, and he nodded in acknowledgment. That meant it was my turn to ask a question. "You know something about what happened—to Mariela. And to Laurel, too."

To my surprise, he winced. For a moment, he even looked away, as if he could take off through that window into the gray sky beyond. "I may have some ideas," he said finally. "Some thoughts about what happened to those two young women."

"And?" To me, the next step was obvious.

"It's not in my interest to make waves." He gazed down into his own drink. It looked like embarrassment to me. Submission. I was beginning to not care.

"Look, Bill—Gregor—whatever your name is. If you know something, you have to tell—" I stopped short. "That's what you brought me here for. Why you agreed to meet me. To tell me what happened."

He raised his eyes, a different man. Older, in pain. "Bill, please. Tell me." This time my voice was soft.

"I don't like the idea of involving you, Pru." It seemed easier for him to talk if he stared out the window. "I don't like it at all. But I believe you are already on the right track. You've got the scent, so to speak."

He wanted a hound. Spot, not me. Unless… "That hunter, Stu, he said his name was?" It was a guess, but it felt right. "He works for you, doesn't he?"

He inclined his head at a slight angle. Another acknowledgment.

"But why do you need a hunter?"

He lifted his glass and took a drink, a big one. Even as he started talking, he kept staring out the window, as if the answer were in those clouds.

"Some people become bored more easily than others." His voice was as even as ever. The light from that window, though…it wasn't kind. Harsh, as the overcast thinned, it showed every line that time had drawn, and some that may have been etched by sorrow or by grief. "Some people require more…" His pauses didn't seem strategic anymore. He was having trouble voicing his thoughts. "…more stimuli in order to enjoy themselves. If those people have the means to acquire such stimuli…"

He shrugged ever so slightly, and I felt my face grow hot. He was a procurer. I knew that. "And you were arranging some kind of entertainment?"

Another slight movement. Perfect deniability. Perfect outrage.

"You were setting up some kind of hunt." An idea was forming. "But you could have gotten a license. Anyone could…"

I stopped. My own words had caught me up, an echo forming. Something Wallis had said about how she hunted. How she killed. A memory that conflicted with the bloody corpse Spot and I had found only a few days ago.

Mariela had been shredded, her scalp half torn off her head and her chest opened by savage claws. I had known something was wrong. Wallis had tried to show me, but I hadn't seen it. An animal in the wild doesn't tear at its prey like that, not something as soft and vulnerable as Mariela had been. A predator kills quickly: a crushing bite to the skull or the back of the neck. I pictured Wallis grabbing a mouse, shaking it hard and fast.

The image was horrible, but it was real. It was what Wallis had been wanting me to understand all along. Whatever had killed Mariela hadn't been wild, not in any true sense. It had been captive—and panicked.

"Home." That one word, I had heard it again and again. Something was out there that shouldn't be. Something as scared as Mariela must have been.

I looked at Benazi as the truth dawned on me. He saw it, read it on my face if not from my thoughts.

"It was a staged hunt. Canned." It helped to put the idea to words. "Whatever mauled Mariela. You brought in something that had been raised in captivity—something that you didn't expect to fight back—an easy mark for personal big-game hunt."

The image that had been haunting me. From the sheltie. From Spot. Not a cougar, native or otherwise. A snow leopard. Beautiful, but deadly. "You brought in—" I caught myself. Whatever Benazi knew about me, I didn't want to confirm it. "Whatever it was that killed Mariela. You're responsible."

"I am trying," his voice was low and steady, each word carefully enunciated, "to set things right."

"Do you know how many laws—" I stopped myself. Keeping so-called exotic animals is illegal in our state. Hunting an endangered species added more violations—federal ones, too. Not to mention trafficking. It didn't matter. Legalities weren't important to Benazi. I knew that. Logistics, however. "Where did you get—? No, never mind." My mind was racing. Richard Haigen couldn't be the client. He couldn't hunt. Who else had that kind of money? "Who—" He shot me a look that should have shut me up. At least it made me change tack. "What happened?"

He shrugged, a most eloquent shrug. "Something that should not have."

"I gather." I sat up, glad that I'd not let him refill my glass. "And now you need my help."

Traps. That's what I needed. I also could use an expert. Someone familiar with big game rescue. With tranquilizers, and...

"No." Benazi had leaned over and put his hand on mine. His palm was cold and leathery, his eyes gray steel. "Absolutely not."

"Are you kidding?" I jerked my arm away, no longer concerned with the niceties. "You set up a hunt, but the prey has gotten away from you. That's why you brought me here, isn't it? I'm the animal expert."

"I did not want you involved in this." He hadn't raised his voice, not much. Clearly, he was used to being obeyed. "I have been trying to warn you, Pru. Leave this alone. The situation is under control."

"Is that what you told Laurel?" I was on my feet.

Clearly, the shrink had put this together. "Did she figure this out? Did she confront you about Mariela?"

"We are done talking about this."

"I'm not." I turned toward the door. It was getting late. I didn't care. I'd walk till I could get a signal. Creighton would come. He'd come to hear this.

"You do not understand the implications." He was standing too. Great, he could walk me to the door. "For yourself—and for others."

I whirled to face him. "So, what? More people are going to die?"

"I'm not threatening anybody." He held both palms up, as if in surrender. "But don't you see this is a complex situation, Pru? Please, be reasonable."

"What I see is illegal procurement and sale of an exotic animal for a horrible purpose. A dangerous animal that got loose and when Laurel found out…" I stopped, stumbling over the words. "Wait. Mariela wasn't killed in the woods. Neither was Laurel. Someone put Mariela in with…with whatever." I stopped. The outbuilding. The one that had set Spot off; the one that had burned. How could I have missed it? The leopard had been kept on the Haigens' property, where poor Mariela had worked. "And someone killed Laurel and tried to make it look like the same thing, then dumped them, both, out in the woods."

There were too many blanks to fill. Too many missing parts, and I looked up, blinking. "Why?"

"As I've said…" He reached forward and took my hands again. His voice had grown softer now. The voice of reason and restraint. "…this is a complicated situation. It is being handled, and you've got to let it go."

"But—"

"No, Ms. Marlowe. No more questions." With that, he gestured toward the door. "Shall we?" His voice, as courtly as ever, wasn't really offering any options, and when I opened my mouth again, he simply shook his head. Creighton could be like that—the comparison flashed through my mind as I let him show me out. The thought wasn't particularly comforting. Nor was the flash of a smile I glimpsed as he locked the door behind us, as if I'd spoken aloud.

He drove me back to my car in the fading light. It didn't matter. I wasn't looking at the scenery. Instead, I was thinking about two women, both dead.

"Look, Laurel, I get." I didn't. I was just thinking out loud. "She was asking questions. But how did Mariela get mixed up in this? Tell me that." I turned toward Benazi. The dying light made the lines on his face deeper, more like scars. "Was she in on it? Was Raul?" My mind raced over possibilities: a smuggling ring. The ways in which a young undocumented person could be abused—and discarded.

"Was she…?" I swallowed hard. "Was she some kind of bait?" The idea that that beautiful young woman might have been exploited in such a way made her death even more obscene.

Benazi scowled, and I kept on. "They use cats, you know. Kittens, sometimes, in dog fights." I was spitting out the words. They were all I had to hit him with. "They throw them in with the dogs to stoke the killing instinct. To wake the taste for blood."

I saw his hands tighten on the steering wheel. I knew he had a soft spot for women. For cats, too. Good, let him stew on it.

"She wasn't—" His voice croaked, as if he hadn't

spoken in weeks rather than a few minutes. "That was an accident."

"And Laurel?" I was too angry to stop. "Was her death an accident, too?"

His mouth was set in a thin, grim line again. I didn't care.

"I would have thought you had more finesse." I chose my words with care. "More style. Not about murder, but in the cover-up. Trying to make *that* look like another 'hunting accident'? Sloppy."

When that didn't get a response, I gave up. By the time we'd arrived back in town, I was thinking of where else I could go for answers. Even as Benazi slowed, I was reaching for the handle.

"Pru, please..." His fingers grazed the back of my hand. I fought the urge to slap it away. "I want you to be safe."

I looked over at his sad and tired face. For a moment, my anger flickered and dimmed. It's hard to live outside the lines. Then I thought of Laurel, of Mariela, and it came roaring back. "I'll be fine." I opened the door.

"Be careful." His voice was soft but audible. "She's not what you think. She's dangerous, Pru."

I nodded, eager to be away. Not until he left, the Maserati growling like a cat, did I realize he'd driven me down the side street to my car, where I'd thought I'd left it unobserved over an hour before.

FORTY-SIX

WALLIS WAS HAVING none of it, and she wasn't holding back.

"Are you insane?" She'd jumped up on the window-sill to be at eye level with me, and her twitching tail kept banging against the wall. *"Going up against something that...something that large?"*

"I'm not 'going up' against a leopard, Wallis." I'd raced home to gather some supplies as well as, finally, get something to eat. If I'd been hoping for support, I'd have to look elsewhere. "I want to initiate a humane search. That's all."

"Humane." Sarcasm dripped from her voice. I didn't think it was at my intent so much as the word. Wallis has a dim view of anything human. Even me, she barely considers functional most of the time. *"Huh."*

"You know what I mean, Wallis. It's not used to being out there, alone. You're the one who showed me that." I turned away from her and found myself staring at my phone. I should call Creighton. I knew that. I should have called him the moment I'd made the date with Benazi. When he'd shown up early. Creighton would be angry, but this was more important than our relationship. I had information that directly related to two murders.

I would call him, I promised myself. The only problem was how to explain away the evidence I shouldn't have had. I pulled the letter from my jacket. A receipt for the value of a car. The Haigens' Benz.

"Don't trust her," Benazi had said. "She's dangerous."

In retrospect, it made perfect sense. I'd suspected Dierdre Haigen from the start. The jealous wife, consolidating control during a husband's decline. The only questions remaining were about how she had managed it, but I thought the donation letter was probably key.

As I assembled a hasty sandwich, ignoring Wallis' glare, I tried to put it all together.

Creighton, I knew, was no slouch. I'd seen the techs at Laurel's. I had no doubt he'd had a team over at the Haigens, too, once he knew for sure that Mariela's body had been moved. They'd have been looking for a crime scene—for traces of her blood. He'd have checked Dierdre's little sports car, but the SUV would have been already gone. At the dealers, Richard had said. But not sold. No matter what someone had told Tracy Horlick.

I had wondered about that, as I'd slopped mayo on the stale bread. Had wondered, as I tore up the rest of the chicken... Why lie? Why not say that the big Benz was a white elephant: more valuable as a tax write-off than an asset?

Now, I thought I had the answer: Someone had used it to transport Mariela's body, that's why. And then someone had to get rid of it, fast. Could Dierdre Haigen have engineered that?

"Oh, please, Pru." Wallis was losing patience. I couldn't. I had to consider all the options.

"I don't think she acted alone." I bit into my sandwich, more concerned with refueling than taste. "She could have signed the car away. Maybe even dragged

Mariela into it. But how would she have picked the car up out in Amherst, or wherever it was? How would she have carried Mariela into the woods? No, she's in this somehow, but not alone."

Wallis blinked once, slowly. Coquettishly. *"Some kinds of women are not made to be alone."*

I started, hearing my own words repeated back to me, and it hit me. Nick. Nick Draper. Richard's right-hand man had teamed up with his wife to kill Richard's mistress and poor Laurel Kroft, who may just have come asking the right questions at the wrong time.

It was time to take my lumps: I dialed Creighton's number.

"Jim? It's me." I didn't know whether getting voice mail was a good thing. I did know it made my role easier. "We need to talk. I saw Benazi. He—he surprised me. I'm going over to the Haigens, Jim. I think I know what happened to Laurel and Mariela."

FORTY-SEVEN

I GAVE CREIGHTON a good ten minutes, but when my phone didn't ring, I was done with waiting. It hadn't been totally lost time. I'd packed a flashlight and my warm fleece, in case I needed to do some snooping outdoors. My black raincoat would be useful if the rain started up again and would give me some cover if I did have to poke around. Finally, I'd checked that my knife was still sitting, secure, in my back pocket. I always carry it, but a girl likes to be sure.

As I drove over to the Haigens, I tried to formulate some kind of a plan. I didn't need an excuse to be there. Dierdre herself had basically invited me. It was evening. Time to walk the dog. That fire would have taken care of the outbuilding where the leopard had been caged, but some evidence might have survived. A sign of the big cat—or of either woman. That was lower priority, though. Creighton would soon be on the rest of the estate, now that he knew what to look for. No, what I wanted to do was confront Dierdre Haigen.

THE DRIVE OUT to the Haigens seemed longer in the dark. The rain had started up again, making the road slick, and the cloud cover kept any moonlight under wraps. Driving past the preservation land, I was aware of that darkness. The trees, still leafless and skeletal. And in there, somewhere, a bringer of death. As lost and alone as any poor soul, doomed to roam the night.

I wasn't in the best of spirits by the time I reached the house. The tang of wood smoke, barely perceptible, didn't help. I don't like people who hide things, and I like even less being played for a fool. Still, I tried to calm down as I climbed the front steps. Better to have the advantage of surprise.

That moment spent working my grimace into something like a smile paid off. From the front stoop, I could hear raised voices. A man and a woman arguing. This was going to be interesting.

"I can't believe you'd do that." The man. It could have been Richard. Then again, I'd already cast him as the injured party. "I loved her."

Richard, for sure.

"You're not listening!" Dierdre, it had to be. But as I leaned forward to hear more, I heard another voice. A bark. *"No! No! You've got it wrong!"*

"What's that?" Richard again. "Is someone out there?"

Poor honest Spot must have been trying to stop the fight from getting physical. In the meantime, he'd blown my cover. I rang the bell.

"Pru." Her cheeks flushed, Dierdre looked years younger. Fighting brought out the best in her.

"I came to walk the dog?" I looked in, as if to see Spot. What I saw was Richard, with a face like thunder. "Mr. Haigen?"

"Bah!" he said, and turned to storm off. Only a slight stumble on the edge of a rug ruined his exit. But although Spot had jumped up to stand at his side, the angry man ignored him, reaching instead to feel his way along the wall as he disappeared down the hall.

"I'm sorry." Dierdre saw me watching him. It was hard not to. "Things have been difficult lately. It's hard for him to accept some of the changes."

Now it was my turn to look surprised. "Changes" was quite a cavalier euphemism for killing, even for Wallis. "I can imagine," I managed to say. "Would you like to take some air with us?"

If Dierdre thought she was getting away from a scene, she had another thought coming. I waited while she donned a jacket, and let her set our path toward the road. The smell of the fire was much fainter now and faded as we walked away from the house. Still, it served as my cue.

"Interesting thing about fires," I said, as Spot sniffed a tree trunk where a raccoon was nesting. "You'd think they destroy all the evidence. But they don't."

We were too far from the house for the porch lights to reach us, but this close I could see her respond.

"Excuse me?" She was straining to keep her voice level, her smile in place.

"The evidence," I repeated, as I laid it out. "You killed Mariela. Your rival." I watched as her smile faded, then I delivered my kicker. "To throw her in with a leopard, though. That's cold. I bet that really taught Richard a lesson."

"It was an accident." Dierdre's eyes were wide with shock. "I never meant for her to…"

"To what? To wander into the leopard cage?" I was furious. Fed up with her assumed helplessness. "Was she one of Richard's pretty toys? His newest diversion?"

"No, it wasn't like that. Richard always…" She colored and turned away. Turned toward Spot, who was watching us both, a low whine rising in the back of his throat. "I knew what he was like when I married him."

"He was going to trade you in for a newer model." It was cruel. I didn't care. I thought about Laurel, about Creighton. I hadn't killed anyone. She had.

I had to hand it to her. She faked confusion very well, looking up so fast she startled Spot. "No, it wasn't what you think. Mariela wasn't supposed to be there...." Her voice was shrill, but not hysterical. I looked at her.

"But she was. And she saw. You had someone on the side, too." It all made sense. "Richard's friend, Nick."

She gulped. I had her. She opened her mouth to speak, but when no words came out, I supplied them.

"Richard could have his dalliances, but I bet he wouldn't want you to," I said. Spot's whine was getting louder. In a confrontation like this, he wouldn't know whom to protect. "Not when he'd already paid for you."

It was cruel. I didn't care.

"Maybe that's what happened." I went on. "Maybe she was the one who really loved Richard. Maybe she caught you with your lover and that's when you pushed her in."

"Lover? I don't—" She was pulling herself together, and I felt Spot shift to her side. "I've been faithful to Richard since the day we met."

"Stow it." I could admire Spot. He was protecting the weaker of the two of us from the aggressor. But I really had no time for this. "Infidelity is the least of your sins."

"But I wasn't..." She grabbed my arm. "I love him. I was trying to save him."

What happened next, happened fast. She'd reached for me, but I was expecting that. I stepped back pulling my arm away in a move that was part reflex, part calculated, as I went for my knife. Only in the dark, it didn't work. I tripped and stumbled. Spot ran to my side barking. *"No! No!"* And Dierdre? The woman I'd thought a killer? She didn't follow up on her advantage. Instead, she stood there, her hands over her mouth and tears springing from her eyes.

"No! No!" This time, I felt that Spot was talking to me.

"Quiet." I picked myself off the wet leaves. "Heel."

Spot looked up, concerned, but I didn't have time. *"No?"* I asked silently, just to be sure. He wagged his tail, and I looked at the woman, now openly crying in front of me.

"Maybe I got it wrong, Dierdre." I didn't know what was going on, but I trusted Spot. "Why don't you tell me?"

I had to wait while she had her sob. When she did start to talk, it didn't make sense.

"We've been... Richard's money, it's all gone." Her voice had sunk to a whisper. "All the treatments. All the so-called miracle cures. That's why he let everyone go."

I'd thought the lack of staff meant something. Still, I wasn't buying it. "And I'm sure your upkeep was all done on a budget."

She colored, the flush showing through her makeup. "I didn't know, not at first. And Richard, well, he insisted on having me look a certain way. It wasn't until I took over the books that I saw how far in debt we were. How far we are. That's when I knew I had to raise some funds. I had to sell some of his treasures."

Benazi the dealer. The middle man. "You were sell-

ing the leopard, weren't you? Did you get him from
Benazi? Was he not willing to take it back?"

"It wasn't that. Mr. Benazi was trying to broker
something. He was trying to set up an arrangement.
But Nick didn't want to pay his fees, pay for the animal to be boarded when it was just going to be killed."

Nick. I'd known he was involved. "So, what, Nick
arranged a private sale to a canned hunt?"

Without a word, she nodded. Her face a mask of
horror. "It was supposed to be drugged, supposed to
be delivered all doped up. He got our gardener to help
him—Raul, Mariela's brother. Raul was supposed to
help get it out of the barn. They had a cage they were
going to load into the SUV. Only the drugs hadn't
worked. Not yet. And the animal was—it was still fighting. Screaming. Nick had Raul poking at it, trying to
get it into the cage. Pushing it with a rake, of all things.
Mariela must have heard it. She was on her way out for
the evening, and she must have heard it—it sounded
like it was crying. She started yelling at her brother.
Yelling at Nick that he had to stop. That he had to stop
hurting it. That she was going to call Richard, call the
police. And Nick—Nick grabbed her. He shoved her. It
all happened so fast."

Dierdre fell silent, the tears starting again. It didn't
matter. I didn't need the details. I'd seen them for myself. Nick didn't know how to drug an animal. The cat
had been panicked. The woman, simply in the way.

After a moment, Dierdre wiped her eyes. I found my
voice had grown gentle. "And after?"

"Nick said…he said we had to make it look like an
accident. That we were responsible. That she was dead
anyway." She put her hand up to her mouth. Maybe

her own words made her sick. They should have. "The leopard was out cold by then, and so he had Raul load it into the SUV. With…with Mariela. After—after, he said he'd swear that the car was on his lot. He said he could do that much for us."

I nodded. The last pieces were falling into place. "Did Laurel figure it out?"

"I wasn't here when she—when she came over that last time. I needed to get out. Richard has been increasingly distressed. He's—he missed her." She bit her lip, but I didn't interrupt. I no longer thought she'd been jealous of any attention her husband had given the pretty maid. Relieved, more likely. "Laurel must have gone directly to the back. When I got home, the building— the one where Richard kept the panther—was on fire. I don't think he knew she was there."

"Nick was trying to destroy any evidence." I filled in the blanks. "He knew Richard's clout could only hold off Creighton's lab techs for so long. But Laurel didn't need a warrant. She saw the cage. She figured it out— figured out enough anyway."

Now it was Dierdre's turn to nod. "I think so. I think she made Nick mad."

Dierdre was shivering by then, exhausted by her confession. I was feeling the cold, too. So with Spot leading the way, we headed back to the house in silence. It had been a lot to digest. I still didn't understand why Richard Haigen had the animal. Denial, I told myself, as we made our way up the walk. The macular degeneration had come on more quickly than he'd thought. He must have planned a last adventure—a hunt was never going to happen.

"Halt!" I nearly fell over Spot, who had stepped in

front of me. *"No."* He was using my commands back on me, I realized. Seeing as how I'd already tripped once in the dark, I could only assume that he was being careful, that the training was working. Dierdre, a few steps ahead, turned back toward me, waiting, a slight conciliatory smile playing on her lips. How often, recently, must she have taken that pose with her husband? She must love him, to put up with his bullying. And more. "He missed her," indeed.

Sometimes, I'm slow on the uptake. More often than not, Wallis would say. This time, she'd be right. *"It's okay,"* I urged Spot. *"I can think and walk,"* I tried to let him know. Finally.

Dierdre hadn't been talking about Mariela, I realized as we climbed the stairs, Spot watching my every move. Mariela had never been Richard's focus. He liked toys. *Pretty toys.* Not women, not even fancy guns. That's why Richard had the snow leopard. Not as a trophy. Not to hunt. But as a "treasure"—one of the "pretty things" he collected.

That fascination, I thought as Dierdre held the door open, was what saved the snow leopard's life. If he hadn't been afraid of angering Richard, Nick would have killed the cat right then. I had no doubt that Nick Draper would have been happy to shoot an unconscious animal if a gun had been handy. Probably would have tried to sell the pelt, too.

I stepped into the foyer. He had a gun now.

FORTY-EIGHT

"NICK." I NODDED, even as my hand tightened on Spot's lead.

"Pru," he responded. "Dierdre."

"Nick, I didn't say anything." Dierdre's voice was rising in pitch. "Nothing!" Her hands were fluttering around her face. Desperation turning to panic. I could use that. Spot knew it, too. He was trembling, every muscle ready to go.

His excitement was obvious. "Watch the dog." Nick angled the gun down. "One move and I'll shoot it first."

"I'm sorry." I let my eyes flick over to Spot. *"You tried to warn me."*

"This is my job." He heard me. He saw the gun and understood what it meant. Spot would attack to protect me anyway. *"My job."*

"Sit, Spot. Stay." I couldn't risk it. Not while there were any other options to consider. Slowly, every fiber battling to revolt, the dog sat. Dierdre, meanwhile, had collapsed against the wall. I could hear her whimpering.

"So, Nick." I tried to sound normal as I could. "What's your game plan here? Another fake mauling, like you did with Laurel? Did you sweep up some cat hairs to put on her? Some scat?" I spit the words out, more disgusted than afraid. "Do you have another car you can get rid of?"

"I don't think I need one." He was actually smiling.

"You're the type of gal who likes trouble. The kind who sometimes disappears."

This was getting worrisome. I shook my head. "Detective Creighton knows I'm here." I hate to play the white knight card. Right now, however, his appearance would be welcome. "I called him close to an hour ago to tell him I was on my way."

Nick smiled, and in a moment I knew why. I'd said too much. "On your way," said the man with the gun. "What a pity. I'm sure Dierdre here will swear up and down that you never showed."

I looked over at the quivering mess propped against the wall. I suspected he was right.

"You can disappear into the forest," Nick was saying, "just like that pretty cat of Richard's."

That's when I heard it. A howl like a soul possessed. A wordless yowl coming down the hall. Nick couldn't help himself, he turned. We both did. I don't know what I expected. The snow leopard, maybe. A demon. What I saw was an elderly man, overcome with rage.

"You killed her!" Richard's choking cry finally found the words as he charged. "You killed my beautiful girl!"

"Richard, no!" Nick shook his head, confused, and put up his arms to ward off his onetime benefactor.

"Go!" I don't know who gave the command: me or Spot. It didn't matter. We both jumped. I threw myself against Nick's body. Spot had his arm in his teeth as Richard's bulk hit. All four of us went over in a jumble of bodies as the gun went off.

"Spot!" I yelled. He growled, Nick's beefy arm still in his mouth, as we all lay in a heap.

"It's good to see where your priorities lie," said Jim Creighton, standing in the open door.

FORTY-NINE

IT WAS NEAR dawn by the time we got out of there. Somehow, nobody had been shot, but we needed the EMTs anyway—first to bind Nick's arm and then to sedate Dierdre. They took Richard, too; he had shrunk, after that last desperate run, collapsing into himself in exhaustion or in grief. It had been hard to see his eyes, sunken in that lined face, but even I could feel the cold hate when he glared at his onetime wingman. Nick may have thought he was stepping up, chipping in when things had gotten tight, but he'd gone too far. And really, he was only the help.

The floodlights made the grounds bright as noon, if noon had a harsh whiteness to it. Under their glare, I finally got to take Spot out to the smoldering embers, where the snow leopard had been kept and where both Mariela and Laurel had been attacked. The techs wouldn't let him close at first, but when Jefferson started asking about his breeding—speculating about Spot's lineage—I knew my canine companion had found a friend.

I left Spot there, leashed, but under the lead tech's care. While they were working, Creighton took my statement. I realized, then, how smart Benazi had been. I really had nothing concrete to say about him. What I suspected—what Dierdre had intimated, I held back. Why, I wasn't exactly sure. Habit as much as anything, maybe. That and a sense that I might need something to barter with later.

Creighton knew it. He always did, but as he poured us both more coffee from a thermos that was going around, he also gave me my out.

"You must be exhausted, Pru." It wasn't a question. I nodded anyway. "So I'm going to let you go. But I may have more questions for you, in the days ahead."

I nodded again and then cleared my throat. Words, it seemed, were called for. "You know where to find me, Jim."

"Indeed I do." He smiled. And that was it. We were back on.

I drove slowly, for me, once he let me go. The combination of bad coffee and adrenaline had left me feeling shaky. I almost swerved off the road as I was passing by the preservation land. That's when it hit me. I needed to pull over. Not for safety's sake, but to touch base. Maybe say good-bye to something that had been lost there.

It felt odd to pull into the parking area without Spot by my side. I knew he was in good hands: The hound part of him loved working with the techs. But I felt naked as I got out of my car and walked to the edge of the clearing. Mariela had been dumped here. Laurel had died here, bleeding out from Nick's brutal attack. And the snow leopard? Well, she was alone, in unfamiliar territory. And unless I missed my guess, she'd been raised in captivity with no experience on her own. She was about as vulnerable as they had been.

It made me sad, all the waste. The lives, the beauty. I walked back to my car, and leaned back on the hood, the slight warmth of that big engine the only comfort I could expect.

I don't know how long I sat there. Too tired and too jacked up to sleep. But I thought I was in a dream state when I first saw it. A rustle in the underbrush. A play in the shadows as the sun broke over the hills.

What happened next took my breath away. It—*she*— was a beauty. Not that much larger than Spot, maybe a hundred pounds, but with a stealth and grace that marked her as a wild thing. Stepping into one of the first shafts of sunlight, I saw the play of muscles under her thick fur. The power in her low-slung body and those heavy jaws.

"Home?" She turned her big, round head to face me, and I caught the sadness in those eyes. She was as lost out here as I would be.

"I'm sorry," I whispered. I didn't know how much she'd get from me, if anything. I had to try. Staring into those pale green eyes, I thought of the preservation land. How it stretched to the border, to the mountains beyond. Here might be familiar, but here there was a highway. People. The high grounds would be safer. There'd be snow at the higher elevation still, and it would stay cool up there, even in summer. I pictured deer and opossums, and smaller prey, too. She held my gaze as I pictured this and, even without Spot, I got that scent: strange and fierce. Then she turned away, those big paws moving silently over the wet earth. Her tail, as long and thick as a boa, was the last to disappear, its beautiful mottled spots fading into the shadows under the trees.

"Spectacular, isn't she?" I turned with a start. Benazi had parked at the other end of the clearing, but I still thought I'd have heard him walk up, if it weren't for my fatigue and that glorious distraction. "It's a pity she's so dangerous."

I turned to appraise the man beside me, unsure, exactly what he was discussing.

"You are talking about the leopard, right?"

"What leopard?" He asked, his bushy eyebrows rising slightly. "There are no such animals in these woods."

"You know, Nick wanted to sell her for a canned hunt." I wasn't sure why I told him this. Maybe so he'd know what a sleazebag he had almost done business with. For a cat-lover, he'd had a close escape.

It didn't seem to make him happy. "My way will be kinder," he said, his voice so low I barely heard him.

"Wait, what?" I was too tired. I hadn't put this all together. "You can't mean, Stu... Gregor, you've got to call it off."

He turned toward me. "He's very good at what he does," he said. "It will be quick, and it must be done."

"You can't." I met Benazi's eyes. "I won't let you."

His heavy eyebrows rose slightly at that, but I had the bit in my teeth.

"The Haigens are going to be prosecuted for keeping a big cat illegally. There are going to be questions about how it was obtained. About who is trafficking in endangered animals. They may be scared of you. Scared into silence." I paused as I heard my own words. "I'm not."

His voice went soft. "Are you threatening me?"

"I am doing what is necessary." I thought of the animal I had seen so briefly. She was beautiful. Wild. Scared. "I want your promise that you won't let Stu kill her. I'll work with you. Help you with any resources I have." I let that one sink in; he knew what I was offering. "We can trap her. We can relocate her—to a sanctuary if she's not fit for these woods. But I won't let her be hunted down and slaughtered."

"You won't," said Benazi. His face was a mask, showing nothing. I felt my stomach clench, but I held his gaze.

His eyes were like stones. I swallowed. And much to my amazement, he smiled. "No, you won't, will you?"

With that, he took out a cell and punched in a number. "The hunt is off," he said. Then he nodded to me, and walked away.

FIFTY

THE HAIGENS HAD enough money left to hire good lawyers, not that it helped. The exotic animal infraction—keeping a big cat as a pet without the proper permits—might have gone away. The wrongful death of Mariela Gomez was not going to be brushed under the rug, and Laurel's murder, a savage stabbing, had been committed in an attempted cover-up. Richard's blindness was nearly total by the time their case came to trial, and that might have helped with the sentencing. But his complete lack of regard for the human life lost worked against him. He was taken away wailing about how much he loved her. He didn't mean any of the women.

Nick Draper was another matter entirely. He didn't have money of his own, and all the rich "friends" he'd helped over the years deserted him when they heard of his latest escapade. Once Raul had been located—he'd gone into hiding, traumatized by the death of his sister and threatened with deportation—the case was sealed. Covering up an affair, or even an illegal pet, would have been one thing. Killing two women? Quite another. He was convicted of second-degree murder, with no mitigating circumstances.

Dierdre got off lightly, all things considered. She faced the same charges as her husband, but it wasn't hard to convince a jury that she was under his sway. As an accessory, she would still do time. The difference was, unlike her husband, she'd probably live to walk in the woods again. If her nerves could stand it.

That left the leopard. But as spring turned to summer, she didn't surface, and no sightings were reported. I wanted to think I could trust Benazi. Trust the deal we'd made. As the months passed by, I realized he wasn't going to take me up on my offer. I'd have asked Spot for his impressions, but he'd moved on by then, going to a young mother in Worcester who'd lost her sight in an industrial accident. When I asked Wallis what she thought—about the snow leopard, about her chances—she tended to act smug. Sometimes, I thought, she was jealous.

"So you're worried about another cat, out in the woods?" She'd been staring out the window, the last time I'd brought the leopard up. *"Wondering if she can make it?"*

From the way her tail twitched, I thought Wallis was looking at a bird. The hills were fully green by then. The road obscured by a veil of leaves.

"Life in the wild is harsh, Pru. You know that." A bird or a squirrel, definitely. *"A female alone? Doesn't stand a chance."*

A flash of red in the distance. A cardinal, or a bright red Maserati.

"Unless, of course, she's made some friends."

* * * * *

ACKNOWLEDGMENTS

The EASTERN COUGAR—aka panther, puma, or mountain lion—is a mystery in itself. I had great fun playing with the concept of this great cat, and for guidance in all things panther, my heartfelt thanks go out to IFAW media contact Kerry Branon and animal rescue officer Kelly Donithan. In terms of writing, I'd like to thank my usual stalwart crew: Lisa Susser, Vicki Constantine Croke, Colleen Mohyde, Sophie Garelick, Frank Garelick, Lisa Jones, Annette Rogers, and, as always, Jon S. Garelick. Jon not only read multiple revisions of this mystery, he took great care of me while doing so. Thanks, my love. Thank you, my friends. Enjoy!

REQUEST YOUR FREE BOOKS!
2 FREE NOVELS PLUS 2 FREE GIFTS!

ⓗ HARLEQUIN®

INTRIGUE

BREATHTAKING ROMANTIC SUSPENSE

HI15

REQUEST YOUR FREE BOOKS!
2 FREE NOVELS PLUS 2 FREE GIFTS!

H HARLEQUIN®

ROMANTIC suspense

Sparked by danger, fueled by passion

YES! Please send me 2 FREE Harlequin® Romantic Suspense novels and my 2 FREE gifts (gifts are worth about $10). After receiving them, if I don't wish to receive any more books, I can return the shipping statement marked "cancel." If I don't cancel, I will receive 4 brand-new novels every month and be billed just $4.74 per book in the U.S. or $5.49 per book in Canada. That's a savings of at least 12% off the cover price! It's quite a bargain! Shipping and handling is just 50¢ per book in the U.S. and 75¢ per book in Canada.* I understand that accepting the 2 free books and gifts places me under no obligation to buy anything. I can always return a shipment and cancel at any time. Even if I never buy another book, the two free books and gifts are mine to keep forever.

240/340 HDN GH3P

Name	(PLEASE PRINT)

Address	Apt. #

City	State/Prov.	Zip/Postal Code

Signature (if under 18, a parent or guardian must sign)

Mail to the **Reader Service**:
IN U.S.A.: P.O. Box 1867, Buffalo, NY 14240-1867
IN CANADA: P.O. Box 609, Fort Erie, Ontario L2A 5X3

Want to try two free books from another line?
Call 1-800-873-8635 or visit www.ReaderService.com.

* Terms and prices subject to change without notice. Prices do not include applicable taxes. Sales tax applicable in N.Y. Canadian residents will be charged applicable taxes. Offer not valid in Quebec. This offer is limited to one order per household. Not valid for current subscribers to Harlequin Romantic Suspense books. All orders subject to credit approval. Credit or debit balances in a customer's account(s) may be offset by any other outstanding balance owed by or to the customer. Please allow 4 to 6 weeks for delivery. Offer available while quantities last.

Your Privacy—The Reader Service is committed to protecting your privacy. Our Privacy Policy is available online at www.ReaderService.com or upon request from the Reader Service.

We make a portion of our mailing list available to reputable third parties that offer products we believe may interest you. If you prefer that we not exchange your name with third parties, or if you wish to clarify or modify your communication preferences, please visit us at www.ReaderService.com/consumerchoice or write to us at Reader Service Preference Service, P.O. Box 9062, Buffalo, NY 14240-9062. Include your complete name and address.

REQUEST YOUR FREE BOOKS!

2 FREE NOVELS
FROM THE SUSPENSE COLLECTION
PLUS 2 FREE GIFTS!

YES! Please send me 2 FREE novels from the Suspense Collection and my 2 FREE gifts (gifts are worth about $10). After receiving them, if I don't wish to receive any more books, I can return the shipping statement marked "cancel." If I don't cancel, I will receive 4 brand-new novels every month and be billed just $6.49 per book in the U.S. or $6.99 per book in Canada. That's a savings of at least 19% off the cover price. It's quite a bargain! Shipping and handling is just 50¢ per book in the U.S. and 75¢ per book in Canada.* I understand that accepting the 2 free books and gifts places me under no obligation to buy anything. I can always return a shipment and cancel at any time. Even if I never buy another book, the two free books and gifts are mine to keep forever.

191/391 MDN GH4Z

Name	(PLEASE PRINT)
Address	Apt. #
City	State/Prov.	Zip/Postal Code

Signature (if under 18, a parent or guardian must sign)

Mail to the **Reader Service:**
IN U.S.A.: P.O. Box 1867, Buffalo, NY 14240-1867
IN CANADA: P.O. Box 609, Fort Erie, Ontario L2A 5X3

Want to try two free books from another line?
Call 1-800-873-8635 or visit www.ReaderService.com.

* Terms and prices subject to change without notice. Prices do not include applicable taxes. Sales tax applicable in N.Y. Canadian residents will be charged applicable taxes. Offer not valid in Quebec. This offer is limited to one order per household. Not valid for current subscribers to the Suspense Collection or the Romance/Suspense Collection. All orders subject to credit approval. Credit or debit balances in a customer's account(s) may be offset by any other outstanding balance owed by or to the customer. Please allow 4 to 6 weeks for delivery. Offer available while quantities last.

Your Privacy—The Reader Service is committed to protecting your privacy. Our Privacy Policy is available online at www.ReaderService.com or upon request from the Reader Service.

We make a portion of our mailing list available to reputable third parties that offer products we believe may interest you. If you prefer that we not exchange your name with third parties, or if you wish to clarify or modify your communication preferences, please visit us at www.ReaderService.com/consumerschoice or write to us at Reader Service Preference Service, P.O. Box 9062, Buffalo, NY 14240-9062. Include your complete name and address.